I0760898

ZANDRA VOORHIES

and the PIASA WAND

ZANDRA VOORHIES

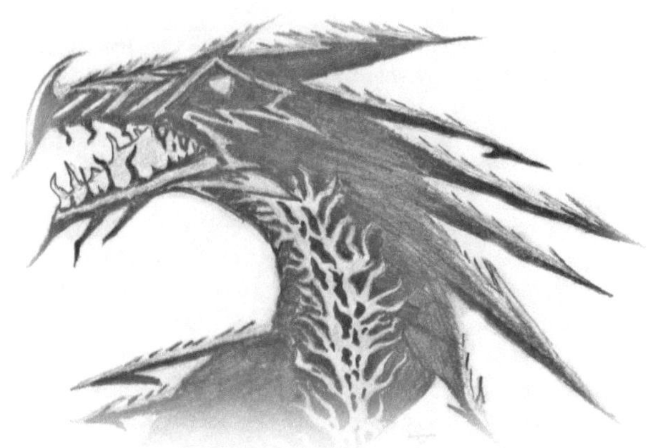

M. T. FISHER

EMPYREAN PUBLISHING

The text of this book was set in 11.5-point Baskerville Old Face, and the chapter headings were set in 24-point Algerian BasD.

Book design by Sam Fisher

Empyrean Publishing

Library of Congress Control Number:2019908682

ISBN: 978-1-7332462-0-0 (hardback)

Summary: Zandra Voorhies, wandmaker, goes on various adventures to acquire wand infusion materials, eventually creating the most powerful wand ever made in the New World, and defeating a power-hungry wizard bent on domination.

ISBN: 978-1-7332462-1-7 (paperback)

Dedicated to all the poor, the minorities, the misunderstood, the misfits: the ones who don't fit in to society. The ones who bravely pull on their tattered coats every day and head out into the cruel, cold world.

That tattered coat is a crown. Wear it proudly.

CONTENTS

Across the fields of yesterday,
He sometimes comes to me,
A little lad just in from play;
The lad I used to be.

And yet he smiles so wistfully,
Once he has crept within;
I wonder if he hopes to see
The man I might have been.

-Brother Nelson, Hobo Evangelist

Voorhies' Wands
VW
Since 1780
Old World Quality at New World Prices

1

PROLOGUE

April 28, 1780

Yet another wave crashed over the bow of the L'Hermione,[1] throwing the ship to the side like a fly tossed in the wind. Zandra hugged her knees tighter, trying to hold back her nausea.

It had been a long journey.

Her seasickness was an inconvenience in more ways than one; on top of the discomfort, it was harder to keep up her concentration on her Transverto spell. The spell disguised her as General Lafayette's[2] assistant, Jean Luc, but if her focus wavered, the spell would drop, and she would be exposed. It didn't help that Lafayette's demands on her had been so rigorous that she could barely keep up.

If it hadn't been for her quick thinking, they might not have ever made the crossing. During a nasty storm, Zandra had saved Latouche,[3] the commander of the L'Hermione, from going overboard when a wave almost swept him away. Luckily no one had seen her pull her wand out to put him back on board.

They would have been talking about that for years if I'd been seen, she thought to herself as the wind roared by outside. Zandra was very used to hiding her powers. Her people had to be.

She had been training with wand makers from all over Europe since the age of nine. Being very bright, with a steely determination that belied her looks, she felt she was ready. So at twenty-three years of age, she decided that she could learn no more and chose to head to the New World. With the war between England and the colonies, she thought it would be easier to merge into the community.

So she had set off to make a name for herself in the New World. The prospect of new wand woods and the possibility of new creatures excited her. What would she find, what combinations would produce the best wands? Could she come up with wands to rival those of the masters of Europe?

To Zandra's relief, the storm eventually subsided. Once she had her seasickness under control, she went up to the deck to see if land was in sight.

As she rose up out of the hatch, she squinted her eyes—and, there, in the distance, she could faintly make out a thin stretch of green on the horizon.

"Terre devant!" came a shout from the crow's nest above her.

As Zandra gazed into the distance at the strip of land on the edge of the sky, the promise of solid ground beneath her feet, new places to explore, and with the start of her new life just within sight, she couldn't help but smile.

In just a few hours, the ship was tied up on the dock at Boston Harbor. Once Lafayette had departed to go into Boston for the afternoon, Zandra pulled Jean Luc's tiny body out of a little box in her trunk, laying it on the bed. She gathered her remaining things after setting her trunk down in the hall, then she stuck her wand through the crack of the door and reversed the spell she had placed on Jean Luc at the beginning of the voyage back in France. He quickly grew back to his normal size and came out of the deep sleep he had been in, looking around with a very confused look on his face.

As she walked down the gangplank of the L'Hermione, Zandra's head spun with excitement. Quickly finding a secluded corner of the waterfront, she pointed her wand at herself.

"Aversa pars," she said, shrinking back to her real height of five foot three, the clothes hanging loosely off her petite frame. She shook out her long blond hair; her beautiful milk-chocolate brown eyes shone for the first time since her journey began.

Pointing her wand at herself once more, she changed her clothes into a tight black dress with flares at her wrist. Looking around to make sure she had not been noticed, she headed into Boston proper to start her new life.

CHAPTER 1

The O'Malley Inn

April 28, 1780

Zandra's boots crunched on the streets, her legs still wobbling as if she'd never left the ship. She had become so accustomed to the swaying of the deck that it was hard to walk now that she was on land.

She searched the streets of Boston for several minutes before she found what she was looking for: a livery. She hoped to buy a horse with the money she had brought with her from the old country.

As she entered the stables, a beautiful black horse whinnied at her.

The owner of the livery walked up to her. "Can I help you, madam?"

She nodded. "I'm looking to buy a horse and a wagon. Is this horse for sale?"

"'S a good one there, madam. A Belgia Black. Not many around. Have to get a good bit of gold for him." He shook his head, patting the horse on the back. "It be a draft horse, though, madam. Don't think you'll be needing this kind. Maybe one of these down here." He gestured down at the other end of the livery.

As Zandra looked at the horse and stroked his neck, she thought she felt something; a connection she couldn't quite identify. "No," she said. "I think I'll take this one. Do you have a wagon that I could buy?"

The man nodded. "Right this way, madam."

After getting her horse hitched up and tying it to a post on a side road, Zandra headed toward Salem Street.[4] All new arrivals went there to meet up with her kind. Turning onto the street, she grabbed her wand under her cloak and muttered, "Propinquitas."

Removing her hand, she proceeded to walk down the street.

It was midday and the thoroughfare was busy with people coming and going. She cut through through the crowd slowly, waiting for a reaction from her wand.

After about ten minutes, her wand began to vibrate, signaling that another witch or wizard was nearby. She moved more slowly now, and she scanned the faces along the street. Finally, she saw a middle-aged man looking around the same as her. She moved closer—her wand began to vibrate with increasing vigor—and their eyes met.

He was a tall, lanky man with red hair, razor stubble of gray and red covering his face, and wearing very clean clothes that had nonetheless seen better days. His eyes were green, and gave her a feeling of safety and acceptance.

He gave her a smile. "New to Boston?" he asked, patting her on the shoulder with a large bony hand.

Zandra nodded. "Could you help me?"

"That's what I'm here for. Come back to the inn with me; we'll get you a room for the night."

"I have a horse and wagon tied over there." She gestured toward the side road.

Returning to her horse, they weaved through the streets of Boston until they came to a small house. As they passed through the front door, the home opened up into a larger space than Zandra would have expected from the outside. Chairs were gathered around a large field-stone fireplace, and a long table with many chairs took up the rest of the room. A staircase opened into the room at the far end.

The man gestured around. "We have a Dissimulato Fenestra charm on the house, and I also recently placed an Auris Silentium charm of my own making, so anyone looking in only sees or hears what we want them to. Just so you know you don't have to worry about hiding your magic here."

An elderly woman walked in, short and slightly round, with brown hair pulled back in a bun. "Got another guest, do we?"

Zandra stepped forward. "My name is Zandra Voorhies," she said. "I'm a wandmaker. Or, at least, I'm aspiring to be."

The woman looked intrigued. "Wandmaker? Well, we could sure use one. Getting wands from the old country can be a bit of a problem. The wandmakers here in the colonies seem to only want to cater to the elites."

"What are your names?" Zandra asked.

"So sorry, forgot to introduce ourselves," the man said. "I'm Cormac O'Malley, and this is my wife, Finnghuala."

"Are you of the Grace O'Malley[5] clan?" Zandra asked.

"Why, yes! You know of Grace?" Cormac said, looking delighted.

"A little," Zandra said. "She seemed like a pretty interesting lady for a non-magical person."

"That she was," Cormac said, "but we in the family refer to her as Granuaaile. Ireland's great pirate queen she was. Even met with Queen Elizabeth I. Pleaded her case to the Queen and won the release of her imprisoned family members."

Finnghuala walked off to the kitchen. "Well, would you like something to eat? I imagine the ship food wasn't all that great."

"No, it wasn't," Zandra said.

"Go ahead and have a seat," Finnghuala called from the kitchen. "I have a stew on the fire."

Cormac walked to the door. "I'll go and tend to your horse."

7

Finnghuala stepped back into the room with a bowl of stew and a chunk of bread.

As Zandra sat down, Finnghuala set the cup of stew and the bread down on the table in front of her. Zandra took a whiff. “Smells wonderful.”

“Me mother’s recipe,” Finnghuala replied. She sat down as well. “So where do you plan to start your trade?”

“Well, I thought about moving closer to Salem,”[6] said Zandra. “I was thinking the experiences that the witches there have had might lead me to some creatures that would provide good infusions for my wands. I couldn’t bring many infusions with me, and I was hoping they might lead me to find some interesting specimens.”

“That they might. Those witches had a hard go of it back during those trials. They learned a lot.” Finnghuala leaned back in her chair. “You seem pretty young to be a wandmaker.”

“I’m a fast study.”

“Where are you from?”

“My family is Dutch. My father was the first in his family to have magical powers. He was shunned by his family. My mother was of an old magical family, the Visser.”

A rather large, balding man came down the stairs clad only in his underclothes. “Dinner time yet? I’m starving.”

“Flanagan, you march right back upstairs and put some clothes on!” Finnghuala said. “How many times have I told you I don’t want to see your filthy behind down here? Besides, we have a new guest.”

“Well, if you didn’t keep it so infernally hot in here—”

“Well, if you would move along, you wouldn’t have to sweat yourself over it, would you?”

“Ah, Finn, you wouldn’t know what to do without me around.”

“I wouldn’t have to deal with your scurvy gums bleeding up my sheets!”

"You know I took care of that weeks ago!" Flanagan turned to grin at Zandra. "You'll have to forgive her, madam. She gets difficult sometimes."

"*I* get difficult?" Finnghuala scoffed.

Zandra chuckled.

Flanagan bowed at her. "Griorgair Lomhar Necat Flanagan, at your service."

"Zandra Voorhies," she said. "Pleased to meet you, uh...."

"Just call me Gregor."

Zandra smiled. "Okay."

"Don't you mind us—Finn really loves me, she just has to act as if she hates me so Cormac won't know."

Finnghuala snorted. "You wish." She turned and walked into the kitchen.

Gregor sat down. "So what brings you to Boston?"

"Just passing through," Zandra said.

"Well, if I can help you in any way, just say the word. I know lots of people."

"I'll keep that in mind."

Gregor leaned out of his chair and yelled into the kitchen. "Finn, where's my stew?"

Finnghuala came into the room and slammed a cup down on the table, spattering Gregor.

"Now you went and got my clothes dirty!" Gregor whined.

"Can't see any difference," Finnghuala said stubbornly.

Zandra snickered.

The doorknob rattled, and Cormac came back in from stabling Zandra's horse.

"Look what your wife has done!" Gregor roared.

Cormac looked at Gregor and laughed. "What have you done now, Gregor?"

"Who, *me*?"

"Yes, you," Cormac replied.

Gregor mumbled something unintelligible. Finnghuala looked over to Zandra. "Would you like some more stew?"

"I'm full," Zandra said.

"I can show you to your room," Finnghuala said. "We've already moved your trunk up there."

"That'd be great."

Finnghuala and Zandra ascended the stairs. They rose through multiple floors, each appearing to get smaller and more flimsy.

"Sorry for the appearance, but Cormac's carpentry spells aren't what they used to be, and we've had to add on recently with all the newcomers," said Finnghuala.

The house had been only two stories tall from the outside.

As they hit the fifth landing, Finnghuala opened a door to a room. "It's not much, but it's cozy and clean."

It was a small room, but very nice. The view of Boston was great. Zandra could just see the L'Hermione at the dock on the Boston waterfront.

Finnghuala walked across the room. "Here is your chamber pot. Just give it a tap on the side after you're done and everything will disappear. And this is your washtub. To bathe in it, tap it with your wand and tell it how hot or cold you want your bath water to be, along with what kind of soap you want. Tap it when you're through and it will vanish." She turned back to Zandra. "Cormac is very proud of these spells he created, although, like his carpentry spells, they've gotten a little troublesome of late. The other night, the contents of a chamber pot ended up at the foot of another guest's bed. Caused quite an uproar."

Zandra cringed. "Hopefully that won't happen."

Finnghuala strode toward the door, and Zandra stepped aside to let her through. "Flanagan is harmless," Finnghuala said, "but let me know if he gives you any trouble."

"I will. I'm sure it'll be fine," Zandra replied.

"I'll leave you, then. Good night."

"Thanks for everything," Zandra said.

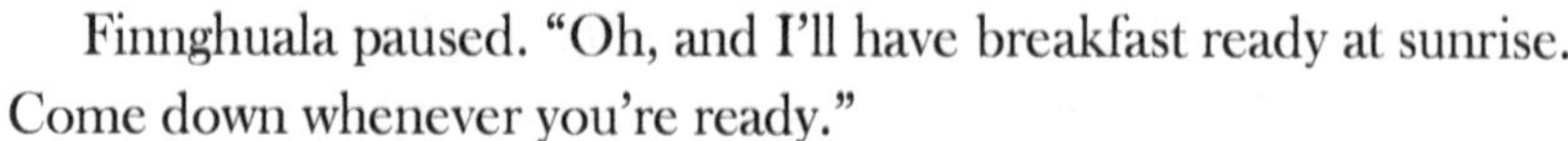

Finnghuala paused. “Oh, and I’ll have breakfast ready at sunrise. Come down whenever you’re ready.”

She closed the door behind her as she left.

Zandra walked over to the end of her bed, opened her trunk, pulled out some fresh clothes, and laid them on the bed. She walked over to the washtub and tapped the side with her wand. “Warm; lavender soap.”

The washtub filled. Zandra removed her clothes and sat down in the tub. It felt so good to soak in the warm water.

She turned her head, looking out the window across Boston and the bay. The sky was streaked with orange, and the ripples in the bay below reflected the colors of the horizon.

The sun was setting on the end of her first day in this new land.

CHAPTER 2

BEGINNINGS

April 29, 1780

When Zandra woke the next morning, the sun was already up. The feather mattress in her room had been so much better than her bunk on the L'Hermione. She dressed and headed down for breakfast.

Gregor was already seated at the table. "Morning, Zandra. Have a good rest?"

"Much better than I did on the ship," she replied.

Cormac entered from the back door. "Been over to Fritz Bohm's shop. He'd like to meet you, Zandra, before you head out."

"Who is Fritz Bohm?"

"He's the owner of our magical supply shop here in Boston. I think he wants to talk to you about the wands that you'll be making. I can take you over there if you'd like."

"I have a few wands that I brought over with me," Zandra said. "Do you think he might be interested in them?"

"I'm sure he will. I have to be getting back up to Salem Street, so let me know as soon as you're ready to leave."

Finnghuala sat a glass of milk and some bread down in front of Zandra.

She took a sip. "Your milk is cold!"

"Yes, I put a cooling charm on it. I find it lasts longer," Finnghuala said. "Would you like me to warm it for you?"

Zandra thought for a minute. "No...it's very unusual, but I think I like it this way."

"I can't stand Finn's cold milk," said Gregor. "Makes my teeth hurt."

"So now that you have your belly full, you decided to speak," Finnghuala said. "Thought maybe you were going to let us digest our food in peace."

Zandra got up from the table.

"Don't you want something more to eat?" asked Finnghuala.

"I'll eat more at lunch," Zandra replied. "Let me get my wands from my room."

She ran upstairs, taking her wand out and pointing it at her trunk. "Recludo!"

A compartment at the bottom of the trunk slid open. She took the seven wands she'd brought over with her from the old country out and put them in a silk pouch. She tied the pouch to her waist and, tapping it with her wand, murmured, "Lateo." The pouch disappeared. With the wands properly concealed so they wouldn't attract the attention of non-magical people, she headed back down the stairs.

Cormac had just finished his tea.

"I'm ready," Zandra said.

Cormac got up from the table, and they headed out the door and down the street.

"Quite a horse you got, Zandra," said Cormac. "I was talking to him this morning."

"You can talk to him?"

Cormac nodded. "You've got yourself a horse with magical powers. He started talking after he saw me use my wand to feed the animals this morning. He doesn't speak out loud, but you hear him in your head. His name is Xavier."

"I knew there was something different about him," said Zandra.

"Xavier said he knew you were a witch," said Cormac. "He hadn't wanted to expose his powers until he was away from the non-magical people."

"Well, I'll have to come out to the stable to talk to him when we get back," Zandra said.

Cormac stopped walking. "Here we are."

They had stopped in front of a cellar door, where a shingle hanging off the side of the building read:

Bohm Cauldrons

They entered and went down the stairs until they came to a low-ceilinged room, where cauldrons of different sizes lined the walls. Another door was open across the room that lead out to street level, and a very large cauldron was being moved out to be wrestled onto a wagon. Zandra watched them struggle to load it on.

Cormac whispered to Zandra, "Fritz sells to non-magical people as well. Does a pretty good business selling those cauldrons to them for rendering pigs."

When they finally got the cauldron loaded onto the wagon, the storekeeper closed the doors and turned to Cormac.

"I'm looking for a special type of cauldron," Cormac said.

"Then you'd better go back and talk with Fritz," the man replied.

The man opened a door in the far wall that Zandra hadn't noticed. It led into a small room. As they entered, the storekeeper closed the door behind them. Cormac took out his wand and whispered "Revelabo Stultitiam."

A blue line appeared at the floor and made its way up the wall like a fuse being lit. After it had outlined the shape of a door, it went out. Then a latch appeared. Cormac grabbed it and opened the door.

This room was much lighter, and many candles hung from the ceiling. All around the room were shelves of potion supplies, vials, magical books, broomsticks, cloaks, a few wands; all kinds of things a witch or wizard would need. And, of course, cauldrons.

Fritz, a blond-haired, blue-eyed man with a stern look, stood behind the counter looking through some papers. He looked up when they entered. “Cormac! Is the new wand maker coming?”

Zandra stepped out from behind Cormac.

“This be Zandra Voorhies,” Cormac said.

“Well, now, you’re a bit younger than I expected!” Fritz said.

Zandra frowned.

“Do you have any of your work with you?” he asked.

Zandra pulled out her wand, pointed it at where she knew the pouch was, and said “Inverto.” The pouch appeared, and she untied it from her waist, opened it, and placed the wands on the counter.

Fritz grabbed a walnut wand, pointed it at Cormac, flicked his wrist, and said “Atollo!” Cormac lifted off the floor and hit his head on the ceiling.

“That is quite enough!” Cormac protested.

“Nice workmanship! Well balanced. How much are you asking for the lot?”

Zandra shrugged. “Make me an offer.”

“Well, I work in Spanish currency. That’s what a lot of people in the colonies use. And since I do business with both sides, it’s just easier. How about five reales?”

Zandra thought for a moment. “What about ten?”

“Seven,” Fritz shot back.

She sighed. “Okay.”

“Seven it is.” Fritz smiled as he pulled the reales from a drawer and counted them out. He handed Zandra seven silver coins.

“Well, it’s getting late, I should have been up on Salem Street by now,” Cormac said. “We’d better get going. Come, I’ll walk you back home.”

15

Zandra went up to her room to put her money in the drawer of her trunk, and headed down to see Xavier. As she passed through the dining room, Finnghuala was cleaning the floor. A rag glided past Zandra's feet, raising at the end of its pass and slashing down into a bucket of soapy water. Then it rose up again, wringing itself out, and started to wipe the floor once more.

"How did your visit to Fritz go?" asked Finnghuala.

"Good," replied Zandra. "I got seven reales for my wands."

"Not bad."

"I'm heading out to talk with my horse."

Finnghuala did a double take. "Your horse?"

Zandra nodded. "Your husband told me that my horse can talk to you in your head."

"Well, now, that is something. Let me know if his feed is acceptable, won't you?"

"I'll see what I can do," replied Zandra.

She headed out the back door and into the stable. She found Xavier in the last stall.

"So I hear your name is Xavier," she said hesitantly. "That saves me the trouble of picking out a name for you."

And it keeps me from having to put up with a name that I can't stand, said Xavier. *I was hoping you wouldn't miss the subtle prompting that I was sending your way. I could tell you were a witch. I'm so tired of not having a human that I can talk to.*

"Well, you have one now." Zandra looked down the length of his back. "You're quite a large boy. Do you think you could come down a little so I could get on your back? I don't want to have to use the wagon all the time."

I might be able to do that. Don't usually let people ride me.

"Well, you wanted someone to talk to, and I don't want to have to deal with that wagon all the time."

You're not going to wear any armor, are you? My great uncle Harrison used to have to carry a knight around, and he told tales about how he hated the way the armor pinched him.

"No, I won't be needing any armor. I don't know that anyone does anymore." She leaned up against the stable wall. "So how did you end up in the colonies?"

I overheard the stable hands talking about gathering up some colts and foals to send overseas. I thought that sounded like fun, so I made sure that I was always front and center when they came around. When the day came, they herded us off to the docks and loaded us onto a ship.

"What did you think of the voyage?"

All my time was spent below deck. I would have liked to have seen the ocean, though I didn't care for the smell.

"I was sick a lot of the time," Zandra said.

What brought you here?

"I'm a wandmaker. I'm hoping to make a name for myself here in the New World. We'll be looking for new woods and new magical creatures together, to procure infusion samples for my wands."

I have no knowledge of how your world works, said Xavier. *I guess I just got my first lesson.*

Zandra headed to the door of the stall. "I have a few things to do. We'll probably head out in the morning. Are you comfortable here? The lady of the inn wanted to know if your food was satisfactory."

It's fine. Though I could go for a bit of rum to wash it down.

"Rum? You drink rum?"

Yeah! Good stuff! You should try it some time.

"Well, I'll see what I can do. I don't know what Finnghuala's going to think about that."

Zandra entered through the back door of the inn.

"Are you ready for some lunch?" Finnghuala asked.

"Yes, I'm starving."

"I'm afraid all I have is the stew from last night."

"That'll be fine," said Zandra.

"I'll get you a bowl," Finnghuala said. "I have a pig on the fire for dinner. We've had several new arrivals today."

Zandra looked over at the fireplace, where a large pig was rotating over the fire on its own. "Xavier said that his feed was fine, though he would like some rum to wash it down with if you could."

"Your horse wants rum with his meals? I've never heard of such. I'll see what Cormac can do."

"Thank you," Zandra said. "I'm going to hitch Xavier up to my wagon and go for supplies after lunch. I'd like to head out in the morning. Do you know anyone near Salem that could help get me started and introduce me to our community up there?"

"We have a guest that comes in from Danvers[7] now and then to get supplies from Fritz. You can talk to him at dinner."

Over the course of that afternoon, Zandra bought all the supplies she needed–axes, shovels, hoes, saws, wood planes, hammers, pots, pans, and all the things to set up a home. She returned to the inn later than she had planned. Cormac helped her to unhitch Xavier, and then gave Xavier the rum he had brought out for him.

"The meal should be ready by now," Cormac said once they were done getting Xavier set up. "We should head in."

The air smelled wonderful inside the inn. The incredible aroma of roasted pork filled Zandra's nostrils, accompanied by a warm, appley smell. Plates were flying through the air, and steins of hard cider followed silverware, which clanked as it landed on the table. A knife was floating above the fire, carving slices of meat off the roasted pig. Plates of johnny cakes, still steaming, floated along with bowls of hominy, squash and onions. Then came the pies, all landing on the table without a crumb being dropped.

18

Finnghuala stepped into the room. "Hmm—forgot the coffee." Pulling out her wand, she flicked her wrist. In flouted a pot and cups for all.

Finnghuala walked over to a small gong, lifted the mallet, and struck it. A huge ringing resonated from it so loud that Zandra wondered if the Auris Silentium charm would contain the sound.

The first one down was Gregor.

Finnghuala looked up. "Well, I'm glad to see you put some clothes on. Have you been anywhere or done anything, or have you just laid around soiling my sheets all day?"

"For your information, I've made great progress on my many tasks today. I have to be moving along to Philadelphia soon."

"Won't be soon enough," Finnghuala muttered irritably. "Save some food for the rest of the guests."

Witches and wizards of all kinds came down. One young wizard, dressed in typical Boston attire, with black shoulder-length hair, blue eyes, and looking very uneasy at the gathering, walked up to the table.

Finnghuala gestured to him as he approached. "I have someone that needs your help, Phineas. This is Zandra Voorhies. She's a wandmaker looking to set up shop near you. See what you can do for her, won't you?"

Soon other guests started to come down, until there were about thirty people around the table. Food was passed around, and soon the room was loud and boisterous.

"You seem uncomfortable," Zandra said to Phineas.

"Don't like crowds," he responded nervously.

"I didn't catch your last name."

Phineas looked down at his plate for a moment. "Phineas Osborne," he said in a low voice.

"Well, Phineas, have you lived up in Danvers long?"

"Yes, I—I suppose. All my life."

A tall, slender wizard with piercing eyes, a pale complexion, and curly brown hair interrupted from across the table. "So I hear you're a wandmaker."

"Yes," Zandra said.

"Bazel Blackbone."

"Pleased to meet you," said Zandra.

"I've been away for a few days. Have you been here long?" asked Bazel.

"No, I just came yesterday," she replied.

"Where do you hail from?"

"I'm Dutch," said Zandra, "but I came here from France, with Lafayette on the L'Hermione."

"Did you now?" Bazel looked intrigued. "I'm working covertly with General Washington.[8] Lafayette just brought word that reinforcements had been secured. It was great news for Washington's army."

Zandra frowned. "Don't you mean the continental army?"

Bazel's eyes shifted away. "Yes, of course."

She nodded. "Yeah, I know about that. I was General Lafayette's assistant on the trip over."

Bazel frowned. "The general never mentioned that he had a female assistant."

"He didn't."

Bazel grinned. "Oh, I see now. Pretty clever of you. What did you do with the real assistant?"

"I just put him in a deep sleep and shrunk him down to fit in my trunk, then reversed the spells when we arrived." Zandra paused while she swallowed a bite of pork. "What are you doing hanging around the war?"

"Just making sure that it goes well for the colonies. I have hopes that this might be a place where we might eventually not have to live in the shadows."

"Well, good luck with that," Zandra said skeptically.

Bazel frowned and looked like he was going to say something, but just then the witch seated beside him spilled her cider all down his front.

Turning back to Phineas, Zandra said, "I want to leave for Danvers tomorrow."

He took a bite of pork and chewed it for a while before responding. "I'll...send word tonight." Turning back to his food, he picked at it, not looking at Zandra for a long time.

Zandra watched him. "You're not much of a talker, are you, Phineas?"

He looked around the room, avoiding Zandra's eyes. In fact, he had not really looked at her at all except when she was engaged in conversation with Bazel. "I don't like crowds."

"So you have said."

"How are you traveling?" Phineas asked.

"I have a horse and wagon."

Still looking down at his plate, he said, "Take Ipswich road[9] to Danvers. When you arrive, find the baker, and ask to see Zipporah. Tell her Phineas sent you."

"Thank you. Will I see you there?"

Phineas nodded his head, still not looking at her. "I–yes," he said in a low voice.

What a strange, shy boy, Zandra thought to herself.

By now the guest's bellies were full, and some were getting a little drunk. Zandra was a little light-headed herself and felt it was probably time to turn in for the night.

CHAPTER 3

Ot ne yar heh

April 30 - May 3, 1780

The next morning, Zandra packed her things and headed down the stairs to get some breakfast. A few of the guests were sleeping on the floor.

Finnghuala glanced up at Zandra. "I turned in before they were done. Looks like they had a little too much cider."

Zandra nodded. "I'm glad your Auris Silentium charm keeps the noise from traveling throughout the house when there is such revelry going on."

"That's why I had to get that gong. It was the only thing that I could find that could overcome the charm." Finnghuala gestured at the table. "I have some porridge for you, and some food from last night packed up for you to take with you. I've found the cooling charm works quite well for keeping food from spoiling. It's not a long trip to Danvers, but it'll take you half a day by horse."

"Thank you, Finnghuala, for all your assistance. Cormac, too. You've both been very helpful."

Finnghuala smiled. "You're more than welcome."

Zandra finished her porridge and grabbed her stuff. Finnghuala gave her a hug. "Hope to see you again."

"I'm sure I will be staying here from time to time."

Zandra turned and headed for the stable. Xavier was waiting.

So are we off, then?

"Yes. I met a young man who told me who to contact when we arrive at Danvers. We'll hopefully see him when we get there." Zandra set down her stuff on the stable floor. "Let's get you hitched up."

Good. I'm ready to get out into the country, said Xavier.

Once Zandra had everything loaded onto the wagon, they headed out onto the street.

Looking back at the inn, Zandra saw a bird flying over it, but it suddenly slammed into an unseen something. At first, Zandra was confused, until she remembered that the rooms above the inn weren't visible from the outside. She thought people must wonder why birds were always dying in front of the house.

They rode through Boston until they came upon Ipswich road, then followed it out of town.

As they passed through the countryside, Zandra felt they were being watched. After a couple hours on the road, they stopped at a stream so Xavier could get a drink and rest for a bit. Zandra unhitched him, then pulled out the food that Finnghuala had given her. Xavier finished his drinking and stood under the shade of the tree where she was eating.

Something has been following us, said Xavier. *It's off to our right. I can never get more than a glimpse of it.*

"I thought something was watching us. Is it a man or beast?" Zandra asked.

I don't know, but it's large and walks upright. It's very good at concealing itself. I noticed it a little while after we got out into the woods outside of town. Xavier tossed back his head. *I'm going to go into the meadow and graze for a bit. Maybe I'll be able to get a look at it then.*

"I'll keep my wand close at hand. Alert me if you see anything. We'll leave it alone until it makes a move."

Xavier walked off into the meadow and began to eat. As he did, he rotated his ear to detect where the stranger was.

I'm between you and our shadow. Still haven't gotten a good look at it, but my eyes must have been correct. Its breathing is long and deep. It has to be very large.

"Keep a close eye out."

Suddenly, Zandra had an uneasy feeling come over her, down in her stomach, a sense that something was amiss.

Did you hear that? said Xavier.

"Hear what?"

That low rumble.

"No," said Zandra uneasily.

There! Another one, from far ahead of us. Our shadow is talking to something down the road, said Xavier. *A long way down the road.*

"Are you ready to move along yet?" asked Zandra, unnerved.

Yes. I've had enough for now.

Zandra hitched Xavier back up to the wagon, and they headed up the road. They rolled through the countryside for about a half-hour, over creeks and lakes. Eventually, they stopped for a break.

Our shadow has left us, said Xavier.

"How long ago?" Zandra asked.

A few miles back. But I believe we have picked up another. It's on our left side, and it doesn't seem to be as big. It might be the one that our first shadow was talking to.

Xavier stopped, turning his head and listening. Then Zandra felt it again, that feeling of dread in the pit of her stomach.

Yes, it just rumbled a response back to our first shadow.

Zandra was getting increasingly nervous. "Well, we had better get to our destination before dark. Don't know what these things are up to."

They would have to get through me to get to you, said Xavier.

"We don't know what we're dealing with here. It might be more than we can handle. I'd rather not find out just yet."

Well, I can pick up the pace.

"We should have plenty of time, barring any unforeseen trouble," Zandra said.

So they headed on up the road at the same pace. They pulled into Danvers late in the evening, because they had come upon a bridge that seemed to have been damaged recently. They had had to find a place to cross the river that would not draw too much attention to the fact that Zandra had to use magic to get the wagon across. Eventually, they found the baker's shop, but he had turned in for the night.

"Well, Xavier, what do we do now?"

I don't know. You were supposed to be the one who knew what to do when we got here.

Zandra reached into her pocket and wrapped her fingers around her wand. "Propinquitas," she muttered.

Zandra stood there waiting with Xavier, as people walked by.

A man of middle age stopped. "Can I help you?"

Zandra reached into her pocket and grabbed her wand, but she felt no vibration. She repeated the spell in her head. Nothing.

"Thank you, but no," she replied. "I'm here to meet someone. They should be along any time."

"It's not common for women to travel alone around here, especially not at this hour," he said. "You should have a man with you."

Time to use her cover story. "My husband is off fighting in the war," she said. "I'm coming to stay with some relatives while he is away."

The man looked appeased. "Well, good luck, then." He smiled and strode off down the street.

As she scanned the area, Zandra noticed another woman across the street. Her wand began to vibrate. She nudged Xavier. "Looks like we might have found a friend."

The woman walked up to her. Zandra smiled. "Hello. I'm Zandra Voorhies."

"Zipporah Osborne," replied the woman. "Sorry about this. Don't know what Phineas thinks sometimes. He should have known that the baker would have been in bed by the time you would get here."

"That's okay," Zandra said.

"Well, you can stay with us tonight, and we can take you out to a house that might suit you in the morning."

"Thank you," said Zandra. "Climb on my wagon. This is my friend, Xavier."

Hello, Zipporah, said Xavier.

Zipporah looked at Xavier with a cross look. "That is Miss Osborne to you."

Well, I can see we're going to get along wonderfully, said Xavier.

"Xavier, mind your manners," Zandra said.

Xavier gave Zandra a look that let her know he was not happy, but he started pulling the wagon and said no more.

Zandra turned to Zipporah. "So you're related to Phineas?"

"Yes," Zipporah sighed. "I'm afraid I'm his mother."

"He seems like a nice boy."

Zipporah sniffed disapprovingly. "Oh, he's nice enough. Just seems to ball stuff up a lot."

Zandra left it at that. She didn't know what to say, but she had the feeling that she was not going to like this lady much.

I agree, said Xavier. *She's a bit of a snob.*

"Get out of my thoughts."

"What?" said Zipporah, looking confused.

"Oh, nothing," said Zandra.

She can't hear me when I'm talking only to you, said Xavier. *You need to learn to talk to me without speaking.*

Zandra sighed.

Zipporah spoke up. "Our house is just past the edge of town, on the right."

Once they arrived at the house, Xavier turned up the lane, stopping in front of a small barn. Zandra and Zipporah got down off the wagon.

"I will go in and make sure Safferon has dinner at hand," said Zipporah. "You can leave your wagon here. Find an empty stall for your horse. Feed is in the bin at the far end of the barn. We'll have dinner ready when you're done." Zipporah went into the house.

I'd like to poop on her front porch, said Xavier.

"We have to be nice," said Zandra. "We need her help."

Okay. For now.

"Do you want a stall, or do you want to spend the night in the pasture?"

I'll stay in the pasture. I lost track of our shadows, and I'd like to keep an ear out for them.

"Okay, then." Zandra opened the gate and closed it behind Xavier. "I'll see you before I go to bed. Be careful."

Zandra headed for the house. She knocked on the door and walked in.

"It's going to be a few minutes," said Zipporah. "Have a seat."

A young girl of about twelve was working at the stove. Zipporah introduced her. "Safferon, this is Zandra."

Safferon looked back at Zandra and waved. She set the table and brought the food over.

"It's not much, but it's been a busy day," said Zipporah.

"It'll do fine," replied Zandra.

Just then, Phineas walked in the door.

"Good! Have a seat, food is going on the table. How did you do on your errands?" asked Zipporah.

"Everything went fine," he said nervously.

"Good."

They all sat down to eat. Zipporah looked over at Phineas. "I can't believe you sent Zandra to the baker to contact me. You should have known that he would have turned in for the night before she could get here. What were you thinking?"

Phineas looked down at his food. Turning red, he said in a low voice, "I'm sorry. I should have known better."

Zandra spoke up. "It's okay, everything came out all right. I think the big crowd at the inn was too much for him."

"Most likely it's from being around the Ordies," said Zipporah.

"What does that mean?"

"Ordies is the word we use around here to describe non-witches and -wizards. Comes from 'ordinary.' You see, my great Aunt Sarah was one of the first people accused by the Ordies of witchcraft. She died in prison. All for some girls having fun! We had done nothing to attract their attention. Maybe if their religion wasn't so strict and the girls had a little bit of freedom, the trials wouldn't have happened. Seems to me that the religion of some of these colonists causes a lot of trouble. Magical and non magical people alike suffered because of it."

"I've found plenty of people that are good and kind," said Zandra.

"Very few, in my experience," Zipporah said irritably. "Phineas will take you to the house in the morning. It was owned by an old hag who died recently. We take care of all the land of our people in this area."

"Thank you for the meal. I would like to go out and check on Xavier before I turn in," said Zandra, standing up. "Phineas, would you like to come with me? Maybe we could get to know each other now that there is no crowd."

"Uh, okay, I suppose I could," Phineas said quietly, staring down at the table and looking uncomfortable. He stood up.

Safferon's wand swiped over the table, and all the dishes flew up in the air, landing softly in a tub. A pot of hot water came off the stove and poured over the dishes.

Zandra and Phineas walked out the door to the side yard. Phineas was lagging behind, so Zandra circled around and came up beside him. Grabbing his hand, she said, "Come walk with me. You've never met my horse. He's quite amazing."

She could feel his pulse pounding fast. They walked up to the fence.

Xavier came up to them. *Hello, Zandra.*

"Xavier, this my friend Phineas Osborne."

Hello, Phineas.

Phineas looked startled. "H-hello. How do you do that? How are you in my head?"

I don't know. Just something I can do. Xavier turned to Zandra. *By the way, our shadow is off in the woods over there,* he said, turning his head to look off into the forest behind the house.

"Phineas, do you know what's been following us?" Zandra asked. "It's very elusive, and we think it walks upright. There was more than one of them, and they apparently switched off following us. They seem to communicate with low rumbles that only Xavier can hear, although it gives me a weird feeling whenever they communicate."

Phineas nodded. "It's what the natives call Ot ne yar heh, or as we translate it, Stonish Giant."[1]

"Have you ever seen one? And why are they following us?"

Phineas shrugged. "Can't say why they're following you. They just do that sometimes. I've caught glimpses of them. They're very large, ape-like humans. The Kanohsionni—or, as we call them, the Iroquois—say that the Ot ne yar heh are dangerous and will eat humans. I've never heard of one attacking a person, but a lot of people who are new to this country head off into the woods and are never seen again. We don't know if they were eaten or just keep heading west."

Zandra shivered. "We will have to be careful until we find out more about these beings. Do they have any magical powers?" she asked.

"Don't know for sure. But they seem to be very good at hiding. Some say that they can disappear. I can't say for sure."

---

[1] Commonly known as Sasquatch or Bigfoot.

Zandra let go of Phineas' hand and touched the sides of Xavier's face. "Will you be alright out here?"

They'll be sorry if they come messing around me, said Xavier.

Phineas shook his head. "I wouldn't be so sure if I were you. I've heard of some pretty big things being moved by them—trees broken, boulders moved. They're very strong."

Zandra grabbed Phineas' hand once more. "We had better get back to the house. It's been a long day." She turned back to Xavier. "I'll keep my wand close. Make a lot of noise and I'll come quickly. Good night." They turned and headed for the house.

When they entered, the meal had been all cleaned up and a bed had been made on the floor. Zipporah looked up. "You'll sleep in here tonight, Phineas. I've given Zandra your room for the night."

"I could have slept here, no need to put him out," Zandra said.

"It's fine," said Phineas.

"Well, the sun has set," said Zipporah. "Get some rest. It will be an early morning."

The morning came too soon. Though there hadn't been any trouble in the night, Zandra was still tired.

She woke to the smell of salt pork frying. When she made it out of Phineas's room, everyone was already seated.

She sat down at the table. "Sorry I'm late."

"We just sat down. Phineas just came in from tending to the animals."

"Did Xavier have any trouble last night, Phineas?" said Zandra.

"No."

"Why would there be trouble?" asked Zipporah.

"Zandra had some Stonish Giants follow her yesterday, and one was lurking about in the distance last night," said Phineas.

"Don't like those things," Zipporah said. "You never know what they're up to. Did you get the Integumentum charm back up over the chickens this morning like I asked, Phineas?"

Phineas sighed. "No, I didn't."

"You had better get out there. If I lose a chicken to that hawk again, you will be paying for it." Zipporah shook her head. "Can't trust you to do anything."

Phineas just hung his head and said, "Yes, Mother."

He left the table and headed out the door. Zandra got up, thanked Zipporah for taking care of her, then grabbed her things and headed out to help Phineas. She packed her things into her wagon before following after him. She found him out by the chickens, throwing rocks into the air to test his shield spell.

Zandra walked up to him. "I'm sorry your mother talks to you the way she does," she said softly.

"It's alright," Phineas said in a low voice, not looking at her. A sad look was on his face.

He turned away from the chickens. "Well, we had better get you over to your place. I'm sure it will need some work," he said.

Zandra gave him a hug, then took his hand. They got Xavier out of the pasture and hitched him up to the wagon. Phineas saddled up a horse, and they headed west.

It took about a half hour to reach the home. It wasn't much to look at, but the house was surrounded by a pasture fence. Xavier would be able to have access to the house without raising the suspicion of passers-by. It had a room attached to the back side that could be used as a shop. Zandra had already been thinking that turning spindles for chairs, tables and banisters could be a good cover for her and an extra way to make a living. She could do her wand turnings by hand like she preferred to do, and run the chisels with magic to turn the others when she was busy with other chores, or when she was sleeping. This way she could get a lot done and make the money she needed quickly.

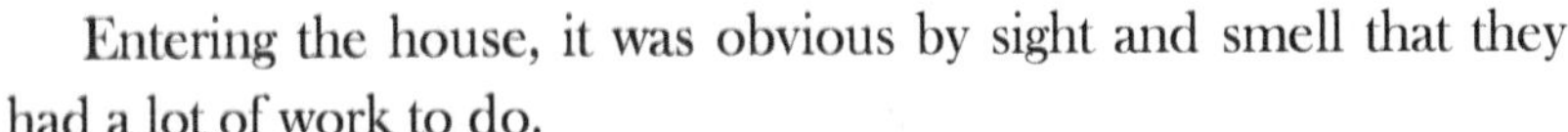

Entering the house, it was obvious by sight and smell that they had a lot of work to do.

"Wow," said Phineas. "Guess we need to do some cleaning. I can help."

Zandra looked up at the ceiling. "Yes, but first we need to get this rock out of here, and we had better fix that hole in the roof."

"It looks like it was thrown," said Phineas.

"Better get Xavier unhitched and watered, then get my tools in here so we can get shingles shaved with magic while I get up on the roof and assess the damage. You can get the rock out of here. Better use Xavier so if anyone passes by it doesn't look suspicious. Don't want the witch trials to start up again."

Zandra got up on the roof and looked it over. When she came back down, she looked in on Phineas.

"Are you alright, Phineas? Need any help?"

"No, I'm doing fine."

"I'm going out into the forest to get some wood to fix the roof. I'll be back in a little bit."

Zandra got her ax and wand and took off across the pasture, headed for the woods. A good distance into the forest, she found some trees that had fallen. She chopped a length of a branch long enough to fix the roof, and bent down to pick it up.

Just then, out of the corner of her eye, she saw it.

A dark figure stood behind a pine tree about one hundred feet away. It was hard to see, but she could tell it was massive. It appeared to be about nine to ten feet tall, and as it moved behind the tree, she got the opinion that it must be close to four feet wide.

Zandra grabbed her wand and stood there gazing intently at the pine, her body trembling slightly, trying to get a better look at it.

Just then, Xavier came crashing through the woods with Phineas on his back. Zandra glanced over at them, then looked back to see the creature, but it was gone.

Phineas hopped down off Xavier. "I wasn't thinking when you said you were heading into the woods. As soon as it hit me that the

Stonish Giants had been following you yesterday, I jumped on Xavier and headed out to find you."

"There was one of them right over by that pine just before you rode up. You seem to have scared it off."

Good thing we came, said Xavier. He walked over to the tree where it had been. Zandra watched as Xavier walked around the back of the trunk.

"Looking at you standing there, Xavier, I'd say it was close to ten feet tall," Zandra said.

You should see these footprints, said Xavier. Zandra and Phineas walked over to him.

"That must be over a foot long," said Phineas. "I wonder if that rock in the house could have been thrown your friend here."

"That's a good possibility," said Zandra. "We'd better get back to the house before it decides to come back."

It took a couple hours to repair the roof, even with the use of magic. Phineas had the house passable by the time Zandra came back down to the ground.

"You'd better be getting home, Phineas," she said. "It'll be getting dark soon."

"Will you be okay here tonight, alone?"

"I think between the two of us, we'll manage." Zandra gave him a hug and walked him out to his horse.

"Thanks for your help today, and for scaring that Stonish Giant away." She gave him a kiss on the cheek.

Phineas blushed. He turned and struggled to get on his horse, then quietly said goodbye.

Zandra waved. "You're welcome here any time."

Phineas didn't look back, but waved as he rode off.

Zandra went back into her new house and started to prepare something to eat. After she got the fire going and all the fixings in the pot, she got the spoon stirring the stew and headed out to see Xavier.

I think we're still being watched, said Xavier.

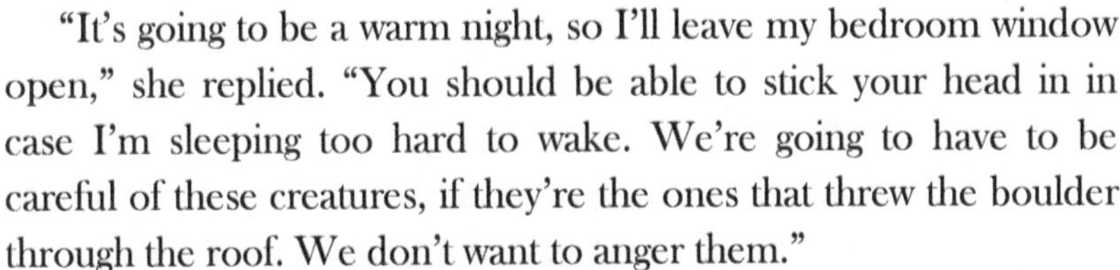

"It's going to be a warm night, so I'll leave my bedroom window open," she replied. "You should be able to stick your head in in case I'm sleeping too hard to wake. We're going to have to be careful of these creatures, if they're the ones that threw the boulder through the roof. We don't want to anger them."

Xavier nodded fervently. *I agree.*

"I think we'll go into Danvers tomorrow and see about getting some chickens, and whatever other supplies I can get there."

They both walked around the property.

"Looks like the former owner had got some crops in before she died." She bent down to examine the plants. "I see corn, squash, cabbage, carrots, and beans. I think we'll do alright once I get the weeds out of here."

The night was uneventful, and they woke the next morning well-rested. Zandra hitched Xavier up to the wagon, and they headed into town. As they passed the Osborne place, Zandra saw nothing of Phineas.

It took a while until she found some chickens that she could buy. On her way back, she picked up some bread from the baker and some nails from the blacksmith. Then they stopped by the sawmill to get some planks for the sheds she needed to build, for workbenches, and to build her lathe.

It was afternoon when she came back by the Osborne house. Zandra pulled up to the barn, and Zipporah came out of the house.

"So how was your first night in your new place?" Zipporah inquired.

"It was fine," Zandra said. "I've been in town to get some things, and thought I would stop by. Is Phineas around?"

"He's around here somewhere." Zipporah waved a hand around vaguely. "I'll be having some people over Saturday for a meeting. If you'd like to come over, it'll give you a chance to meet some of our people, and we'll talk about how you can pay us for your property."

"That would be great."

"Be here about twelve," Zipporah said.

Phineas came around the barn with a basket full of eggs. Seeing Zandra, he smiled shyly.

"Hi, Phineas," said Zandra.

"Hello. Did everything go well last night? Did you have any trouble with the Stonish Giants?"

She shook her head. "No, it was a quiet night."

They seem to have backed away from what I could hear, said Xavier.

Zipporah frowned. "That horse of yours should learn his place."

"He's my friend, and he's allowed to talk just like everyone else," said Zandra.

Zipporah gave her a disapproving look. "I'll have food on Saturday for all." She walked off to the house.

I'm still going to poop on her porch, Xavier said.

"You behave yourself," said Zandra.

Phineas smothered a grin. "Mom can be a bit difficult sometimes."

Zandra smiled. "Phineas, I could use your help. I need to build a shed to keep my lumber in so it can dry. And I need to extend my shop so that I can mill the dried lumber down with magic to the sizes I need for the lathe, without unwanted eyes noticing."

Phineas nodded. "I'm sure I can help with that."

"Today's tasks have taken me longer than I had planned, so it'll be the day after tomorrow before I'll be ready."

"I'll be there as early as I can," Phineas said.

Zandra leaned forward and kissed him on the cheek. "I'll see you then."

Phineas nodded his head as she climbed back on the wagon and headed down the lane.

You know, you really get him in knots when you're around, said Xavier.

"He's not accustomed to someone behaving like that. I think he enjoys it. And he needs to have someone make him feel good about himself," said Zandra.

They headed off down the road to their home. It was coming onto evening when they made it back. Zandra let the chickens loose in front of the coop, unloaded the small things from the wagon, and stored them away. She left the lumber on the wagon—she would unload it after dark with magic.

Heading into the house, she worked on all the cleaning, and began setting things right so she could function more efficiently. Xavier spent most of his time grazing at the far end of the pasture.

Zandra heated some water for a bath, at the same time making more stew for dinner.

After she bathed and had eaten, she headed out to get the lumber unloaded. She called Xavier to hitch him up so she could move the lumber as short of a distance as possible.

As they pulled the wagon up to unload the lumber, Xavier said, *Our shadows are back. It took me a while to locate them, but they're off to the north back in the woods.*

She waved her wand and the lumber started unloading itself. "Great. I had hoped they had just moved on."

She heard a twig snap off to their right.

"What was that?" Zandra asked nervously.

We have another visitor.

"Not another one!"

This one is human.

"Hopefully they didn't see me unloading the lumber."

I'll move closer to see if I can get a glimpse, said Xavier.

Zandra unhitched him, then headed back to the house. After a bit, Xavier came up to the window.

It was a native man. He has moved on for now.

"Well, I hope he didn't see anything."

All we can do is hope.

Midway through the night, Xavier woke Zandra.

Our shadow is back.

A sudden noise came from outside, eerie and guttural. "AHHHHR WAKA WAKA ALALALALAL RRRRRRRRR!"

"It sounds like it's talking."

I believe it is. And it doesn't sound happy, Xavier said darkly.

A sudden thumping and rumbling noise came from the roof.

Zandra jumped out of bed. "Is it throwing rocks at us?"

Xavier ducked out of the way as a particularly large one crashed down next to him. He looked down at it. *Yes, I'd say so.*

Zandra grabbed her wand and ran outside. Pointing it at the sky, she shouted: "Integumentum!"

A green ribbon erupted from the end of her wand, reached into the air, then extended out like an umbrella until it came into contact with the ground outside of her house and barn. Then it disappeared. Rocks hit the now-invisible shield and bounced off.

The voices from the woods became more agitated. "AHHHHHHHRH RRRRRR AHHHHHHHRH RRRRRRRR HUMMM ARHAACH!!!!"

The rocks coming in became larger.

After about an hour, the assault began to wane. Near dawn, Zandra fell asleep. Her charm held all night, and she awoke well after the sun had come up.

Their visitor had given up, for now. She walked around, inspecting the damage. Some of the rocks were pretty large. Xavier had been listening intently for signs of their unwanted visitor, but heard nothing.

He sidled up next to her. *Seems it has left for now. Don't know what it was so mad about.*

"I don't know either, but we'll have to find out," said Zandra. She reversed the shield spell and went in to get something to eat before starting her day.

After breakfast, she started weeding the garden. She did it by hand, as the plants were too small to hide the fact that she was doing magic. She now kept her wand with her at all times, in case their shadow returned.

She finished in the garden, then was beginning to organize her lumber in preparation for Phineas the next day, when Xavier walked up.

Our other visitor from last night is coming out of the woods.

Zandra looked up and saw a young Mohawk man. His head appeared to be shaved, except for a tuft of hair that Zandra could see just barely poking out from under his hat. His cap was made of buckskin and decorated with feathers, with three long quills poking out of the top, far above the others. He wore a shirt and leggings made of broadcloth, and he had a buckskin coat slung over one shoulder.

"Sekoh," the man said, then he gestured with his hand, pointing at one of the piles of lumber she had unloaded last night. Zandra looked at him for a moment with unease. He had seen her use her wand the night before.

The man bent over and picked up a stick. Gesturing again with the stick in his hand, he moved it from right to left.

Zandra pulled her wand out and said, "Transferendum." She pocketed her wand again. "Hello. My name is Zandra."

The man looked surprised that he could understand her. "I'm Broken Arrow. I saw you move the wood without touching it last night."

Zandra nodded warily.

"We have people like you, but I didn't know the white men had them as well." Broken Arrow set down his buckskin coat on the ground. "Why do you live so far away from the town?"

"My kind keep our power hidden," said Zandra. "Most people are afraid of us. They hunt us down and kill us. We're called witches, and the men are wizards."

"The white man is so strange."

"Yes, they can be," Zandra said.

"Why do they kill your kind?" Broken Arrow asked.

"They believe that what we do is dark and evil. They think we should be eliminated."

She sat down on the pile of lumber. "Why are you by yourself?"

He sighed. "My tribe is fighting on the side of the men in the red coats. I don't trust them. I don't trust too many of the white men. I don't think we should be on either side of this war. The white man has done nothing but take from us. We tried to help the white man when they showed up on our shore. We gave them the means to survive. But they threatened us; they destroyed our villages, killed the women and children, if we did not become their slaves. They treated us as if we were less than them. They took our warrior's heads as trophies, scalped our people for profit. It is obvious they cannot be trusted."

Zandra nodded. "That's probably true."

Suddenly, a thought struck her. "Do you know anything about the creature your people call Ot ne yar heh? They have been following me, and last night one yelled and threw stones at my home. What are they mad at me about?"

"You might be encroaching on one's territory. I've seen their structures around your place."

"What type of structures?"

"Trees that have been pulled from the ground roots and all, with the tops stuck in the ground, and the trunks intersecting high in the air. Other big trees balance in the top of the intersection, and there are large saplings bent over in an arch with their tops stuck in the ground. You would do well to appease the Ot ne yar heh. They can be very dangerous."

"And how do I do that?"

"You'll have to find a way to negotiate with them. Just be very careful."

There was a pause as Zandra thought about this. She would have to try. *Maybe they're intelligent,* she thought. *I wonder if the Transferendum spell will work?* She put it in the back of her mind to think about later.

"What is all this wood for?" asked Broken Arrow.

"I'm a wandmaker. Wands are the sticks we use to channel our magic. For them to work, we infuse something from a magical creature inside. Do these Ot ne yar heh have powers?"

"It is said that they can travel to other worlds," said Broken Arrow. "I don't know if that's true, but they do seem to be incredibly good at hiding. In my tribe, we have always been taught to leave them alone."

"That's probably wise, if what I've seen of them is anything to go by," said Zandra.

She stood up. "Come, I'll fix us something to eat."

Leading Broken Arrow to the back of the house, Zandra produced a table and chairs, then brought out the soup she had started earlier that day. They sat at the back of the house to eat.

"Are there other magical creatures here that you know about?" she asked.

"Oh, yes," said Broken Arrow. "There are many across the land."

"You'll have to tell me about them."

He looked thoughtful for a minute. "Let me see...well, there is the Azeban. It's a trickster from below. It harmlessly tricks people and animals out of food, and it looks like a raccoon."

Zandra frowned. "What's a raccoon?"

"It's a medium-sized furry black and gray creature, with a striped tale, and a black masked face."

"You'll have to show me one sometime."

"They're not exactly rare around here," Broken Arrow said. "You'll probably see one very soon."

"So what other magical creatures do you know about?" Zandra asked.

"There is the Baykok," said Broken Arrow, "which lives around the great bodies of water that lie inland. It is a skeleton covered in translucent skin that mainly preys on warriors and sometimes sneaks up to sleeping hunters. There is the Mishipizheu, which is an underwater panther. It has the appearance of a panther, but its body is covered in scales and it has spikes up its back. Then there is the Pukwudgie, which is a small, deep-forest-dwelling being that does not like humans. They can vanish and summon fire. They also use a bow and arrow. Rainbow Crow is a crow-like bird with multi-colored iridescent feathers. It can shoot fire from its beak, and burst into flames of any color at will. There is also the Wendigo, which takes many forms, but they're always very thin and their bones show through their skin. They never fill because they grow equal to their prey."[10]

"Thank you for the information," said Zandra. "I'm sure it'll prove valuable soon."

Broken Arrow nodded. "It's getting late. I need to get back to my camp."

"Are you close by?" Zandra asked.

"Not far."

"Will I see you again?"

"I'm going to stay here for a while, until I sort out what to do about this war. I'm sure you'll see me around." And with that, Broken Arrow walked off into the woods.

Zandra took their dishes back in, pulled out her wand, and got them washing while she went out to check on Xavier.

"I'm going put the shield charm up, so stay between the house and barn." She pulled out her wand and said: "Integumentum!" Once again a green ribbon shot out of the end of her wand, turned into a dome over the property, descended to the ground, and disappeared.

When she got back in, the dishes were done and the water was warm for her bath. It was going to be a warm night, so she picked the lightest nightshirt she had. Xavier stuck his head in the window.

Zandra looked up. "Hopefully we'll have another quiet night. Phineas will be here early in the morning."

We'll see, said Xavier.

Zandra lay down on her bed and drifted off to sleep.

Late in the night, she was awoken by Xavier.

It's back. It has been circling around in the woods for a while now.

Just then a huge rock hit the shield above the house and slid down to the ground.

"AAHHHHHHRH RRRRRRRRR ARRRRCH RRRRRRRRRR!" Smaller rocks followed, with more chatter. Zandra grabbed her wand and headed outside. She and Xavier listened.

The rock throwing slowed after a little while. "ARRRRRRCH ARRRRRRRRCH RRRRRR!"

Then the rocks started flying again.

There, to the right of the barn, said Xavier.

Raising her arm, Zandra shouted: "Eum Lux de Caelo!" A ball of white light shot out of the end of her wand and hovered over the forest above where the rocks were coming from. A massive form was just inside the tree line. Zandra could see the creature's face scrunch up and its dark eyes blink as it turned and moved deeper into the woods.

"It was white!" she said, surprised.

Haven't seen that one before, said Xavier.

"Great. We must be dealing with more than one of them."

Zandra reversed the spell, and the ball of white light flew back into her wand.

Near dawn, it was back. But this time it just walked around in the forest and yelled toward the house, keeping Zandra and Xavier up. Just as the sun broke, Zandra fell back asleep.

Phineas showed up at around eight o'clock. Running into the shield charm, he fell onto the ground rubbing his nose, and then slowly stood up. "Zandra! Zandra!"

Xavier stuck his head in and nudged Zandra in the butt. Bleary eyed, she looked up at Xavier. "What?"

Phineas is out front waiting.

Zandra got up slowly and stumbled to the door. Walking out into the yard, she dropped the shield. "Come in. Sorry I'm running late; an unwanted guest kept us up late last night."

Phineas moved toward her slowly, trying not to look at her. She grabbed his hand and pulled him close, putting her arm around him. Once inside, he sat at the table while she made something to eat.

"Would you like some tea?" she asked.

"Sure," he said in a low voice.

A cup floated over to the table, then the teapot floated over and poured steaming water into it.

Zandra sat down with her food. "Phineas, you're looking at me even less than you usually do. What's the matter?"

"You haven't got your clothes on."

"Haven't you ever seen a woman in her nightshirt before?"

"My mom and sister."

Zandra smiled. "I'll get something more on after I've had something to eat. I have an idea on how I may be able to get these Stonish Giants to leave us alone. Do you think you could stay the night to help me?"

"I'd have to send word home."

Zandra gave Phineas some paper, and he wrote a note. Taking out his wand, he tapped the letter.

"Missito," he muttered. The paper folded itself into the shape of a bird and flew out the window.

Zandra stood up. "Could you clean up here, please? I'll go get some clothes on so we can get started."

With a little magical help, they had the shed for the wood storage built by mid-afternoon. After a while, they stopped to have a bite to eat.

"So what's your plan to take care of your night guest?" Phineas asked.

"I thought I'd do things as usual, then when the trouble starts, I'll creep out under the Integumentum charm, put an Auris Silentium charm around each of us, and sneak up on it."

"And do what?"

"I'll put a Resisto spell on it, which will hopefully restrain it. Then we'll cast a Transferendum charm, and see what happens."

"Okay," said Phineas, "but what if that doesn't work?"

Zandra smiled. "That's why you're here. It might take two of us to immobilize it."

Phineas looked startled. "You want me to go out there with you?"

"Yes."

He shook his head disbelievingly. "I don't know that it won't take more than the two of us. Those things are big."

"Well, we'll find out, won't we?"

44

They quit working by late afternoon. Zandra prepared something to eat, while Phineas cleaned up. By the time they had finished eating, it was getting dark. Zandra went outside to set the charm, and Phineas followed.

Xavier came up to the house. Zandra put a hand on his back. "Tonight, when and if we start to have trouble, we need you to locate where the beast is. When you find out, let us know. We'll sneak out so it can't see us. You'll have to keep its attention; we don't know if it can defeat our magic and detect us."

Do you think you have a chance? Xavier asked.

"I think so," said Zandra.

Be careful tonight.

"I'll be fine." Zandra pulled out her wand. "Integumentum!"

The green ribbon came from the end of her wand, and the umbrella descended over the buildings. Zandra and Phineas headed into the house.

"Do you have a blanket I can have to throw on the floor?" Phineas asked.

"No, I don't have any extra. You will have to sleep with me."

Phineas looked nervous. "N-no, I can't."

"It's alright."

They both climbed into bed. They didn't bother changing into nightclothes, because they'd be up soon enough. Zandra cuddled up beside Phineas, and she fell asleep.

Phineas woke Zandra late in the night. He had hardly slept. Between his fear of what was to come, and lying there beside Zandra, he just couldn't.

45

But he had missed his chance for any sleep now. Xavier was at the window.

CHAPTER 4

First Contact

May 3 - 4, 1780

"ARHOOO!"

"OOOOOOOOOOOOOOOOOOOOO!"

The sounds split Zandra's ears, sent shivers down her spine. Xavier reared up and let out a loud snort.

Phineas jumped. "GREAT WARLOCKS! What was that? I've never heard anything so loud!"

"Our unwanted guest is very angry," Zandra said.

Phineas looked terrified. "No doubt. Just what we need; this was already going to be hard."

"It might work to our advantage. The anger might blind it to our movements."

"Hope you're right," said Phineas.

"Xavier, where is it?" Zandra asked.

It's at the edge of the forest, behind your new shed.

"Good! We'll be able to get out the front door without it seeing us." She jumped out of bed. "Xavier, start getting its attention. We're heading out."

Phineas got out of bed, too. "Are you sure you want to do this, Zandra? This might not go well."

Zandra took his hand. "It will be fine. Just trust me." She gave him a peck on the cheek. "Just for luck," she said.

She strode to the bedroom door. “When we find it, we’ll split up and come at it from two sides. I’ll immobilize it, and you stand by in case my spell is not strong enough to hold it.”

They headed out the door, pulling out their wands. “Auris Silentium,” they both said simultaneously. They walked silently across the yard.

Pointing her wand at the ground near the bottom of the shield, Zandra said: “Subterraneis!”

A tunnel opened up that went under the shield. They slipped into it, came out on the other side, and headed into the woods in front of the house, the tunnel filling back in as they walked away. Weaving their way through the woods, they finally came up behind the Stonish Giant.

Zandra peered through the trees. “It’s the white one from the other night,” she whispered to Phineas. “He’s not as large as the dark one I saw the day I was getting wood for the roof.” She gestured off to the left. “You head off that way. When we get within twenty feet of it, I’ll do the Resisto spell. Be ready to join in.”

Phineas took a deep breath, readying himself.

Zandra grabbed his hand and pulled him tightly against her. “It’s going to be alright.”

They parted and slowly moved to each side of the Stonish Giant. Xavier was pacing around, snorting and stomping. The creature was throwing rocks at him, but they were bouncing off the shield. It was yelling angrily in whatever its language was.

Suddenly, Zandra heard a crashing sound. Whirling, she saw that Phineas had tripped and hit a dead tree, toppling it over. Since the Auris Silentium charm only covered his immediate vicinity, when the tree came down, it made a loud crash of broken branches.

The Stonish Giant turned and saw Phineas. It started to charge at him, but Zandra quickly yelled: “Resisto!”

The Stonish Giant slowed as the restraining spell tried to take effect. Its arms were being pulled down to its side. But it wasn’t enough.

Struggling to get to his feet, Phineas shouted: "RESISTO!"

The Stonish Giant slowly came to a stop, arms falling to its side. Zandra flicked her wand. "SUSTRINGO!"

A large rope shot out of the end of her wand with a glowing red halo around it. Quickly, it wrapped around the Stonish Giant, breaking off from the tip of her wand as it bound the beast's limbs. As the creature struggled, the halo around the rope turned orange with the strain.

Just as the air cleared, there came a huge crash from Phineas' direction. Trees were splintering and falling as a massive Stonish Giant burst through the brush. Zandra turned to the house, reversed the shield charm over the house and barn, and Xavier came charging into the forest toward the new arrival. Rearing up and kicking at it, Xavier held it back long enough to give Phineas a chance to realize what was happening.

"PULSO!" he yelled, but the knock-out spell wasn't powerful enough.

It staggered, then Zandra shouted as well. "PULSO!"

The Stonish Giant wavered, and after what seemed like forever, it fell over. Zandra murmured "Sustringo," and another rope with a red halo wrapped around it. She turned back to the white one.

The beast growled at her. "Bak tuh hoon doh wook RRRRRRR."

She flicked her wand. "Transferendum." The translation spell took effect.

In a very deep voice, the white creature spoke. "Let me go."

"After I've had a word with you," she replied.

The Stonish Giant looked bewildered that it could understand her.

"Why are you harassing us? We've done nothing to you," said Zandra.

"You're invading our territory."

"I'm sorry. I had no idea."

The pale beast looked defiant. "We're not going to take your intrusions."

Zandra thought for a few moments. The ropes were turning a brighter orange with the struggles of the Stonish Giant. Apparently even two immobilization charms weren't quite enough. She would have to hurry. Phineas was standing over the larger one, while Xavier was in between, watching over both.

"What is your name?" Zandra asked.

"Shakock," the beast rumbled.

"Well, Shakock, what if I made it so that you had an area that no human could go in? If I did that, would you leave me alone? All I want is to be able to get some wood out of the forest from time to time. I would also like some of your hairs, if you could, when you shed them. I want to see if they're useful in my work. Other than that, I will leave you alone and so will everyone else."

Shakock thought for a while, continuously struggling against the bonds. Finally giving up on trying to get free, he spoke again. "You can do this?"

"Yes, but you will have to walk me out into the middle of your territory. I can't get back land you have already lost, but I can save what is left."

"Okay." He looked resigned.

"We will leave your friend here, and let you go. Then you can lead us to the center of your territory."

I don't think this is a good idea, Xavier said to Zandra only. *We don't know if we can trust him yet. And we don't know how many more there might be.*

We'll have to trust him, she said in her mind. *Anyway, we still have his friend.*

Very good! You're getting better at not using your mouth to talk to me.

Zandra pointed her wand at the stack of broken branches. "Asser," she muttered. Six large branches flew into the air and drove into the ground beside the other Stonish Giant. "Sustringo!"

A rope shot out of her wand once again, twirling around the Stonish Giant and the stakes.

Zandra gave Phineas a look. He pointed his wand at Shakock, and so did Zandra.

"Aversa pars!" she said.

The ropes flew off of Shakock, and he began to move. "Follow me," he said.

Zandra and Phineas mounted Xavier and followed. After about forty-five minutes, Shakock stopped.

"This is the center of our territory," he rumbled.

Zandra and Phineas hopped off Xavier. "Help me with this, Phineas," said Zandra.

They both pointed their wands in the air. "Invius!" they said in unison. A translucent blue light shot out of their wands. As it rose into the air, it became clear. They could just see a distortion, like a mirage, that engulfed the woods.

Looking back at Shakock, Zandra said, "It's done."

Shakock grunted, then turned back towards Zandra's house.

When they got back, Shakock's friend was still asleep on the ground.

"We'll wake him and let you tell your friend of our deal. And you'd better be quick. I don't know how long our magic will hold him," Zandra said, pointing her wand at Shakock's friend. "Excito!"

Immediately, the beast started thrashing and making a roar like they had never heard before. The ropes turned bright orange as it struggled to free itself. They progressed onward to yellow, even almost white with the strain put on them by the Stonish Giant.

Shakock placed his hand on his friend's shoulder. "Stop your struggles," he rumbled. "I'm fine. I've come to an agreement with these beings."

The struggling Stonish Giant turned to look at Shakock.

"I'm your leader; you will obey me," said Shakock. "And I say we will go in peace from here and not bother them again."

The Stonish Giant's look of anger persisted, but he stopped his struggles. Zandra and Phineas were standing at the ready, unsure that their magic could contain it if it started thrashing again.

"You can let him go now," Shakock said.

They let one rope go, then the next. Finally, Shakock's friend was free.

"This is Nook," said Shakock.

Nook stood up slowly. It seemed he was going to top the trees. His girth was unreal, with muscles like they had never seen. He gave them a look that sent shivers down Zandra's spine, then slowly turned and walked into the woods. Shakock followed.

Zandra turned to Phineas and threw her arms around him. She was shaking slightly. "They're so big! I didn't know if we could hold them. I can't believe you thought to use the Pulso charm on Nook. That was quick thinking."

Phineas looked solemn. "I'm sorry I fell. We could have been killed."

"But we weren't." She turned. "Xavier, you were amazing! Thanks for saving us. You were so brave." Zandra walked over and stroked his muzzle. She pressed the side of her face against his.

Well, it's been a night, he said. *We should get some sleep.*

As they passed the place where Nook had been lying, Zandra held up her wand. "Lumino!"

Nook had lost some hairs! She bent down and gathered them up. They were about eight inches long and dark brown. She examined them and put them in her pocket. Then she walked over to where Shakock had been restrained. After just a few minutes, she had recovered a few hairs. They were only five inches long, but they were pure white. The moonlight reflected off them, making them look silvery and beautiful.

When they got back to the house, they both collapsed in bed. Zandra cuddled up against Phineas again. This time he fell asleep almost instantly.

CHAPTER 5

Council of the Salem Witches

May 6 - 15, 1780

The skunk lay there, convulsing on the ground. If Zandra had not stumbled upon it, it would have died alone, and no one would have known. It didn't even know what was going on around it. To have made it through the long, hard winter, and yet to die on the first nice day of spring seemed so unfair.

Zandra was so stunned at what she was seeing that she didn't act in time to put a comforting charm on the poor creature. It faded away quickly. There was nothing she could do but just be there so it didn't have to die alone. It sickened her. She couldn't stand death. It hurt too much to see something leave the world behind. Life was too precious; no creature should have had to go that way. She wished there was something she could do, but not even magic could bring something back from the dead. She so wished it could.

She made herself a promise that she would never kill anything to get infusion materials for her wands, not even if she couldn't get it any other way. She didn't want to take a life for something as trivial as that.

Gasping, Zandra sat up in bed. She tried to calm her breathing. *It happened a long time ago,* she told herself. *There was nothing I could have done about it then, and there certainly isn't now.*

Getting up out of bed, she walked over to the window and gazed out at the starlit pasture. It had been a long time since she'd had that dream, but it still troubled her as much as it had when the real events had occurred.

But the one thing the dream did was remind her of her resolve to never kill. She could easily kill for her wand infusion materials, as many wandmakers did, but she would never be like them.

Eventually, she went back to sleep, hoping the nightmare would not resurface.

By the next afternoon, Zandra and Phineas had finished the extension onto the shop, and Phineas had returned home.

Zandra spent the next day building her lathe so she could start turning wands and other parts to sell to furniture and cabinet makers. The nights had been uneventful; the Stonish Giants had left her alone.

Tomorrow was Saturday. She would be heading to Zipporah's to take part in the Salem Witches' monthly meeting.

On Saturday morning, Zandra saddled Xavier and headed to Zipporah's. She got there early so she could spend some time with Phineas, letting Xavier loose in the pasture.

People started to show up around noon. As soon as they were all in the house, Zipporah pulled out her wand. "Auris Silentium."

Zandra was surprised. Cormac had invented that spell. "You know Cormac O'Malley?" she asked Zipporah.

Zipporah gave her a look. "Of course I know him. Everyone stays at the O'Malley Inn when in Boston."

There was plenty of food for everyone. Before the meal, Zipporah introduced everyone to Zandra.

"This is our newest resident witch, Zandra Voorhies. She is a wandmaker, and has trained with the masters of Europe."

Pointing at a young man and woman across from Zandra, Zipporah moved around the table.

"Zandra, this is Zadoc and Esther Gloyce. Zadoc's grandmother, Sarah, was accused of witchcraft, but never convicted." She gestured toward an older couple. "Azariah and Dorcas Jones. Dorcas' great uncle John Willard was hanged." She pointed at a middle-aged couple to Zandra's right. "Jasper and Susanna Livingston. Susanna's grandfather George Burroughs was a reverend in the Ordies' church. He was killed." Zipporah gestured toward a couple to Zandra's left, who looked to be in their late sixties. "Theophilus and Phoebe Martin. Theophilus' great aunt Susannah Martin was killed in the trials also." She pointed at the couple next to the Martins. "Kenelm and Aphra Adair. Aphra's grandfather, Giles Cory, would never plead guilty or not guilty, so he was pressed to death." She came to the end of the table. "And, lastly, Duncan and Amity Cowgill. Amity's grandparents were both accused of witchcraft. Her grandfather, John, was killed. Elizabeth Proctor, her grandmother, was pregnant, so her execution was held off and she was pardoned later." Zipporah sat down at the head of the table. "And, of course, Sarah Osborne, my great aunt, was one of the first to die in the trials.[11] All of us here today are surviving families of the witch trials. So now you know a bit about us, let's have our meal, then we will start our meeting."

They began to eat.

"So, Zandra, are you getting set up at your new place?" asked Phoebe Martin.

Zandra nodded. "I've got the house in order, my shop set up, and I just finished my lathe yesterday. I'm ready to start my work."

Kenelm Adair spoke up. "I hear you had a talk with the Stonish Giants the other night."

"Yes, it was quite an adventure. If it hadn't been for Phineas and Xavier, I don't know if I would have made it through. Phineas was so quick with his Pulso charm, he saved both of us."

Zipporah made a disbelieving smirk.

Zandra gave her a look, but Zipporah didn't notice. "I also talked to a Mohawk man, Broken Arrow. He told me of some of the magical creatures that I might be able to use for my wands. I'd be interested to find out if any of you know of any."

"I'll have to come over and talk to you sometime. I know of one you might be interested in," said Theophilus.

When they had finished their food, they started the meeting, covering the same mundane stuff that was usually handled in this type of organization: how they covered up old Odphior's flying pig, what should be done with Epbaris's spring at the back of her house that was now bubbling up rum, drawing the attention of the Ordies.

Once this had all been covered, Zipporah spoke up. "The old hag Dyhione had no heirs, so what are we going to do about Zandra taking over the property? And should we defer payment till she gets on her feet?"

Susanna spoke first. "I think there's no reason we couldn't wait for payment on the property until Zandra is on her feet. We're in no need of money at this time."

"As long as Zandra takes care of the place, I have no problem with it," Jasper interjected.

"I think she should give us a deposit," said Zipporah.

"Let's take a vote," said Phoebe. "All in favor of letting Zandra pay us when she is on her feet, say yea."

Everyone said yea except Zipporah.

"Well, I guess that does it," said Zipporah irritably. "Next month's meeting will be at the Cowgill's home."

They all got up from the table, and the witches all helped clean up from the meal. Then they all walked out on the front porch and talked for a bit.

Zipporah went to step off the side of the porch, but slipped and fell, landing in a pile of horse manure. Phineas stifled a laugh.

Zipporah got up, looking irate. "Whose horse pooped on my porch?"

Everyone started laughing except Zandra. She, of course, knew which horse had done it, and she suspected Zipporah did too. Phineas went to get a shovel and Zandra got a pail of water to clean up the mess.

Once they were done, Theophilus walked up to Zandra. “Would it be alright if I stopped by tomorrow to talk with you?”

“That would be fine,” said Zandra.

“I’ll be there sometime in the afternoon,” said Theophilus.

It was getting late, and everyone had to get going. Zandra and Phineas walked out to the pasture to talk to Xavier. They found him at the far end trying to reach the grass on the other side of the fence.

Zandra walked up to him. “Xavier, I told you not to poop on Zipporah’s porch.”

She had it coming, he said stubbornly.

“I don’t care! You can’t do things like that; it isn’t good to make enemies. Especially when we know so few in the community.”

Xavier ignored her. *So where is this spring that’s bubbling up rum?*

Zandra stomped off across the pasture.

Phineas followed. “It’ll be okay. I found it pretty funny. You need to lighten up a little on Xavier,” he said.

Zandra said nothing. They stood there in silence for a moment.

“Okay, I admit it,” she finally said. “It was pretty funny.”

Xavier came to the door of Zandra’s workshop the next afternoon to let her know Theophilus was there. Having just finished a wand, Zandra came around front.

“Making wands already?” asked Theophilus.

Zandra nodded. “My first one off my new lathe. Hickory, twelve and a half inches, with hair from one of the Stonish Giants. I found some of their hairs after our encounter the other night. I decided I was going to give it a try.”

Pointing it at a rock, she said: "Atollo!" The rock rose off the ground.

"Well, it seems to have worked," said Theophilus.

"Yes," Zandra smiled proudly.

"Can I see it?" asked Theophilus.

Zandra handed him the wand.

He examined it. "Very nice work. Well balanced and elegant."

"Thank you." She smiled. "Let's go to the porch; we can talk in the shade. Can I get you something to drink?"

"Do you have any coffee?"

"Yes," she replied.

After a few minutes, she came back out onto the porch carrying a pot and some cups.

"So you said you knew of a creature that I might be able to get some wand infusion materials from?" she inquired.

"Yes," said Theophilus. "I have relatives in Philadelphia, so I have to travel there from time to time. They tell of a creature that prowls the Pinelands[1] of New Jersey. They call it the Leeds Devil. They say it has the body of a horse, but it walks on two legs. Its arms are short, with sharp claws. It has the head of a goat, with deer horns, wings like a bat, and a forked tail."

Zandra was intrigued. "Is this an indigenous magical creature?"

"Well, the story the Ordies tell is that when Mother Leeds[12] found out she was having her thirteenth child, she cursed it, saying it would be a devil child. And when it was born, that was what she got."

Zandra nodded. "And what's the real story?"

"Well, it seems that the Leeds family were living with the Quakers, pretending to be one of them. Old man Leeds got tired of masquerading. He was an astrologer and was using the stars to predict events. Then he started publishing some of his work and was ostracized from the Quaker community. Since he was free from his charade, he started doing more with his magic. He

---

[1] Known as the Pine Barrens in modern times.

decided at one point that he wanted to breed a new magical creature. That is what is known as the Leeds Devil."

"How far is the Pinelands from here?" Zandra asked.

"By broom, eight hours. It's an eleven day trip by horse."

"Well, that *is* a long way away," said Zandra. "I think I'll have to wait for a while to do that kind of a trip."

"You'd better be careful," Theophilus said warningly. "No telling what kind of magic you might run into. We've known of a few wizards who have headed out to investigate this land and have never returned."

"Thank you for your concern," she said. "I'll be careful."

"I'd better be moving along," said Theophilus, getting up and stepping down off the porch. "We're still having problems with Odphior."

Zandra grinned. "More flying pigs?"

He nodded. "Don't know what we're going to do with him," he said.

"Well, thank you for the information," Zandra said. "Stop by any time."

Theophilus got on his horse and rode off.

Over the following days, Zandra kept herself busy with chores and wandmaking, and Phineas would stop by from time to time. She was doing as she had planned–wands during the day, things for furniture at night with magic. She had found furniture makers in the neighboring towns to sell her turnings to.

One day Xavier disappeared. Zandra called for him, but he never came. She gave up and went back to her work, figuring he would return soon enough. Toward evening, she was sitting on the porch eating her meal when Xavier stumbled through the pasture gate. Setting her food down, she walked out to talk to him.

"Where have you been?" she said sternly.

His words were slurred. *Just been out for a walk.*

She could smell the rum on his breath. "You've been drinking from Epbaris' spring!"

She's a nice lady, said Xavier. *We talked for quite a while. She let me have as much as I wanted to drink.*

"Yes, I can tell. You should at least have let me know that you were leaving."

Xavier stumbled and finally decided to just lay down. Zandra left him there to sleep off the rum.

Xavier woke the next day not feeling too well. Zandra left him alone with his hangover.

About midday, Broken Arrow came up to the house. "Sekoh," he said.

Zandra smiled and pulled out her wand. "Transferendum," she said. "It's been a while. I was wondering when I was going to see you again."

"I've brought you whiskers of the Azeban," Broken Arrow replied. "He's been stealing my food, so one night I set a trap. I placed food very near to me and pretended to go to sleep. When the Azeban came near, I reached out and pulled the whiskers from his face. He yelped and ran off into the woods. He hasn't been back since."

Zandra grinned. "Thank you. I'm needing more wand materials. I'll see what I can do with this."

She went into the house and placed the whiskers in a bowl. Returning to the porch, she told Broken Arrow of her encounter with the Stonish Giants and all the progress she had made setting up her shop.

"I was wondering if you'd be willing to help me track down some of those magical creatures that you've told me of," she said.

"I suppose I could," he replied. "I've decided that I will not fight with my people for the Redcoats any longer." His eyes drifted down to his feet. "I've heard that the white man's sickness is still killing the Arikara.[13] I don't know if they intentionally gave it to them this time, but I know that the white man has done that in the past."

"They've intentionally spread sickness to your people before?"

"Yes," said Broken Arrow. "They give us blankets and clothes of people that have had the sickness."

"What are the symptoms of the white man's disease?" Zandra asked.

"The sick become hot and they vomit. A rash breaks out on their skin, and the rash becomes pockets of fluid. Those that don't die sometimes become blind. It has killed many of us."

"Smallpox," said Zandra. She thought for a moment. She had a load of spindles turned, she would have more than enough to pay for a broom. If she could get back to Fritz's shop and get some potion supplies, she might be able to save some of the Arikara.

"Xavier," she said, "we leave for Boston tomorrow."

"What are you thinking of doing?" asked Broken Arrow.

"I'm going to help the Arikara."

"You can do that?" he asked.

"I can't cure them, but I may be able to help strengthen their immunity to it."

Zandra went into the house and got some paper, a quill, and some ink. Coming back out onto the porch, she wrote a letter to Finnghuala, telling her she would be there the following evening. Tapping the paper with her wand, she said, "Missito." The letter folded itself and flew off toward Boston.

"When I get back," Zandra said to Broken Arrow, "I'll send you one of those. It will find you wherever you are. I know you can't read our language, but when it comes to you, you'll know that I'm back and ready for your help."

Broken Arrow said good-bye and departed. Zandra climbed onto Xavier and headed off to the Osbornes' to see if they could watch over things while she was away. Phineas was not happy with her plans to head west. He felt that it was a dangerous idea, but said little to change her mind. They agreed to watch over her place while she was away.

The next day, Zandra was off for Boston. Finding a carpenter that built houses for the wealthy of Boston, she sold her spindles. She then went to Fritz's. He bought her new wands, as the last batch had proven to be well-liked by his customers. Then she bought the best broom she could find, and all the potion supplies she would need, and headed to the inn. She took Xavier to the stable, where some rum had been left for him. Walking up to the back door of the inn, she knocked and entered.

Finnghuala was preparing the evening meal. She turned to see Zandra enter. Wiping her hands on her apron, she said, "Zandra! How ye be?"

"Good, Finnghuala. How about you?"

"Fine, fine. What brings you back so soon?"

Zandra told Finnghuala of her plan to help the Arikara. And, of course, Finnghuala told her it seemed like a dangerous plan. But Zandra wasn't swayed.

Cormac soon came with a new arrival. Dinner was served, and she told of her encounter with the Stonish Giants, and of meeting Broken Arrow.

The next morning, she woke early and headed back to Danvers to get ready to leave.

CHAPTER 6

The Journey

May 10 - 29, 1780

"I'll be fine!"

"We don't know much about what is out there," said Phineas. "I wish you weren't going alone."

"I'm not going out looking for trouble, I'm just going to help those people, possibly save some lives," said Zandra.

Phineas sighed. "I know."

"Take care of Xavier. Please keep him away from Epbaris's spring."

Xavier snorted. Zandra walked over to him. She rubbed his snout. "You take care of yourself, big guy."

She had her warm cloak on; she would be flying at night as high as possible to avoid unwanted eyes seeing her. Placing all her supplies in her flight bag, she threw it over her shoulder.

She swung her leg over her broom. "I'll be back in a fortnight or so. I'll write when I can."

Zandra gave Phineas a big hug and a kiss on the cheek. Setting the wand on the palm of her hand, she said: "Ad Designandum Arikara." The wand spun and stopped, pointing almost straight west.

Pocketing her wand, she kicked off into the night.

Zandra flew higher and higher, over the trees, hills, and rivers. The wind made her eyes water. She stopped and hovered every so often to pull out her wand.

"Lumino." The tip of her wand would light up, then she would say: "Ad-Designandum Arikara!" Getting her bearings, she would head off again.

Just before dawn, Zandra landed on the east bank of a huge lake.[I] Casting an Invius charm so no one would be able to stumble upon her camp, she pulled a tent out of her flight bag, set it up, and started a fire to heat up some food.

The mosquitoes were bad. She put up a repellent charm to keep them away. Sitting there by the fire, she watched the sun rise as the lake became illuminated.

At sunset that evening, she broke camp and headed off for another night's flight. Flying over the lake, she noticed steam rising from a ripple in the water. Something was gliding along the surface. Zandra dropped down to get a better look.

It was a large reptilian creature, of a dragon-like form. The creature looked up at her.

She climbed rapidly. There was no time to get entangled with it now.

Zandra was surprised at the size of the lake. It seemed like it took forever to cross.

It was close to dawn again when she came to the shore of another massive lake.[II]

The following night would find her on the eastern shores of yet another giant lake.[III] When she broke camp, she noticed thunderheads in the sunset. Not thinking much about it, she waited until dark and departed.

The lightning was increasing as she neared the west shore of the lake. Zandra decided to turn south to try and dodge the storm.

[I] Lake Ontario
[II] Lake Huron
[III] Lake Michigan

However, the squall line raced toward her, and she soon found herself climbing higher and higher to try to get above the storm. The lightning was making it hard for her to see and the rain was getting heavy. The wind was so strong that she was having a hard time keeping her broom under control. Hail was pounding her as she tried to climb even higher. Soon she was getting light headed, as the air was getting too thin. Pulling her wand out, almost dropping it, as she was soaked and freezing, she yelled: "Aer Bulla!"

A bubble of air enveloped around her head so she could breathe. The winds were now so strong that all she could do was ride them. She was going faster than she ever had, and was at the wind's mercy as to where she ended up. She soared on the winds for what seemed like forever.

When dawn finally broke, she was still in the air.

Beneath her, she saw an amazing site. Mounds of earth of differing shapes spread over the land. Just to the west was a great river. She decided that she had better land, as it would be very easy for someone to see her.

She touched down in a clump of trees about a half mile from the biggest of the mounds. Starting a fire to dry her clothing, she heard rustling in the brush. She spun around just in time to see a man raising a rifle. Pointing her wand at the man, she shouted: "Pulso!"

The man fell to the ground. Walking up to him, she could smell liquor. The man was dirty and unkempt. Thinking for a moment, she remembered noticing what seemed to be a trading post near the large mound. It would be nice to see what the post might have that would be of use to her.

She pointed her wand at herself. "Transverto."

Once she had transformed into the man, she cast another spell to replicate his clothes. She was not going to wear his filthy ones to go to the trading post.

Looking the man over, she saw a jug in his hand. She picked it up and pulled the cork off. It was the alcohol he had been drinking. Zandra splashed some on herself and headed for the post.

As she got close to the mound, she was astonished at the size of it. She walked up the south side. If this was built without magic, it must have taken forever. Obviously, there had been a civilization here in the past.

She spent a little while there, on top of the mound, just thinking of what must have been. Walking back down, she headed for the trading post. It was a small, one-room shack. She entered. The room was very dark; only one small window illuminated the interior. A stack of animal furs were piled in the corner, and the rest of the room was sparsely populated with goods.

"Claude! Finished your bottle already?" came a voice from behind the counter.

That must be the man's name, Zandra thought. "No, I just needed to get...." She paused as she looked around the room. "I just wanted some jerky. I forgot to get some yesterday."

"Well, go ahead, get yourself some."

Zandra (or Claude, depending on how you looked at it), pulled four sticks out of the tray.

Putting some money on the counter, she asked, "What is the name of that river over there, the big one?"

"How much have you had to drink this morning, Claude? You know that's the Mississippi. You'd better lay off the bottle!"

"Yeah, I suppose I should. Well, thanks." She turned and walked out the door.

Returning to the real Claude, she pointed her wand at him and said, "Atollo." As Claude's unconscious body floated behind her, she headed off into the woods. When she had traveled far enough away from her camp, she lowered him to the ground, then hid in the trees.

"Aversa pars," she muttered, transforming back into herself. Pointing her wand at Claude from behind the trees, she said: "Excito."

Claude woke, scratching his head with a look on his face that seemed to say: *Well, it's happened again.* "Got to lay off the bottle," he muttered to himself.

He stood up and walked off.

The next day, Zandra woke before sunset and prepared herself for another night's flight. Pulling out her wand to get her bearings, she could tell that she had been blown way south of her planned course.

Just after nightfall, she took off and headed northwest.

She was just passing over the bluffs along the Mississippi River when her broom gave a jerk. Looking back, she saw a large, dark creature flying up behind her. It had taken a bite at her, just getting a few bristles off her broom.

She accelerated, but the beast was keeping up with her. Pulling her wand out, she threw spells at the beast while doing some barrel rolls to avoid it, but the spells were not working. Quickly pulling her broom handle up, she climbed straight up till the broom stalled out. Doing a hammerhead maneuver, she headed right back down at the creature, throwing hexes and spells at it.

The beast shot flames, which whizzed past her with a crackle. *Must be a dragon,* she thought, but as she passed it, one of her spells landed close to the creature's face, and with a jolt of surprise, she realized that its face was human. Except, it wasn't quite–it had large fangs protruding from its lower jaw, and what looked like deer antlers on its head.

As it rushed past, its long tail slashed at her. The very tip had a fishtail that hit her in the face. She found she could dive faster than the creature and turn sharper, so she decided to do a Cuban Eight. Her hope was that she could catch it in the middle and get off a good spell. She headed into the first loop of the sideways figure eight, and the creature was right on top of her. When she came out of the second loop the creature was directly in front of her.

"CONCUSSIONE!"

The spell shot out of the end of her wand and exploded near the creature's head. Zandra dived past in a flash. A shard from somewhere on the creature hit her in the chest, and she turned to see the beast falling toward the river.

The creature righted itself just as it broke the surface of the water. The shard was causing Zandra some pain, but she would have to keep fighting.

Heading up a stream that came into the river on the east bank, she flew as fast as she could, hugging the shore, and hoping that the stream would narrow so that the creature would have to break off.

It shot fire at her again, and the trees along the bank burst into flames. Zandra rolled again, trying to be a harder target.

She came to a fork in the river. The land in the middle of the two streams came to a long, sharp point that was about twenty feet above the water. Zandra saw two silhouettes on the point. Two streaks of red light shot from them as she passed, aiming at the beast behind her.

Zandra angled back to the northwest, hugging the tops of the trees and just missing some of the taller ones. She didn't look back for a long while, hoping to get as much space as she could between her and that thing.

After a while, the adrenaline had worn off and the pain in her chest was getting more intense. She would have to land and take care of her injury.

Finding a meadow near a group of trees, she touched down. The pain was shooting up to her shoulders.

After setting her protection charm, she started a fire. Now that she had some light, she could see her wound. Luckily she had not lost much blood. The sliver was about six inches long. Grabbing the shard with her right hand, she pulled it out, dropping it on the ground. Picking up her wand, she cauterized the wound.

Zandra grabbed the shard, and walked over to a small creek, washing it along with her hands. She came back to the fire. It wasn't a cold night, but she was chilled. Between her injury, and what she had just gone through, she was exhausted.

Looking at the shard in the firelight, she could tell it was bone; maybe from a tooth or fang. Deciding she would look at it more in the morning, she took a bite of the jerky she had bought earlier, lay down on the ground, and fell asleep.

Two nights later, she was coming closer to her destination. She now had to check her course more often, as her wand was being more precise. The land was fairly flat; the soil had changed to a dusty tan and became more rocky.

After a few hours, the earth shrank away, many fingers of valleys leading down into a river, where she landed. After setting up her camp, she pulled out her mortar and pestle so she could start crushing the ingredients for the potion that she would need to help the Arikara.

Suddenly, she sensed movement behind her. Quickly pulling her wand out, she spun around. "INTEGUMENTUM!"

The shield appeared just in time–an arrow bounced off and hit the ground. Zandra looked around for the archer. It took her a moment to see him. The warrior was in the tree line a short distance from her, and when she spotted him, he ran off.

Well, they know I'm here now, she thought. Pointing her wand at the arrow, she said, "Uro."

The arrow burst into flames. She didn't want to take any chances.

Turning back to her work, she set up her cauldron in the fire so she could boil the potion for the Arikara. Her injury was still hurting. While the potion was on the fire, she rested. She would head out the next day to give the potion to the Arikara.

When she woke in the late afternoon, she realized that she had not let Phineas know how she was doing. Getting her paper and quill out, she started to write to him, to let him know that she had made it to her destination.

When she was finished with the potion, she bottled up the paste and put it into her flight bag so she would be ready for tomorrow.

When she woke the next morning, she decided to fly around the area to find the Arikara's camps. They already knew there was someone unusual among them, since her incident with the archer last night, so she might as well make it easy. Pulling out her wand, she said: "Are Bulla."

A bubble of air materialized around her; it looked like she was in a drop of water. The spell would keep her separated from the infected natives. Mounting her broom, she kicked off from the ground and started her search.

It didn't take long for her to find a camp. Landing a few hundred yards away, she walked up to it. A warrior that was obviously not doing well came out to intercept her, raising his bow but having a hard time. He was weak.

Zandra pulled out her wand. "Transferendum," she said. "I'm here to help."

The warrior fell to the ground. She could not help him up, as that could get her infected. An elderly man came out to them. As he came close, she said, "I'm Zandra Voorhies. I'm here to help."

The elder stopped. "My name is Spotted Pony. You're not wanted here. We have many sick. We know this is the white man's sickness. Go away!"

"I'm what the white man calls a witch. I have some medicine that can help. It won't cure the ill, but can help those that are not sick yet to fight the sickness off."

Spotted Pony looked sceptical. "I'm a medicine man, and yet I can do nothing for them. How do you think you can hope to help them, and why should we trust you? We've heard many stories of your people's treachery: how you'll say you're a friend, then come and kill us the next day."

"Like I said, I'm a witch," Zandra replied. "I have magical powers. You saw me fly in, you see the bubble that I'm using to protect myself. The normal white men are afraid of us, and try to kill us. Not much different than the way the white man treats you. I'm not like them, even though I'm pale-skinned and golden-haired. I care for life, and only want to help save some of your people. I've traveled far to do this and I've seen great danger in coming here. Please give me a chance."

Spotted Pony looked thoughtful, but didn't say anything.

Zandra took off her flight bag and pulled out the container. "Are there any of your people who have survived the sickness, who would be able to take this to other camps?"

"Yes," said Spotted Pony.

"Could you get them so I can tell them what needs to be done?"

Spotted Pony went into the camp and came back a short time later with a young man. "This is Running Deer. He has agreed to take this to the other camps."

"Come as close as you can to my bubble," said Zandra, pulling out a spoon. "A young person gets one spoon, adults get two. Only give this to the healthy ones."

Running Deer nodded.

"I will be back in a few days to see if you had enough." Zandra left the container and spoon on the ground and backed away. Running Deer picked up the container, and he and Spotted Pony walked back to the camp.

Zandra climbed on her broom and kicked off, flying back to her camp. She would have a few days to explore the country while she waited for Running Deer to get back from his travels.

The following morning, she took off to the northwest. The ground was undulating with no discernible landmarks. It seemed to be an endless ocean of grass and sagebrush, sporadically broken by a few trees along dry creek beds. The gently rolling hills all looked alike. As she flew, there began to be sandstone bluffs, low and indiscernible from each other.

With no help in navigation, a person could easily get lost out here. As soon as you found what you thought you could use as a landmark, it would seem to disappear right before your eyes. The waves of the land all seemed to look alike, and the sky seemed to go on forever. She could travel for hours and seemingly still be where she started. If it weren't for her wand pointing north, she would be hopelessly lost.

But this land did have an empty, lonely beauty about it. She felt that except for the antelope and bison that she saw, she was the only living thing within hundreds of miles.

Finding a tree-covered creek bed, she landed to set up camp for the night.

When night fell, she walked out away from her camp. Staying within sight of her fire, she laid down on the ground, looking up at the stars. It was a moonless night. The longer she laid there, the more stars there seemed to be. The sky was so immense.

The next morning, Zandra decided to make a large arch to the southeast, back toward the Arikara.

She had only been in the air for a couple of hours when there appeared a change in the land. It became even more arid, keeping its same dusty tannish color. The hills became covered with what looked like veins in leaves that had fallen from a giant tree. These veins appeared to have been carved in the hills from what little rain this land got. Not much grew here.

Then green mountains rose above the dull, tannish-white land. Gliding over the trees, she saw a very large, gray column of stone, rising out of a bed of red and maroon rock that was covered in trees, seeming out of place. When she got closer, she could see that it was a bunch of separate columns that had been combined. It looked like the stump of a mammoth tree.[I]

The butte rose more than a thousand feet above the river that meandered along its east side. Zandra could feel a spiritual power surrounding this place.

She flew to the west face of the butte to get the afternoon sun that was illuminating it. She felt that this place deserved respect, so she landed at a distance and walked up to it.

As she walked, she came across a native camp. They had not heard her come up, and she was concealed behind a tree. Watching them for a while, she finally decided to approach them.

She got as close as she could, before pulling out her wand. "Transferendum." Then she stepped out.

The natives jumped up, grabbing their weapons.

"I'm not here to hurt you," said Zandra.

They all looked astounded that they could understand her.

"I'm Zandra Voorhies. I'm here helping the Arikara."

One of the natives spoke up. "Why can we speak with you?"

"I'm a witch," said Zandra.

They looked puzzled.

Zandra turned to the side and took out her wand. Pointing it at a log, she said: "Atollo."

The log rose into the air.

The natives lowered their weapons. One looked quizzical. "How can you help the Arikara? Our best medicine men can't do anything."

[I] Devil's Tower, SD

Zandra explained that she couldn't cure them, but could only strengthen them against it.

"Why would you do this for them?" one of the natives asked.

Zandra explained her feelings about death and her need to do something to help. She asked about the butte.

They told her that they were Lakota, and there were many names for the mountain: Ghost Mountain, Bear Lodge, Grizzly Bear Lodge, Mystic Owl Mountain.[14] These mountains were where their people were created. They were sacred to many native peoples. They said they were there to take Hanbleceya."

"What is a Hanbleceya?"

"It is how we find our purpose in life."

Zandra found this very interesting. There was a lot that she needed to learn about this land and its people.

They talked for a while, then she said goodbye and moved on up the trail.

She set up camp at the base of the butte. Zandra could feel the spiritual power all around her.

She slept outside of the tent so she could look at the butte in the starlight. She thought that she could see wisps of colored light shooting off the top of the rock.

In a dream that night, she saw a large, majestic bird, with silvery-tinted feathers. When it flapped its enormous wings, the scene behind it would change. As its wings rose into the sky, it appeared as though a thunderstorm poured heavy rain and streaked lightning over a body of water. When the wings whooshed down, it was a clear, blue day over an arid land of beautiful maroon-orange and red buttes, along with immense valleys with unusual rock formations and arches of stone. She felt as if she was rising, floating into the air.

The dream faded. She tried, in her sleeping mind, to pull it back, but could not.

When she woke in the morning, she lay there puzzling over the dream. Had some spirit tried to communicate with her? Was it the magic of this mountain, or just her mind dealing with what she felt in this place?

She broke camp and headed back to the Arikara. When she got there, she went to Spotted Pony's camp. Running Deer had made it back. He had had enough potion. She made another batch for them to share with other natives, and the next day she packed up and headed back east.

CHAPTER 7

Thunder on the Water

May 31 - June 3, 1780

"I was skimming the surface of the stream, hoping that the trees would close in enough that it would have to break off. Then the trees burst into flames. As I started doing barrel rolls to evade its fire, I came to a fork in the stream. Taking the left fork, I saw there was a long finger of land, about twenty feet high, that stuck out into the fork. Coming closer, I could see the silhouette of two figures standing on top of the point. Just after I passed, two ribbons of red light shot up at the creature. They must have at least slowed it enough to let me escape. I didn't look back, I just banked up, hugged the tops of the trees, and headed northwest."

Zandra paused for a moment. Her wound had healed, but still caused her pain sometimes.

"Seems that you found some friends out there. If you could find out who they were, maybe they could tell you more about this creature," Phineas said.

"I've heard of it," said Broken Arrow. "It's called the Piasa Bird. It lives in the bluffs over the Mississippi River."

"Do you know anything else about it?" asked Zandra.

"It is said that the Piasa Bird feasted on the people of the Illini Confederation,[15] which encompassed the Kaskaskia, Cahokia, Tamaroa, Peoria, and Michigamea tribes, among others. The bird raided villages, snatching up people for its meals, until a great medicine man of the Cahokia managed to communicate with the creature. The tribes of the Illini promised to supply the Piasa Bird with bison, and would let the bird feast on the fallen warriors of their many enemies in exchange for the bird leaving the Illini alone.

"Paintings of the Piasa Bird were put on the cliffs over the Mississippi River to warn warring tribes of their foolishness at attacking the tribes of the Illini. This ultimately lead to the demise of the truce, as the Piasa Bird craved humans, and the fact that warring tribes strayed away from fighting with the tribes of the Illini Confederation lead to a shortage of humans for the bird to feed on.

"So the Piasa Bird began feasting on the Cahokians, and their society fell before the arrival of the of the white man. The age of the beast is unknown, and it seems to have an indefinite lifespan."

"Well, this sounds like a formidable creature," said Zandra.

"Your unknown friends must be very powerful," said Broken Arrow.

"I also saw a large, reptilian-looking creature while I was flying over the first huge lake," Zandra said.

"You might have seen a Gaasyendietha," said Broken Arrow.

Zandra gave him a quizzical look. "What's that?"

"It's a large serpent that dwells in deep waters. It spews molten rock and can also fly on a ribbon of fire."

"Sounds like a dragon," said Zandra. "But all the dragons I know of don't live in the water."

"That reminds me–I've found a Mishipizheu in a lake not too far from here," said Broken Arrow.

"The Mishipizheu...that's what you called the underwater panther, right?"

"Yes. I was camped near the lake, when I heard a loud roar. I turned to see it not far from me. It didn't see me, but continued to roar. Soon a terrible storm came upon me and I was forced into my shelter."

"Could you take me to it?" asked Zandra.

"I could, but this is a powerful magical creature," said Broken Arrow.

Zandra shrugged. "I've already faced one."

"Yes, but remember, if it hadn't been for your unknown friends, you might not have survived," said Phineas.

"I wasn't prepared for that one," she said stubbornly. "Besides, is this creature even as powerful as the Piasa Bird?"

"I don't think so, but it's nothing to mess around with," said Broken Arrow.

"No magical creature is," said Zandra. "Broken Arrow, give me two days to get some work done around here, then meet me at my house and we will try to find this Mishipizheu."

By this time, it was getting toward evening. Phineas and Broken Arrow headed out for their homes.

I'm glad that bird thing didn't get you, said Xavier.

"I am, too. I'm ready for a few calm days, and I need to get some turning done to get some more money. See you in the morning."

With a handful of wood shavings, Zandra pressed them against the wand as it turned on the lathe, polishing her newest creation. Finally satisfied with it, she rubbed a finish onto it as it spun. Pulling it off the lathe, she held it in her hand. It felt good in her hand; a simple but elegant design.

Deciding to put a whisker of a the Azeban in it, she laid the whisker beside the new wand, then, taking out her personal wand, she said: "Indo!"

The whisker melded into the wand. Taking the new wand outside, she pointed it at a stick and said: "Uro!"

Instead of bursting into flames, the stick sprouted and produced a leaf.

Hmm, that's not good. She returned to the shop, and set the wand aside. Putting a piece of hackberry on the lathe, she started to turn another wand.

An hour later, she was pulling it off the lathe. She sat it down on the table. It had a nice light tan color, with a smoky gray clouding to it. She pulled out the shard that had stuck her in the chest from the Piasa Bird and cut it into thin slivers. Setting one down next to the hackberry, once again she pulled out her wand. "Indo!" she said. The Piasa Bird sliver melded into the new wand, oozing into all the pores of the wood.

Walking out to the sprouting stick that was now a small sapling, she pointed the wand at it. "Uro!"

The sapling exploded into flames, setting the pasture on fire. Quickly, she yelled: "PERFUNDO!"

Copious amounts of water poured onto the fire, putting it out immediately.

"Wow, that's a powerful wand," said Phineas as he walked up.

She nodded. "I melded a Piasa Bird fang into this one. I think I need to use a smaller amount. This one's uncontrollable and unstable."

"Yes, I think so," Phineas said fervently. "Broken Arrow was right. This is a very powerful creature."

Zandra stuck the wand in her pocket. "So, what are you up to today?"

He sighed. "Just thought I would stop in."

"Zipporah being difficult again?"

"Yes, and I just wanted to see you. I know that you're leaving tomorrow with Broken Arrow to do some magical creature hunting, and I wanted to spend some time with you before you leave."

Zandra smiled. "I missed you, too." She grabbed his hand and pulled him into a hug. "Come back with me to the shop. You can help me with my work."

They walked back around to the shop with their arms around each other.

Zandra offered to let Phineas spend the night. She had bought some fabric and made a hammock that she strung between the walls, so that Phineas would not be so uncomfortable staying with her. They had just turned in for the night when—

"Whoop! Whoop!"

Xavier came to the window. *We have a guest.*

Zandra and Phineas hurried out of the house. Xavier nodded toward the tree line. It was Shakock. They walked up to him.

"Transferendum," Zandra said. "Shakock! How are you doing? Is our spell working for you?"

Shakock's deep voice came thundering back. "We're not having any intrusions. I've brought you some of our hairs, as you asked." Shakock handed them to Zandra.

She smiled. "Thank you."

Shakock just looked at her, not saying anything. Then, finally: "Watch the places you go."

"What do you mean?"

"There are a lot of very powerful things in this land." Shakock turned and walked back into the woods.

Zandra looked at Phineas and Xavier. "Do you think he knows of my travels?"

I think we know very little about these Stonish Giants, said Xavier. *The distances that they were talking to each other when we traveled here tells me that they could be in a position to know what is going on all over this land.*

"I think you're right," said Phineas.

"Well, it'd be more helpful if they weren't so secretive," said Zandra.

That's just their way, replied Xavier.

Soon after breakfast the next morning, Broken Arrow came up to the house. Zandra hitched Xavier up to the wagon, and Phineas helped them load supplies onto it. Zandra gave Phineas a hug and told him goodbye.

They climbed onto the wagon and headed northeast. The lake was only a few miles away, but it was large enough that it might take a night or so to catch up with the Mishipizheu.

That evening, they sat around the campfire they had set up near the lake. It was getting late, and there was no sign of the Mishipizheu. Xavier had headed out to a patch of grass a little way down the road for a snack.

Then Zandra saw something in the woods behind them. "What was that?"

Broken Arrow looked over where she was pointing. "I don't see anything," he replied.

"There it is again! Off to the right."

It was a small, gray humanoid creature, with porcupine quills over its head and down its back, giving the appearance of long hair.

"That's a Pukwudgie," said Broken Arrow.

The creature disappeared, then reappeared a little farther away.

"He's trying to lure us into the woods," Broken Arrow said.

Zandra stood up and headed into the woods after it. Broken Arrow grabbed his bow and followed her. The Pukwudgie kept reappearing at a distance, until they lost sight of it.

They were deep in the woods when a fireball came flying at them from behind, just missing Broken Arrow. Zandra shot a Pulso spell in that direction, hitting an opossum, which promptly fell out of the tree it was in.

The Pukwudgie reappeared to their left, throwing another fireball, but falling short. With increasing speed, it kept appearing in different places. Luckily, the Pukwudgie's aim got worse the faster it moved. Zandra hit it in the back with a Pulso spell, but it bounced off. Finally, Zandra put up a shield spell. This infuriated the Pukwudgie, and gave them time to come up with a strategy.

There was a tree stump behind them. Zandra got an idea. She turned to Broken Arrow. "I'm going to make this tree stump into a likeness of me. Then I'll cloak myself, drop the shield, and put up another shield around you."

Arrows began to bounce off the shield. The Pukwudgie had decided to switch tactics.

"You keep its attention, and I'll sneak up to it. I will try to come at it from the front; my spells seem to bounce off its back. Maybe I can stun him at close range. Stand in front of me to block his view. Hopefully he won't see me."

Broken Arrow nodded.

Zandra pointed her wand at herself. "Nubes!"

A wave of dark green and black poured over her like paint spilled from a can, starting at her head. When it came to her feet, it took on the appearance of the forest behind her. She pointed her wand at the nearby tree stump and said: "Commuta Habitum!" The stump shimmered and took on a likeness of her.

Broken Arrow dodged a shot from the Pukwudgie as Zandra pointed her wand at him and reset the shield charm. Pointing the wand at herself again, she said: "Auris Silentium!"

Silently, she started to outflank the Pukwudgie. Working slowly, she tried to anticipate its movements. Broken Arrow started shooting arrows at it.

It took a couple tries to get in front of the Pukwudgie. And then it happened—the Pukwudgie sprang out of thin air, directly in front of her. She raised her arm to cast the stunning spell. The Pukwudgie saw the movement, and it turned to run away. Zandra reached out and grabbed a handful of quills from its head as it disappeared.

Then the attack stopped. Zandra decloaked and returned to Broken Arrow.

"Well, he was a tough one, wasn't he?"

They walked back to the camp. It was about one in the morning. Zandra put up a shield charm so they could rest without worry for the rest of the night.

When morning broke, Zandra was still asleep. Broken Arrow woke her after cooking some breakfast.

She ate sleepy-eyed, not saying much till she finished. "I've been thinking that we should take that log and hollow it out to make a canoe. We might have better luck out on the lake."

Broken Arrow nodded. "That might be a good idea."

Should you be out there on the water with this creature? asked Xavier.

"I think it will increase our odds greatly." Zandra walked over to the log and took out her wand. "Cavo!"

Wood shavings began to fly as the center of the log hollowed out. In no time, they had a canoe. Broken Arrow smiled in wonder.

"That will do." Zandra grinned.

"We'll have to wait until tonight," said Broken Arrow. "That's when the Mishipizheu shows itself."

When night fell, they climbed in their new canoe. Xavier stood by the shore as they departed.

I won't be able to help you if you get in trouble. Try not to make this thing too mad.

"We'll do our best." Zandra pointed her wand at the shoreline. "Truso!"

The canoe slid out onto the lake.

When they came close to the center of the water, she pulled her arm back around. They slowed until they were drifting, sitting there silently, the water sloshing against the canoe.

After a while, ripples appeared on the surface, as if something was moving away from them just under the water.

Then the back of a great, dark head appeared. It glimmered in the moonlight, black in color, with scales that reflected purple and aqua, like oil on dark water. A great spray of mist came from its nostrils.

Slowly, the head turned, and its dark, reflecting eyes met theirs.

Without a sound, a tail came up behind them. Lifting up out of the water, it wrapped around the canoe between Zandra and Broken Arrow, picked it up, and tossed it into the air.

Zandra and Broken Arrow hit the water. With a swat of its giant webbed paw, the creature swept at Broken Arrow. Shooting across the water, he glanced off a rock and slid up the shore, unconscious.

The Mishipizheu sprang up out of the water: a great cat bounding after prey. Its muscular body glistened in the moonlight, jagged flat spikes protruding from its back.

Zandra gasped at the impressiveness of the creature. The Mishipizheu let out a roar that sounded like thunder. The wind picked up, and rain started to fall. Zandra started throwing spells at it, but, like any cat, it moved so fast that she could not hit it. Leaping and diving, its long prehensile tail whipped at Zandra.

The wind was getting very strong, and the rain had become heavy. Finally, she hit the Mishipizheu with a glancing blow, but it didn't seem to slow the attack.

The Mishipizheu charged, leaping up to pounce on her. She swam to the side, throwing a curse at it as it hit the water. The intensity of the storm increased drastically.

Suddenly, the Mishipizheu rose up behind her, slapping at her wand with its tail, knocking it out of her hand. Then it raised its giant paw over her head, and pushed her down under the water.

Everything went blank.

Above the lake, lightning began to cross the sky as giant, silver wings descended upon the water, and claps of thunder broke the night. An enormous bird dove at the Mishipizheu, talons extended. The storm had become furious. The Mishipizheu swatted at its airborne attacker as it passed, but missed.

The silver bird lifted it out of the water, tossing it across the lake. With a mighty flap of its wings, it came back over to where Zandra was now sinking and snatched her out of the water.

Zandra looked up briefly, then passed out.

Depositing her on the bank, the bird returned to battle. It glided out over the lake as the storm continued.

Suddenly, the Mishipizheu leaped up from the waves, grabbing the bird around the neck. The giant, silvery-feathered head hit the water. Rolling head-over-heels, the bird's back hit the surface of the lake. The Mishipizheu was now on top of the great bird, out of the water, holding the silver raptor's head under the surface.

The massive bird thrashed and flailed under the water, its talons digging into the Mishipizheu, cutting a deep gash into it. The giant cat let go and headed to deep water.

The silver bird rose up out of the lake. Flying over to the shore, it looked down at Zandra. She moved her head, opening her eyes slightly.

She could just see it flap its great wings and fly off to the west as she fell back into unconsciousness.

Broken Arrow knelt beside Zandra. They were both soaked. Zandra stirred, gazing up at him with a dazed look.

"Are you all right?" asked Broken Arrow.

She didn't answer for a moment. "Yes, I think so. Did you see what happened?"

"No," he said worriedly.

"The Mishipizheu had pushed me under the water, and the next thing I knew, I was flying through the air under a giant, silver bird."

She paused. "I hadn't told anyone, but when I was at Ghost Mountain, I had a dream. There was a giant silver bird, just like this one, and when it flapped its wings, the scene around it would change. When its wings were up, there was a storm over water. When its wings were down, there was a land of orange-maroon and red buttes, a dry land of incredible beauty. Then there was the feeling of rising through the air. It must have been a premonition of things to come."

Broken Arrow looked thoughtful. "Or maybe the Thunderbird was letting you know what was to come."

"Thunderbird?" she asked. "That's what it's called?"

He nodded. "The Thunderbird and the Mishipizheu both can bring on storms, and they're enemies. You're lucky that you have the protection of such a great creature."

Just then Xavier showed up, soaked, and panting very hard.

Do you remember me saying something about not making it too mad?

"Well, it was in a wee bit of a snit before we got introduced," said Zandra.

Xavier nickered. *What was that bird that came to your rescue?*

"It was a Thunderbird," replied Broken Arrow.

Well, that's a fitting name if I ever heard one, said Xavier. *Hop on. I'll take you two back to camp.*

Zandra looked off to her left. Lying on top of a patch of cattails were two large silver feathers. She picked them up.

Broken Arrow turned to see. "Well, at least tonight wasn't a waste."

Zandra grinned excitedly. "There are enough vanes and barbs to make several wands from these two feathers."

Zandra and Broken Arrow climbed onto Xavier's back and headed off to camp. Starting their fire back up, they dried themselves off and drifted to sleep lying there in front of the fire.

First thing next morning, Phineas showed up.

"I headed out soon after the storm let up last night. I was worried about you, Zandra. That was a very unusual storm. Did you have anything to do with it?"

Zandra recounted the story of the battle to Phineas, and showed him the Thunderbird feathers.

Phineas shook his head disbelievingly. "I hope it's worth it to you. You could have died. I'm worried that one of these times, you might not be so lucky. I don't want anything to happen to you."

"I know you don't, but this is what I'm here to do. If I'm going to create a wand to rival those of the old country, I have to collect as many new wand infusion materials as possible to find the right one."

Zandra grabbed Phineas and gave him a hug. Tears welled up in his eyes as they stood there, but he tried to hide his upset. Zandra just hugged him tighter and left it at that.

Soon afterward, they broke camp. Just before they left, Zandra walked over to the shore to look across the lake. Broken Arrow and Phineas walked up beside her.

"Do you think the Thunderbird killed the Mishipizheu?" asked Zandra.

"I doubt it," said Broken Arrow.

Zandra noticed something on the water. Wading out into the lake, she found three scales that clearly came from the Mishipizheu. She grabbed them up and returned to shore.

"Looks like luck is with me," she said, holding up the scales and smiling.

CHAPTER 8

The Three Devils

October, 1785

The leaves were just beginning to turn. Zandra's wand business had been doing well, and she was heading into her sixth winter in her new home. The Thunderbird feathers and Mishipizheu scales had made very good wand infusion materials, and she was getting exceptional prices for them. Zandra had made herself a new wand of bird's-eye maple, with a Thunderbird feather infusion.

She had had some luck making friends with the local Pukwudgies, and had been regularly getting their quills. Shakock delivered hairs regularly, and the Stonish Giant wands had become the mainstay of her business. Her reputation had grown, and she had finally been able to pay for her property.

Zipporah was still not treating Phineas very well; he was spending increasing amounts of time with Zandra to get away from her. Zandra and Phineas had become regulars at The Chalice, the local gathering place for the witches and wizards in the area. Broken Arrow stopped in often and brought magical creature materials that he had had an opportunity to get his hands on.

Zandra had found a store in New York that wanted to sell her wands. She had decided to deliver the wands to New York herself. Phineas was with her, and they planned to travel on to the Pinelands to check out the Leeds Devil that Theophilus had told her about.

I hate cities.

"We know, Xavier," said Zandra wearily. "We won't be here long. Soon we'll be off to the Pinelands."

They turned down an alley.

This town smells.

Zandra sighed. "Xavier, *we know.*"

They stopped in front of a three-story stone building, with a sign that read *Las Squelette.*

Don't be long in there. I'm thirsty; I want some rum, said Xavier.

Zandra waved him off, and she and Phineas entered the building.

The room was dim and gloomy, even though there were ample windows. The shelves were lined with bottles of perfumes.

A small man came out of the back room. "May I help you, ma'am?"

"Yes," Zandra replied. "I'm looking for Rodrigue Boneapart."

"I'm Rodrigue." The man smiled.

"Zandra Voorhies," she said. "I wrote to you about selling some of my products."

The man's eyes flashed with recognition. "Ah, yes. Come with me."

They passed through the door which Rodrigue had just entered through. A woman was in the next room.

"Please take care of the shop for me, Genevieve," Rodrigue said.

The woman nodded as they passed through the room.

They headed up a flight of stairs. The room at the top was a magical store, but unlike most stores in the colonies, there were a lot more exotic items.

Zandra gestured to Phineas, standing next to her. "This is my friend, Phineas Osborne."

Then there came footsteps on the stairs. Bazel Blackbone stepped into the room.

"Ah, Mister Blackbone!" Rodrigue walked over to him.

"Rodrigue!" said Blackbone. "Do you have my package?"

"Yes, right back here. I'll be back with you in a moment, Miss Voorhies."

Bazel seemed to notice Zandra for the first time. "Zandra! It's been a while. You're making quite a name for yourself."

"How's your mission going?" Zandra asked.

"Not well," he said, shaking his head. "Not well at all."

"I'm sorry."

"I'm trying a new strategy. Hopefully things will improve."

Bazel headed up to the counter, and Rodrigue handed him a package. Zandra watched them as she walked around the store.

After he had paid, Bazel headed to the stairs. "Good day, Zandra."

Zandra smiled as he passed. "He's up to more than he lets on," said Zandra. "I think we might need one of these Voodoo dolls someday." She gestured towards a display of medium-sized cloth dolls. Phineas grinned.

"Do you have your wands, Miss Voorhies?"

Zandra put her bag on the counter, and Rodrigue examined her wands. Zandra and Phineas continued to look around the store. After a while, he had inspected all the wands, and they agreed on a price.

Zandra and Phineas walked back out onto the street.

Did he buy your wands? asked Xavier.

"Yes, we got enough that we can buy you a keg of rum."

Well, at least that makes waiting here worth it.

After picking up the rum for Xavier, they headed for the Pinelands.

They were on the second day of the journey to the Pinelands. It was near twilight, and Zandra, Xavier, and Phineas were still on the road. The sky was blue, with a few thin, high pink clouds.

They rounded a bend in the road, and there in front of them was a huge creature, standing on two legs. It had red hair, and looked like a Stonish Giant, but unlike Shakock or Nook—both of whom had a face between a human and an ape—this one's face was more like a flattened version of a baboon.

Startled, Xavier reared up. The creature grabbed his underside and threw him, breaking the traces of the wagon. Phineas pulled out his wand and cast a spell, slowing Xavier's fall.

Zandra pointed her wand at the creature. "Resisto!"

It slowed slightly for a split second, then came at them. Phineas turned his wand on the creature, and they both yelled: "Resisto!"

"Sustringo!" Zandra shouted, but the creature broke the rope she had conjured like it was nothing.

Phineas yelled: "Uro!" Flames shot out of his wand, and the creature raised its arm to protect its face. The smell of burnt hair filled the air. It roared, the sound echoing across the land around.

Phineas jumped down off the broken wagon and came at the creature, flames still shooting out of his wand, but the beast would not retreat any further than just beyond the flames. It was raging mad, and not giving in.

Zandra came at it from a slightly different angle. "Pulso!" she shouted.

Nothing happened.

Zandra looked at Phineas. "Pulso on three!"

Phineas nodded.

"One, two, three!"

They both raised their wands and yelled: "Pulso!"

Still, nothing happened.

Then Zandra shouted: "Fulgur!"

A bright light flashed intensely, temporarily blinding the creature. It rubbed its eyes, then dropped onto all fours and ran at an incredible speed away from them.

Zandra ran over to Xavier. He was just getting up. "Are you alright?"

Yes, it just knocked the wind out of me. What was that thing, anyway?

"I don't know for sure," said Zandra. "It appeared to be a Stonish Giant, but it looked different, and was much more aggressive. Plus, our magic barely worked on it."

They walked back to the wagon.

"Come around and back up to the wagon, Xavier. I'll repair the damage," said Phineas. "Exsarcio," he muttered. The traces raised up to meet their ends and molded back together.

"We'll have to ask Shakock about this creature when we get back," Zandra said.

They stayed on the road for about half of the night, to get as much distance between them and their attacker as possible.

Two days later, they had made it deep into the Pinelands. Setting up camp, they started a fire and cooked some food. There had been strange wailing sounds the night before, but they had come from way off in the distance. Zandra and Phineas had both brought their brooms so they could fly at night, to make searching for the Leeds Devil easier.

After dark, they heard the wails again. Zandra and Phineas grabbed their brooms and flew off into the night.

There was a harvest moon, huge and orange in the eastern sky. The sounds were coming from in front of them as they flew into the moon.

They had only been in the air for a few minutes when they saw it, rising up out of the pines and into the harvest moon. It was flying erratically, its head bobbing around as it flapped its wings. Zandra and Phineas gained altitude so they could dive down on it.

As they closed in on the devil, they threw random spells, making sure not to hit it, trying to drive it to the ground before they stunned it. But its flying was so bad that Zandra struck it with a Singultum Charm by accident. The Leeds Devil started hiccuping, which made its flying even more erratic. It still didn't even seem to notice that Zandra and Phineas were there.

"Great," said Zandra, shaking her head.

Phineas laughed. The devil was a crazy thing to see in flight. "This thing doesn't seem to be very intelligent," he said.

"No, it doesn't," Zandra agreed.

"Let's stop throwing spells at it and force it down with our brooms," Phineas suggested.

Zandra and Phineas flew up on either side of the creature, and it started to head for the ground. Just as they neared the forest floor, Zandra pointed her wand at it and said: "Resisto."

The devil fell to the ground, motionless. Zandra and Phineas landed.

"What an unusual creature. No wonder it flies so bad. I can't even tell how many different magical creatures it's bred from," said Phineas.

"It's quite a conglomeration," replied Zandra.

She bent down and took some shavings from the devil's horns, and stored them in her flight bag.

When she released it from the Resisto spell, the devil wobbled onto its feet, stood there a moment, wailed, then flew off into the night.

"Well, that was the easiest infusion material I've ever collected," Zandra said.

"Well, they don't all have to be dangerous, do they?" said Phineas.

Zandra smiled. "No, I guess they don't."

CHAPTER 9

SHAY'S REBELLION

Winter 1786 - 1787

Zandra was on her way back from the Ohio Country, where she had been helping the natives. The Washington Administration was implementing a scorched earth policy against them. They wanted to break them so that they could not support the British. Rangers and mercenaries were wreaking havoc on villages, killing women and children, destroying crops and stores of food. Zandra had been doing all she could to minimize the destruction they had wrought.

As she passed through the town of Pelham in Massachusetts, she stopped at the Conkey Tavern[16] to give Xavier a rest, and to get a drink and something to eat. She got a lot of looks as she sat down at a table.

A man came in behind her. "Are you alright, ma'am? It's unusual to see a woman traveling alone."

Zandra used the story that she had fabricated for these kinds of incidents: that her husband had died, and she was traveling to relatives.

"I'm sorry," the man said. "You be careful. Good luck." He moved on to where a group of men were in the corner talking.

"They're going to take my land!" one of them was saying adamantly. "I fought in the war and was never paid for my service; they do nothing to help. I don't know that we wouldn't have been better off not ever having fought that war and just letting Britain stay in power."

Another man across the table from him spoke to the man that had talked to Zandra. "Daniel Shays,[17] you were a captain in the army. What do you have to say?"

Daniel Shays sighed. "I'm suffering the same as the rest of you. I left the army because I was not getting paid. I had to sell the sword that General Lafayette gave me to help pay my debts that the government would not even help with. What they're doing to Luke Day[18] and the others is wrong."

Zandra listened as he went on. *So this new nation is not paying or providing for the well-being of the people who fought for it?*

"I think we should gather as many men as we can and march on the Supreme Judicial Court in Springfield next month," said Daniel Shays. "I will deliver a message saying that we feel that no indictments can be issued, or the court set again, until the grievances of Luke Day and his Regulators have been addressed. If no one stands for them, we will all suffer."

"I think that sounds like a good plan," another man said agreeably.

"Well then, let's all gather as many men as we can. We can meet in front of the tavern here and march on Springfield before the trial next month."

As they all finished their drinks and said their goodbyes, Zandra thought, *I will have to be in Springfield to see what happens.* She finished her meal.

Asking for her bill, she was told that it had been taken care of. Surprised, she said, "Tell whoever it was thanks." Turning, she walked out the door.

Patting Xavier on the snout, she climbed onto the wagon and headed on up the road.

"Shakock, this is my friend Broken Arrow," Zandra said. "He's in danger. His people are being hunted by mercenaries and rangers, unethical killers. Killers of women and children. I ask you if he could set up a home here, just inside the tree line so he can live without fear. His people and yours have lived in this land together for a very long time. Broken Arrow's people have respected you. I've respected you and I've helped you. Can you help us now?"

Shakock stood there silently. A female Stonish Giant was there, with an adolescent one that was already five feet tall.

After a few moments, Shakock's booming voice broke the silence. "I know of what is happening. These invaders, these men of pale skin—they kill just because they seem to enjoy it. Other troops of my kind have encountered them. They rip apart very nicely, some say."

Zandra cringed. "Well, back to the question: could you let Broken Arrow live here?"

After the usual long silence, Shakock answered.

"I will allow him, but he had better not take advantage of our kindness."

"Thank you," said Zandra. "And one more thing: Phineas and I were attacked on our trip to the Pinelands, by a creature with red hair, and a face something like a baboon or a dog. But its snout didn't stick out very far from its face. It was very aggressive. We just came upon it in the road. It threw Xavier, and we almost didn't get away. Was that one of your kind?"

"There are a few different subspecies. We leave the ones you speak of alone. They're very unpredictable."

"I think you're understating them," replied Zandra. "Are your kind all over this land?"

"Mostly."

Shakock and his friends turned and walked off.

"You didn't have to do this for me," Broken Arrow said to Zandra.

"You're my friend," Zandra said. "I'm afraid for you. It was no problem."

September had come. Zandra set off on the night of the eighteenth to see how things played out for Shays' group. She set up camp in the woods, putting up the usual spells to hide her presence.

The next morning, she woke to drums and fifes, and men marching along the road near her camp. Zandra thought there might be seven hundred or more. They were what had become known as the Regulators.

She grabbed something quick to eat and headed off.

When she arrived at the courthouse, she found that some nine hundred soldiers were there, waiting for Shays and his followers. Shays spoke with General Shepard,[19] commander of the troops, as his followers waited.

Zandra could not get close enough to hear what was going on. Grabbing her wand and keeping it under her cloak, she murmured "Subausculto." The voices of the two men came to her ears.

"These are your brothers!" Daniel Shays was saying. "They have all put their lives in peril for this government, and yet they have been cheated of their money and cannot pay their debts. This could have been you, or any of your men. Let us try to stop this trial of Luke Day and his Regulators so their grievances may be heard."

"I will let you through to march," replied General Shepard. "But don't cause any trouble, or we will take action."

As the former soldiers moved forward, Zandra noticed a dark figure standing to the side of the marchers. She looked closer, and realized it was Bazel Blackbone. He was holding something in his hand, which he tossed up into the air over the crowd.

Without really even knowing what she was doing, Zandra pointed her wand at the object and said: "Averto!"

The object stopped, then shot off in the opposite direction with much more force than Zandra expected.

Bazel gazed at Zandra with an enraged look as the Regulators' march passed them.

A woman in the crowd of onlookers was staring at Zandra with a terrified look. *Oh, no!* Zandra thought.

"WITCH!!!" the woman shrieked. "SHE'S A WITCH!!!"

The noise of the former soldiers marching past was so loud that no one heard her. Zandra ducked into the crowd to distance herself from the woman. Bazel rushed after her through the marching soldiers until he caught up to her.

"What do you think you're you doing, casting spells like that in the middle of public?" Bazel yelled.

"Stopping you," replied Zandra. "What was that thing you threw?"

"The Amulet of Kronack. It boosts any spell that hits it. I was using it so that my Ambiguus spell would affect all of the rioters, in the hope that if I was able to get them confused, they would disperse. I'm still trying to make this a land a place where we don't have to live in the shadows."

"By holding back honest people that are just trying to be treated fairly?" Zandra replied coldly.

"If rebellion is allowed to rise from this revolution, all the work that I've done will go to waste," he said.

"I don't see how what you're doing here will help us live in the open. Seems to me that you're allying yourself with the powerful, so you can gain power yourself."

As Zandra and Bazel argued, the Regulators became more feverish. Some of the soldiers under General Shepard joined the Regulators in marching. Things were quickly reaching a point of danger. Shays and Shepard agreed to give the judges safe passage through the crowd to leave unharmed, as long as they did not bring the cases to trial, per Shays' request.

"See what you've done?" Bazel shouted. "You let the rioters win the day!"

Zandra cut him off. "You cannot get power at the expense of the masses. You'll pay a high price in the end."

Bazel stomped off.

The rebellion's victory was short-lived. Though Shays did not want to shed blood, they needed weapons to put pressure on the government. And if they could deny the army access to the arms, the possibility of aggression against the Regulators would be diminished. Not to mention, they needed shelter from the winter weather, as it was now late January.

Shays met with Captain Luke Day and Eli Parsons,[20] both of whom had lead groups of Regulators in early January. They decided to march on the armory at Springfield.

When the day came, only Parsons' men met up with Shays.

As they marched through the snow towards the armory, General Shepard ordered a warning shot fired over their heads. The Regulators ignored it. Shortly, Shepard ordered his men to open fire, and the Regulators fled.

Bazel Blackbone arrived with General Benjamin Lincoln[21] and some reinforcements two days later. Joining forces with Shepard's men, they crossed the frozen Connecticut river after the Regulators.

Word had reached Zandra by this point, and she foolishly grabbed her broom and flew off in the daylight, heading for the armory to see if Bazel was up to no good.

Upon arriving, she found only a small contingent of troops there. Night was falling, but the snow leading away from the armory told of the soldier's departure. Casting a Commuta Habitum charm on herself to hide her presence, she took off.

Flying through the woods at a hurried pace, she weaved in and out of the trees, finally catching up to the troops. She moved in closer to see if she could spot Bazel.

Bazel's wand was vibrating; he had cast a Propinquitas Charm to alert him if Zandra came near. Looking over to his left, he could see a distortion moving through the woods.

"I thought you might show up," he mumbled to himself.

As they came to a clearing, Bazel rode out in front of the column, lifted his left arm, and, using his cape to hide his wand from the troops, he murmured "Detego," just as Zandra flew a bit too close to the clearing.

Her cover was blown. Bazel grinned, then pointed to her, raising everyone's attention to her presence. She was close enough that they could see her clearly. Quickly, she broke off to the south as the soldiers gasped at what they were seeing.

"Was that a witch?" asked General Lincoln, astonished.

"It appears so," replied Bazel.

"Should we send some men after her?" asked the general.

"Give me five men, and I will track her down," said Bazel.

General Lincoln turned and yelled: "Captain!"

A man rode up. "Sir?"

"Five men on horses. Report to Mr. Blackbone."

"Yes, sir!"

A few minutes later, the men rode up. Bazel lead them off in the direction that Zandra had flown. The rest of the soldiers continued on their search for the Regulators.

As soon as they were out of sight of the other soldiers, Bazel turned on his men. "Pulso!"

All five men and horses fell to the ground.

Bazel started murmuring a complex enchantment, and after a bit it began to snow. In just a short while, the snow was coming down heavy, and the wind was becoming strong.

Bazel pulled his rifle out and waved his wand over it. "Detego!"

The gun turned back into the broom that it really was. Mounting it, he kicked off to search for Zandra.

The storm soon increased to a fairly powerful nor'easter. The snow had become mixed with sleet. Zandra's cheeks burned from the cold sleet and wind. Night had fallen; the forest was a cold blue.

Finally, she had made it back to where her cover had been blown, continuing up behind where the troops had gone. Bazel saw Zandra pass and took off after her, closing the gap between them. He pointed his wand at her.

Just as he let his spell go, a big snowflake hit him in the eye, making him close it. His spell narrowly missed Zandra, knocking her off her broom. She tumbled into a deep snowdrift.

Bazel landed near Zandra, leaning his broom against a tree. She could only see his boots as he walked up to the drift that contained her, his dark cape flapping in the near-blizzard wind.

She raised her snow-covered head to see him standing over her, her body still buried in the drift.

"Miss Voorhies." Bazel frowned. "I've had enough of your intrusiveness."

"Are you helping your powerful friends again, Bazel?" she managed to say through her chattering teeth.

Bazel gave Zandra a snarl. "This little rebellion stops today."

"What are you getting out of this?" Zandra asked.

"*Everything.* The minds of the powerful are a sharp tool, Zandra."

"Pushing others down is not a way to help us to be able to come out of the shadows. If that's even your real intention."

As she said this, she raised her wand under the snow. Her spell hit Bazel in the chest, knocking him back.

Zandra jumped up out of the drift as Bazel threw a spell back at her. She deflected it with ease.

"All those soldiers saw you!" Bazel shouted. "You will be a hunted witch!" He ducked a spell from Zandra and threw one of his own back at her. "You're not going to win this one. I would suggest you move on before something bad happens. This is a big country, Zandra!"

Zandra threw another spell at him. Bazel deflected it, then, in the same movement, he hit her with a spell that tied her to a tree, making her drop her wand in the snow.

"You'd best take my advice."

Walking back over to his broom, he threw his leg over it and kicked off, leaving Zandra bound to the tree.

Bazel flew back to his horse and the men he had knocked out with a Pulso charm. Landing next to them, he turned his broom back into a rifle, then reversed the spell on the men. They slowly rose out from under the snow which had fallen over them.

"The witch ambushed us," he told them. "Luckily, she missed me, and I was able to get a shot off at her," he said, raising his rifle. "I don't think I hit her, but I also don't think she'll be coming around again."

The men mounted their horses.

Bazel led the way. "Let's head out and join back up with the column."

Late the next day, Bazel's spell finally failed and Zandra, weakened from exposure to the cold, fell to the ground.

As night fell, a female Stonish Giant found Zandra lying in the snow. Picking up a branch, the Stonish Giant began banging on a nearby hollow tree. Soon one of the massive males, carrying the carcass of a female deer under his arm and being followed by the rest of the troop, came upon them. After a discussion, the big male stripped the hide off the deer, and, as the troop ate, the female wrapped Zandra up in the hide to warm her.

Phineas had not heard from Zandra in a couple of days. He had sent word out to all who knew her, and many had shown up to search for her. Xavier had been out searching since the first day. Broken Arrow and Phineas had spoken with Shakock, and enlisted the help of the Stonish Giants. Cormac and Gregor flew up from Boston, and Theophilus Martin, Amity Cowgill, Azariah and Dorcas Jones of the Salem Witches' Council had all joined in the search.

Zandra had been in a coma for a couple of days when Cormac flew up through the forest where she lay. Just before he passed her, the large male Stonish Giant pushed a tree into his flight path. Cormac landed and noticed the snow stained with blood. Looking around and fearing the worst, he spotted the rolled up deer hide and ran over to it. Unrolling it, he fell to his knees and felt for Zandra's pulse. When he was sure that she was alive, he wrapped her back up in the hide.

Holding his broom in one hand and taking out his wand with the other, he said: "Revoco!" Zandra's broom flew at him from under the snow. Laying the broom beside the bundle that contained Zandra, he pointed his wand at it. "Sustringo," he said, binding the broom to the bundle and his own broom.

Noticing that Zandra's wand was not on her, he looked around. Not seeing it anywhere, he said "Revoco!" once again. Zandra's wand came flying out from a drift of snow beside a tree, and he caught it.

Looking into the woods, Cormac called out: "Thank you!" Then, in a lower voice: "Those Stonish Giants give me the creeps."

Hopping on his broom, he flew back to Zandra's house.

Phineas and Broken Arrow were there when Zandra came around. Sitting up in bed quickly, her head whirled and she fell back down.

She looked around. "What has happened?" Fear rose up inside of her as she remembered. "Where's Bazel?"

"It's over," replied Phineas. "The Rebellion was crushed. You've been out for a few days."

She sighed with resignation. "How did it happen?"

"The Regulators weren't expecting anyone to be following them because of the storm, so they were caught off guard when the federal troops found them. They weren't all caught, and we don't know their fate."

"It was Bazel," said Zandra. "I'll bet he worked up that storm to give himself the advantage."

"Always had a bad feeling about that one, I did," said Cormac.

The first flowers of spring were blooming. Zandra had been licking her wound from Bazel's defeat of her. Daniel Shays was sought after by the government for high treason and had been in hiding. Daniel and his wife moved every few days and never let it be known who they were. Some of his men had been condemned to death.

It was time for her to move on. It was becoming too dangerous for her here.

"I don't want you to leave," Phineas said.

"I know. But there are a lot of reasons that I need to, besides the fact that I'm being hunted. The natives are suffering; if I move to a more central location I can be of more help. And I'll be closer to that Piasa Bird. Maybe I can figure out how to get more infusion materials from it." She put a hand on Phineas's shoulder. "I'll see you from time to time—after all, you're my East Coast distributor, and you'll be living in my old house."

A long, low voice came from the forest. "ARHOOOOOOO!"

Zandra and Phineas walked out to the woods.

"Transferendum," Zandra muttered. "How are you, Shakock?"

"You wanted to talk to me."

Zandra nodded. "I'm moving to the Illinois territory, near the place where two great rivers come together. Phineas will be living here, and I will be here from time to time to visit. He'll take care of anything you might need. You can leave your hairs with him, and he'll send them to me."

Shakock nodded.

"Do your kind live in that area?" Zandra asked.

"Yes."

"Could you put in a word for me with them?"

"Yes," he said again, succinct as always.

"Thank you," Zandra said. "Take care of yourself."

Zandra had loaded her wagon the day before, and Xavier was hitched up.

"Broken Arrow, you lay low. I want to see you when I come back."

"Be careful," he said.

Phineas was looking very sad. Zandra walked over to him and gave him a big hug.

"I won't say goodbye because this isn't," Phineas said. "I'll miss you."

"No, you're right, it's not goodbye," she replied. "And I'll miss you too. Write me as often as you like."

"I will," said Phineas.

They held the hug for a while longer. Zandra gave him a peck on the cheek, then climbed up on the wagon and headed off down the road.

CHAPTER 10

The Great Valley Road and Beyond

Late Summer, 1787 - Fall, 1788

Zandra and Xavier had made it to Philadelphia and had started down the Great Valley Road,[22] which headed southwest along the front range of the Appalachian mountains. Setting up camp every night, they would head out on the road the next morning.

After a week of traveling, they stopped to rest for a few days in a secluded hollow they had found in the mountains.

As the day turned into night, Zandra and Xavier relaxed around the campfire.

Zandra noticed that Xavier seemed overly alert, and he appeared to be listening for something. "What is it?" she asked.

He shook his mane out. *Nothing.*

"Are you sure? You seem on edge."

No, just new surroundings. There's probably nothing to worry about.

Zandra shrugged. "Whatever. Just wake me up if anything happens during the night."

With that, she rolled over to go to sleep.

The next day, they relaxed and did little. Xavier said nothing about the previous night, but once again, as they sat around the fire talking, he seemed like he was nervous about something.

When Xavier finished the keg of rum that they had got as they passed through Philadelphia, he asked, *When can we get some more rum?*

"Maybe at Harrisonburg,[23] I don't know. We don't have endless money. You need to limit yourself. I think you got too used to Epbaris' spring."

Well, if you hadn't drawn attention to yourself, I could still be visiting with Epbaris, and you wouldn't have to buy my rum. You shouldn't have been so quick to go to the aid of those men. You knew they would hunt you down as quick as anyone.

"It's not about that. I just don't like the wealthy and powerful taking advantage of the lesser in a society."

I understand that, but just slow down and think about what you're doing. I don't want to have to move every time you take up a cause.

While they were talking, unseen eyes were in the forest, prowling around the camp stealthily. Climbing a tree, the creature worked its way onto a limb that overhung the fire–watching the two of them, waiting for the right moment.

They both turned in for the night. Xavier had laid down and began to doze, and Zandra was fast asleep. The creature took its chance and dived down, pinning Zandra to the ground, teeth bared. Zandra was struggling to get to her wand, but was it was taking all her strength just to keep the creature from getting its mouth around her neck.

"XAVIER!"

Xavier woke quickly and got to his feet. Rearing up, he struck at the creature with his front hooves. The creature rolled off of

Zandra, then dashed off into the forest on its hind legs, with great agility and grace.

What was that? asked Xavier, shocked. *It appeared to be a cougar, but it ran on its hind legs.*

"Almost like a werecat," replied Zandra.

She thought back to some of the creatures that Broken Arrow had told her about.

"Wampus cat!" she cried suddenly. "It must have been a Wampus cat! Broken Arrow told me of a part-woman, part-cat creature that lives in this part of the country. It couldn't be anything else. I'd better put up a shield charm so she doesn't get at us again."

Looking down on the ground, Xavier found a chunk of the Wampus cat's fur that he had dislodged with his hooves. *Looks like I've collected some more infusion materials for your wands.*

Bending over and picking up the clump, Zandra smiled. "Well, you've earned that rum you wanted."

Pulling out her wand and pointing it at the sky, she said, "Integumentum!" She put her wand back in her pocket. "That should keep her out," said Zandra.

Zandra added the Wampus cat fur to the box of wand materials on the wagon, and they both laid down and went back to sleep.

Later in the night, they heard claws scraping down the sides of the shield as the Wampus cat tried to get at them once more. When morning came, the cat had moved on.

Breaking camp, they headed out onto the road again.

Four days later, they had stopped for another couple of days near a Aniyunwiya[1] camp. Zandra had been visiting with the women of the group, but hadn't let them know of her powers. She

---

[1] Cherokee.

had made friends with a girl named Rising Sun from the tribe. As they sat down and ate some Ageyutsa,[1] Rising Sun told of her tribe running from the killers that had been chasing her people down and destroying their food stores. Zandra told her that she had known of the rangers, and that she was sorry that her people had to go through this. It sickened Zandra to hear of their plight—it always did.

It was late afternoon by the time Zandra returned to Xavier.

That night, they had been asleep for a short while when they were awoken by screams coming from Rising Sun's camp. Zandra jumped up and headed toward the commotion.

A group of men, apparently rangers, were destroying their camp. One of the men had Rising Sun pinned to the ground on her belly, jerking her head up by her hair. He pulled a knife from his belt, bringing the blade to her forehead.

Zandra whipped her wand out. "Atollo!" she shouted.

The man rose into the air, letting go of Rising Sun. Zandra motioned him toward her with her wand. As he passed her with a look of bewilderment on his face, Zandra said, "You scum."

Then she tossed him into a nearby tree, knocking him out.

Xavier had started charging some of the other men. One lifted his rifle to fire on Xavier. Quickly, Zandra yelled "Atollo!" once more. The spell grabbed the musket ball, and Zandra directed it back at the shooter's head, spinning to a halt just inches away from his face. The man froze in fear.

"Sustringo!" Rope shot from the tip of her wand and wove around all of the rangers, binding them all together. Zandra ran back to Rising Sun.

Falling on her knees, Zandra lifted her up. She had gotten there just in time—there was only a small cut on Rising Sun's forehead.

---

[1] Ground hog sausage.

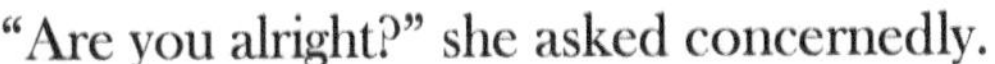

"Are you alright?" she asked concernedly.

"Yes, I'm fine," replied Rising Sun.

Zandra pointed her wand at the cut. "Percuro!" The small cut closed, leaving only a red line where it had been.

"Thank you," said Rising Sun. "Are you a shaman?"

"She's a witch!" one of the rangers said. "When we break out of your demonic ropes, we will burn you at the stake!"

Zandra waved her wand over the destroyed camp, putting everything right.

All the noise had drawn the attention of a troop of Stonish Giants that were now standing just inside the tree line.

We've attracted some attention, said Xavier, gesturing in their direction.

Zandra pointed her wand at the place that the Stonish Giants were standing. "Transferendum," she said. "Hello, friends. I could use your help."

One of the unbelievably large Stonish Giants stepped out. Zandra always found it amazing that something so large could hide so well. The natives retreated back away from it, and the rangers gaped at what they were seeing. No words of defiance came from their mouths.

"I'm Zandra," she said. "I have some men that need to be taught a lesson."

Then the thundering voice came from its huge mouth. "We have heard of you. You're the one who helped Shakock with the intruders."

"Yes, I am. If I do for you the same as I've done for Shakock, would you help me with these men?" she said, placing an Auris Silentium charm over the rangers so they couldn't hear.

"What do you want of us?" it rumbled.

"First off, no ripping them apart."

The Stonish Giant frowned.

"Just scare the life out of them for a few days, then let them go."

The Stonish Giant nodded his head in agreement.

Zandra turned and lifted the silencing spell from the rangers as more Stonish Giants came out of the woods, each grabbing one of the rangers.

Some screamed in fear, another passed out, and there was a definite smell in the air that told of one of them soiling himself. Zandra dropped the spell that bound the men together, and they were dragged off into the woods.

The end was near to their long journey. They had been passing through virgin forests of oak, hickory, dogwood, and maple, in some places thick with wild grapevine. This part of the Illinois country was lush, and at times, hilly. Zandra had even come across a massive salt spring.

Approaching a group of stone hoodoos[I] that rose one hundred feet above the forest,[II] Zandra said, "I think this is it. What do you think, Xavier?"

There would be a commanding view from up there, he replied.

"We could build a house and clear a small meadow for you to graze in."

Climbing to the top, they looked out to the west and could see for miles above the canopy of trees. Zandra set up camp just in time to sit back and watch the sunset with Xavier.

Fall had come. Zandra had set up residence among the hoodoos. Her small home had a porch that looked out to the west. She had built it to carry the weight of Xavier, and they would often watch the sunset from it. Because of its prominence, she had put a charm on it, making it appear like another hoodoo.

[I] Columns of rock.

[II] Now known as Garden of the Gods.

Pukwudgies were thick in the woods around her house. She found Stonish Giant structures in the forest, and she could hear them talking in the night, but they were keeping their distance. She had brought a lot of materials to make wands with from the east. After much difficulty, she had come up with a spell that made the Stonish Giants' hairs collect on her wand as she passed through the forest.

Eventually, Zandra decided it was time to set out and look for new magical creatures. She and Xavier had been out for a week when they stopped to check out the earthen mounds that she had stumbled upon the time she went to help the Arikara. After that, they headed over to the Mississippi River and turned north. The river turned to the northeast, then back to the northwest.

"This looks like the stream that I took to try to evade the Piasa Bird," Zandra said to Xavier.

I don't think I want to run into that thing, he replied uneasily.

They headed onward, coming upon three islands in the river. Zandra heard the flapping of giant wings, and they quickly ducked into the trees.

The Piasa Bird flew over their heads, carrying a large deer. The morning sun shone through the trees behind Zandra and Xavier as the bird landed on the near island. [24]

It's not much to look at, said Xavier.

"It's nasty in more ways than one," replied Zandra.

They stayed hidden until it rose off the island, without the deer, and headed north. Zandra and Xavier came out from under the trees and headed on up the river.

Suddenly, Zandra heard a whooshing sound, and she turned to see the Piasa Bird flying up behind them. It must have circled around the island. Shooting fire from its eyes, it hit the tree next to them, which burst into flames.

Zandra and Xavier dashed off into the forest, running deep into the woods. Zandra pulled out her wand and stood against Xavier.

"Nubes!" she shouted, and a wave of gray and green poured over them.

Stay still, Zandra thought at Xavier. The Piasa Bird dove and clawed at the top of the forest canopy where they had ran in. After what seemed like forever, it flew off.

Then they heard footsteps behind them. Zandra's wand began to vibrate—she had put a Propinquitas charm on it earlier, so she could find any wizards or witches living in the area. Two men came into view. Zandra could see that they were wearing long robes, with turbans on their heads, and both were carrying staffs—one with an ibis on top, and one with an Egyptian ankh. The man with the ibis-topped staff introduced himself.

"I'm Omar Gamal, and this is my friend, Sharif Thabit," he said, gesturing toward the man with the ankh-topped staff.

Zandra stepped forward. "I'm Zan—"

"Zandra Voorhies, and Xavier," interrupted Omar, nodding.

CHAPTER 11

Little Egypt

Fall, 1788 - Spring, 1789

"How do you know my name?" Zandra asked, astonished.

Omar smiled. "There are many things about our magic that you're unaware of. Egyptian sorcery is older even than Egyptian society." He started pacing up and down. "You should try not to get the attention of the Piasa Bird."

"We weren't trying to. We were just traveling upriver."

"I'm sure you had no idea that the bird frequents that island. The Piasa Bird is a formidable opponent. It is a struggle for both Sharif and I to put it at bay. But this is the second time you've had the misfortune of getting its attention. I would not recommend doing so again," Omar said.

"You–it was you two that were on that point in the stream eight years ago!"

Omar nodded. "Very perceptive of you."

Omar's companion, Sharif, spoke up. "You're lucky that you're a good flier, and a quick thinker. You're also lucky that you came across us."

"We need to find a better place to talk," said Omar. "There's a hollow nearby. Come with us."

Traveling to the northeast, they came to the mouth of a hollow that angled back to the northwest. After traveling down it for a short distance, the hollow narrowed.

Stopping for a minute, Omar raised his staff. "Kdeyo!" A clear line, like a stream of water, shot out of his staff and spread above them over the camp, concealing their presence. Now they could start a fire. Sharif told Zandra and Xavier that they still needed to be careful, as the Piasa Bird was very good at detecting them, even through the shield.

As they sat around the low campfire that night, Zandra asked more questions of her new Egyptian friends. Xavier had gone out to graze.

"What are a couple of Egyptian wizards doing in southern Illinois country?" asked Zandra.

"Our people have had contact with the people of this part of the world for a very long time," replied Omar. "We have worked together with many different tribes, primarily the Cahokians in this area and the Aztecs in Tenochtitlan."[I]

"Cahokia...is that the place with the earthen mounds southeast of here?" asked Zandra.[25]

"Yes," replied Omar. "Our architectural methods have proven to be quite popular in this area. Earthen pyramids were the easiest to construct here."

"Are there many of you around?"

"We have three settlements that form a triangle at the southern end of the Illinois country, the point of which is at the joining of the two great rivers. Cairo is there, then about thirty miles to the northeast is Karnak. That is where we live. To the northwest on the Mississippi river is Thebes. We've just started a new settlement, about one hundred miles south on the Mississippi River, named Memphis. We call the triangle Little Egypt."

"You said that your magic was older than your society?" Zandra asked.

Omar nodded. "Egypt was once one of the ten Kingdoms of Atlantis. Our magic came from their priest."

"From their priest?" Zandra inquired.

[I] Mexico City.

"Yes," Sharif replied. "When a witch or wizard becomes of age, they are led into a secret room in the belly of the Great Sphinx. There, a ceremony is performed, and a staff is chosen for them."

"Where is this Atlantis place?"

"It was in what is now western Africa. You can still see the remnants of it if you fly over it at a high enough altitude. The ocean has receded, and the land has risen, leaving it an island in a vast desert."[26]

"Are your spells in Atlantean, then? I don't recognize the language," Zandra said.

"Yes," replied Omar. "All our spells come from a dialect of Ancient Atlantean, a dead language in most of the world these days."

"And you use your staffs to cast the Atlantean spells?" Zandra asked.

Omar nodded.

"Wouldn't that be cumbersome in some situations?" Zandra asked.

Omar picked up his staff. The ibis head was a black reflective metal, with a silver beak, and an emerald green plume off the back of its head. The crescent on its head was gold, and the lunar disk was silver. He put his hand just below the head of the ibis. "Kyrdeza," he muttered.

The end of the staff lifted off, exposing a wand. "We normally use the staff, because it increases our powers, but in close quarters we have the wand. When the wand is exposed, the spells come from the tip. When it's in the staff, the power is focused through the head of the ibis."

Sharif took his staff in hand. The ankh on the end of his was made of silver, with a sapphire in the loop.

"Kyrdeza." His staff separated at the top also.

Zandra was amazed. "I have a friend, Broken Arrow. He told me that there was once a shaman of the Cahokians that came to an agreement with the Piasa Bird."

"Yes, there was," replied Sharif. "Unfortunately, his name has been lost. The indigenous shamans are very powerful."

Xavier returned from his grazing.

Zandra thought for a moment. "During that encounter eight years ago, I managed to blast a sliver of the Piasa Bird's fang off. It caught me in the chest. When I got back from my trip, I infused some of the sliver into one of my wands, and it was immensely powerful. I make a lot of money from them, and I would like to get more infusion materials. Do you think you two could help me get some infusion materials from the Piasa Bird?"

Omar and Sharif looked at each other.

"We've never done more than try to evade it," said Sharif. "I don't know that we could kill it."

"No, not kill," said Zandra. "Just stun it. We could hide out on the island and wait for it to return to eat its prey. Then all three of us could stun it long enough that I could get a sliver from its fang," said Zandra.

"It would be very risky," replied Sharif.

"I agree," said Omar.

Sounds like a crazy idea. But you seem to have a lot of those, and somehow you always survive, said Xavier.

"Do you two have brooms?" Zandra asked.

"We use our staffs," replied Sharif.

"So, first thing in the morning, then?" Zandra pressed.

Omar looked at Sharif and smiled, shaking his head. "Well, we can give it a try," he said.

"Good!" said Zandra. "Then we had better turn in, so we can get to the island before dawn."

It was still dark when they got up.

"Stay hidden," Zandra said, rubbing Xavier's muzzle. "We'll be back as soon as we can."

The three of them kicked off.

Flying into the darkness, they made the short hop to the island. Landing on the sandbar, they walked just inside the tree line to wait for the Piasa Bird's arrival.

Steam rose off the water, giving the island an eerie feeling. The deep blue light of predawn mixed with the steam made it seem even cooler than it was.

Hearing the flap of large wings, Zandra scanned the sky.

"There it is!" said Sharif. Zandra and Omar looked to where he was pointing.

The Piasa Bird was flying over the river from the east. It flew south of where they were standing, passing into the center of the island, a deer in each of its front talons.

As quickly and quietly as they could, they headed deeper into the island. Coming upon a thin water inlet, Zandra got on her broom to hop over it. Omar and Sharif did the same on their staffs.

Landing on the opposite bank, they weaved through the trees. They soon came to a larger body of water, almost like a harbor in the middle of the island. Pointing across the water, Zandra said, "There, on the beach!"

On the west side of the little harbor, the Piasa Bird stood, its back to them, feasting on its prey.

Zandra turned to Omar and Sharif. "I'll kick off and fly toward it. As soon as I have its attention, I'll blind it with a Fulgur spell. Can you two keep it immobilized long enough for me to get a sliver?"

"We can try," Omar responded.

Zandra took flight and headed toward the Piasa Bird. It noticed her immediately. Pointing her wand at its face and closing her eyes, she shouted: "Fulgur!"

A ribbon of light burst from her wand and expanded into a large ball that sent shadows of the trees onto the waters. The Piasa Bird closed its eyes as Omar and Sharif both pointed their staffs at it, yelling: "Kadezon!"

Thick red ribbons of light hit the Piasa Bird in its chest, knocking it on its back. Landing on the beach, Zandra dropped her broom and ran at the creature. Still thrashing slightly, with blood running down its coarse beard from its recent meal, it lay there almost immobilized. Zandra pointed her wand at its fang and said: "Segmentum!"

A sliver of fang came off neatly. She then did the spell again. The second sliver dropped next to the first.

Just then, Omar and Sharif's hold on the creature failed, and it jumped to its feet.

"Ambiguus!" Zandra yelled frantically, as Omar and Sharif tried to re-establish their spell on it. Zandra's spell hit the Piasa Bird, and it stood there looking disoriented for a brief moment.

"Revoco!" The slivers flew into Zandra's hands, and she shoved them in her flight bag. "Revoco!" Her broom flew into her hand and she kicked off, just as Omar and Sharif's spell took effect again. As they saw Zandra rise above the Piasa Bird, they mounted their staffs, dropping the spell.

The three of them headed downriver, with the Piasa Bird in pursuit. As they skimmed the surface of the water, the Piasa Bird was gaining. With his hand, Omar motioned for them to climb higher and split up.

They all rose for a distance, and split in three directions. Looking over her shoulder, Zandra could see that the Piasa Bird had followed her. *Great,* she thought, as she started throwing spells at it. Omar and Sharif came together behind the Piasa Bird and were gaining on it. The wind was whistling in Zandra's ears. Omar motioned his intention to Sharif. Sharif nodded his head.

Ropes shot from their staffs and wrapped around the rear legs of the Piasa Bird. Reversing their direction, they began to pull.

"Faraterum!" shouted Omar.

Electricity ran down the ropes, shocking the Piasa Bird. Sharif joined in. The Piasa Bird writhed in pain as it broke off the chase and fell toward the water, pulling Omar and Sharif with it. As it hit, the electricity spidered across the surface of the water, which frothed as stunned fish floated to the surface. Omar and Sharif broke the spell just in time to pull out of the dive.

Zandra streaked back upriver and flew into camp as fast as she could, landing near Xavier.

Where are Omar and Sharif? he asked.

Before Zandra could answer, they flew in overhead. Omar landed, while Sharif flew through the trees to the top of the ridge to make sure the Piasa Bird would pass them by.

"That was tough," gasped Omar. "It took all we had to hold it for only a short time."

"I think it would take many more witches and wizards from my homeland to do the same. My spells only lasted for a brief second, and that was with my Thunderbird wand," said Zandra.

"You've met a Thunderbird?"

"Yes, it saved me from a Mishipizheu that was in a lake near my home in the Massachusetts Colony."

"The Thunderbird was all the way on the East Coast? I wonder why," said Omar.

"That trip that I was on when we first met, I spent a night at what the Lakota call Ghost Mountain. The Thunderbird came to me in a dream. I didn't know at the time, but it was a vision of things to come. I knew that there was a lot of magic around the mountain, and I didn't know what to think about it: was it just because of the intense magic of the place? Was it a spirit trying to communicate? I just put it out of my mind until the night of the encounter."

"It's very rare for the Thunderbird to contact a person like that. You should feel very honored," said Omar.

"My friend Broken Arrow said I was lucky to have such a protector."

Sharif came out of the woods, having come back down off the ridge. "The Piasa Bird just passed, looking a little tattered and scanning the river banks for us."

"Good. I don't want to fight it again today," said Omar. Turning back to Zandra, he asked, "Did you get your infusion materials?"

Zandra grinned and pulled the two large, yellowish slivers out of her pouch.

Zandra took her latest wand off the lathe.

Omar had been spending some time with her over the winter, and they were becoming close. She had been wrapping her wands in buckskin, and putting a spell on the bundle to make it appear as a bird. Then the wands would fly off to Phineas, so he could distribute them for her.

She had been feeling that it was getting warm enough to make the trip back to Danvers for a visit. She asked Omar if he could watch over things, so she could make the journey. He agreed.

So one evening, in late May, she packed up some belongings and her newest batch of wands, giving Omar a long hug. They kissed, and Zandra flew back east.

CHAPTER 12

PHINEAS

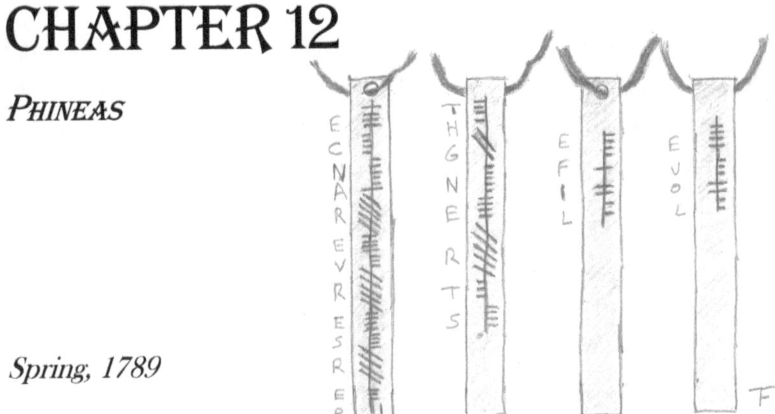

Spring, 1789

The Chalice was busy.

The wood walls gave the room a warm glow in the candlelight. From where he was sitting against the back wall, Phineas had been feeling very out of place. Looking down at the table, he didn't notice Thalia, the barmaid, staring at him. Her long, jet-black hair hung over one of her almond-shaped green eyes, which were outlined in black, exaggerating their shape. Along with her dark lipstick and pale complexion, it gave her a striking appearance, which belied her shy, sweet nature.

Paying too much attention to Phineas, she spilled a drink all over one of her customers. Looking up at the ensuing commotion, Phineas decided it was time to leave. Thalia watched him walk out the door as the enraged wizard yelled at her.

Without Zandra, Phineas's life had become sad and lonely. On his way back to Zandra's old house, he wished that she was there with him. Broken Arrow had been away for some time, visiting with his people. It seemed like sometimes Shakock was the only one that Phineas had to talk with, and he never seemed to say anything more than he had to. Although, one time he did tell Phineas about Zandra's run-in with the rangers, and how Zandra had enlisted the help of another troop of Stonish Giants.

Zandra sent him letters from time to time. He got so excited when a letter would flutter to him. She had told him of her new home among the hilltop hoodoos of the southern Illinois country, meeting the Egyptian wizards, and all she had learned about their settlements in this part of the country, as well as their encounter with the Piasa Bird. When he finished with her letters he missed her even more.

Then, one spring day, one of the rare letters flew up to him.

Dear Phineas,

I'm flying back for a visit; leaving today, should be there in three days. I've sent a letter to the O'Malleys. Thought we would spend some time in Boston and stop by Bohm's shop and then fly down to New York and check in at Las Squelette. Can you get a horse for me to ride? (Xavier isn't coming.) Thought it would be nice to ride to Boston, as it's not that far. Be ready to leave the day after I arrive.

I miss you,

Zandra

Phineas was elated. Deciding that in his depression he had let the place go, he started cleaning and getting the property back in shape.

On the third morning from when he had gotten the letter, a dark-haired woman landed in the pasture. Phineas looked out the window. At first he didn't recognize her—Zandra had changed her hair to brown, with the hopes of fooling anyone that might still recognize her from the Shays' Rebellion incident. He went out to greet her.

Zandra threw her broom down and ran to hug Phineas.

"I've missed you so much!" he said.

She hugged him tighter. "I've missed you too. Do you have anything to eat? I'm starving."

As Zandra put her arm around his waist, they turned and headed into the house.

After they had eaten, the two of them walked out to the edge of the forest. Zandra let out a whoop.

"Broken Arrow has been off with his people for a while now," said Phineas.

"I hope he's alright. It's not getting any safer out there for them."

After a few minutes, Zandra whooped again. Shakock walked up, seemingly out of nowhere, looking down on Zandra as she raised her wand.

"Transferendum," she said. The translation spell took effect, and Shakock's booming voice broke the silence.

"You have come out unscathed twice now with the Piasa Bird. You've been lucky so far. But your luck is running out."

"Have you also heard of those rangers that I had trouble with?" asked Zandra.

"I don't think they will be going out in the woods anytime soon," replied Shakock.

"Good," said Zandra. "Is our spell still working for your troop?"

"Yes."

Zandra paused. "The Stonish Giants in the Illinois country have been...well, elusive. I hear them in the distance, but they never come close."

"They think they're safe, that the pale man will not make it into their territory in any great numbers, so they see no need for your protection."

"Well, I think they'll change their mind. Hopefully before too much of their land is gone." Zandra waved. "Thank you for your hairs again."

Shakock turned and walked off into the woods.

Zandra looked to Phineas. "Do we need to stop by your mother's before we leave for Boston tomorrow?"

Phineas shook his head. "I told Safferon that we were leaving yesterday."

Zandra heard a rustling, and she turned to see Broken Arrow walking out of the treeline.

"We're all here," said Zandra. "Well then, should we go to the Chalice tonight?"

"Sounds great to me," replied Phineas.

That evening, they headed off to the Chalice. Walking into the tavern, Broken Arrow removed his cloak and hung it on a hook at the door. A wizard at the bar gave them a look as they moved to their usual table.

Thalia had an expression of disappointment upon seeing that Phineas had come in with a new witch, as she walked over to take their order.

"Oh, Zandra–it's you! Didn't recognize you; you've changed your hair," Thalia said in a low voice.

"Yes, I put a charm on it to hopefully deceive any enemies who might still recognize me. How have you been, Thalia?"

"Fine, fine. What can I get you?"

After ordering, Thalia went back to get their food. When she came back with three plates, the wizard that had given them the eye when they came in grabbed Thalia by the arm.

"You're not going to serve that?" he asked angrily, pointing at Broken Arrow.

Not knowing what to do, Thalia looked at the large wizard that was behind the bar.

Strozor, the owner of the Chalice, walked down to her like a mountain that had suddenly sprouted legs, his bald head like a boulder balanced on top. Seeing that the strange wizard had hold of Thalia's arm, he asked, "What is the problem?"

"You feed their kind here?" asked the angered wizard.

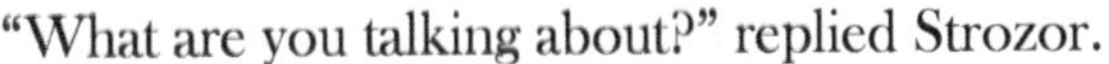

"What are you talking about?" replied Strozor.

"Him!" said the man, pointing at Broken Arrow once more.

"If you have a problem with that, you can leave."

"Not until he does!" replied the man.

Coming around the bar, Strozor spoke in the man's face. "Are you going to leave on your own, or do you need some help?"

Zandra and Phineas jumped up and stood in front of Broken Arrow.

The man pulled out his wand, pointing it at Strozor. Strozor lifted his hand to block the spell, which ricocheted off, hitting the man in the chest and knocking him out.

Reaching down with one hand, Strozor picked the wizard up by the collar, walked to the door, and threw him out.

Then Strozor returned to behind the bar. Everyone was silent. Slowly the murmurs started and the volume rose again.

Walking up to their table, Thalia set their food down.

"I've never seen someone deflect a spell with their hand like that," Zandra said.

"I've often wondered about Strozor–he seems to be different," said Phineas. "You work for him, Thalia; do you know anything about him?"

Thalia shook her head. "He doesn't talk much, but I've heard rumors that he's part Stonish Giant."

"I didn't know that was possible," replied Zandra.

"I don't know, but the story I've heard says a female ancestor of Strozor lived in the Norse settlement L'Anse Aux Meadows[27] up in the far north of this continent. She was kidnapped by a Stonish Giant. She escaped, but not before becoming impregnated. She and her child were accepted back in the community. Strozor is a descendant of that encounter."

"Wow. Poor woman–that had to be a nightmare for her and all of her descendants," replied Zandra.

Thalia shook her head and shivered. "Strozor is very nice and gentle, but there is a great sadness in him." She turned away. "Well, I have to get back to work."

The rest of the night was like old times for Phineas. With Zandra beside him, it didn't matter what they were doing or not doing–he was happy. Broken Arrow told of his people taking their place as Elder Brother of the Haudenosaunee Confederation[28] to stand united against the white man.

"I'm tired of the killing," said Broken Arrow, "but if we do nothing, the white man will kill us all."

It was a beautiful spring day—blue sky with a few fluffy white clouds. Phineas and Zandra rode in silence as they passed down Ipswich road toward Boston. They didn't have to speak as they rode–it was enough for Phineas just to have her there. He wanted to tell her how he felt, but was too scared.

Why should anyone love me? I'm not handsome or smart. I do things wrong all the time. Even my mother doesn't like me much.

But none of that mattered right now.

It seemed that they had been on the road no time when they came upon Boston. They wove their way to the O'Malley's. Putting their horses up in a stall, they knocked on the back door. When it opened, Finnghuala stood there looking at them.

"Well, there ye be!" she exclaimed, stepping out and embracing Zandra with one arm, patting Phineas's cheek with the other.

"So good to see you two! Come in. I'll have dinner after a bit. Can I get you some tea or coffee?"

"Do you have any hard cider?" asked Zandra.

"Sure do!" Finnghuala looked at Phineas.

"I'll have some too."

"Go on in and have a seat. I'll bring it in to you." Walking through the door, they took seats around the large fireplace, setting their packs down beside them.

"This is where it all started," said Zandra. "I'm so glad you were here when I came to Boston."

"Me too," replied Phineas.

Finnghuala came into the room, carrying their drinks. Handing them each their cups, she pulled out her wand.

"I'll send your bags up to your rooms." She waved her wand, and their flight bags disappeared.

"Have you heard anything of Bazel?" asked Zandra.

"No, but I'm sure his hand is in things," said Finnghuala. "Well, I need to go. Food is almost ready."

"Can I help?" asked Zandra.

"No, you relax."

People started to filter down the stairs and in from the street. Food floated in from the kitchen, and in no time, everyone was eating and having a good time. Cormac came in late with a family that had just arrived. After introducing everyone, they continued eating.

When they had finished, Cormac sat down in the chairs around the fireplace, catching up with Zandra's adventures late into the night.

Zandra tapped her wand on the wall, and the blue line moved up. When the doorknob finished forming, they entered Fritz's store.

"Miss Voorhies." Fritz greeted her with a nod.

"Fritz! How have you been? I was in town visiting, and I just thought I would stop by to see how my wands were being received."

"People are wanting more wands with Piasa Bird fang infusions, but that's nothing new."

"I do have a couple new Piasa Bird wands," said Zandra, "but the price is going up. The infusion materials are very difficult to get. It took me and two Egyptian wizards to get the last ones, and I didn't know if we were going to make it out alive."

"How much do you want for them?" asked Fritz.

"Double the old price."

Fritz thought for a while, then said, "I think I'll be able to sell them for that. How many do you have?"

"I can let you have thirty wands—but only half of the Piasa Bird ones. I'm going to *Las Squelette* tomorrow, and I need to save some to sell there."

Zandra pulled her wands out of her pouch, and Fritz went through them. Pulling out a brown wand striped with yellow, he asked, "What's this one made of?"

"That's Devil's Backbone, with Piasa Bird fang. I found it to be a very good combination, though the wood does tend to be brittle, so I put a strengthening spell on it."

Fritz made no comment. He looked it over, then set it on his pile. After a bit, he had set all the wands he wanted aside. Pulling a box out from under the counter, he started to count out Zandra's money while she picked up some things. When she set her stuff down on the counter, Fritz added her total and subtracted it from her payment.

"That should do."

"Thank you," replied Zandra.

"Good day," said Fritz.

Zandra picked up her things, and they headed to the door.

"Fritz isn't the most personable man, is he?" asked Phineas.

"Never has been, it's all numbers with him."

The rest of the morning was spent just walking around Boston. Zandra had not really taken the time to explore Boston before.

Returning in the afternoon, they headed up to their rooms to catch a nap before they flew down to New York that night.

Finnghuala served them a late meal and, after eating, they walked out of Boston.

Once they found a secluded spot and it had gotten sufficiently dark, they flew off on their night's trip. Landing on the outskirts of New York, they changed their brooms into walking sticks and waited for morning.

Making their way through the streets, they found the *Las Squelette*. Upon entering, they found Genevieve behind the counter.

"Is Mr. Boneapart in?" Zandra asked.

Genevieve motioned to the door. They passed through and up the stairs. Entering the store, they found Rodrigue Boneapart stocking a shelf.

Rodrigue turned to look at his new customers, and it took him a moment to recognize Zandra.

"Miss Voorhies! Didn't recognize you at first; you've changed your hair color! It's good to see you," he said, as he lifted her hand to his lips.

"Mr. Boneapart," Zandra greeted him. "How are you doing?"

"Good! How's your new home?"

"It's coming along. I have some more wands with Piasa Bird fang infusions."

"Wonderful! The few I've sold have been very well-liked. People have been asking for more of them for a long time," said Boneapart.

"The price I'm asking has doubled," said Zandra. "The Piasa Bird fang slivers are difficult to acquire."

"Let's see your new work."

Zandra pulled out her bag, and Rodrigue sorted through the wands.

"I'll take them all!" he said.

After they settled on a price, Rodrigue handed her the money.

"Thank you, Rodrigue."

Coming around the counter, he grasped her hand, once more giving it a peck.

"'Till next time," he said amicably. "Be careful!"

"I will."

"Good day," Rodrigue said, nodding to Phineas.

Heading out the door, they walked back down the stairs, through the Ordie shop, and out onto the street.

After a few minutes of walking, Phineas heard a woman scream. Running to find where the screams came from, they turned a corner and saw a man pulling a baby away from her hysterical mother, who was being dragged by another man. The man who had taken the child climbed on to a wagon and quickly left.

Zandra looked revolted. Phineas knew that she had been aware of the Africans' treatment in the colonies, but had never witnessed it herself.

Turning to Phineas, she said, "Get that woman away from that man and meet me back where we landed."

She ran after the man that had the child.

As soon as Zandra left, Phineas pulled out his wand, waving it over his head.

"Pulso!" he said, knocking out everyone around. He ran over to the woman.

"Emarcesco!"

The woman shrunk, still unconscious. Phineas bent over and picked her up, placing her in his pocket. He walked a ways down the street before waving his wand over his head once more.

"Aversa pars!"

Everyone woke. The man that had been dragging the woman looked around confusedly, then got up and ran off to look for her.

Phineas finally reached the spot where they had landed, and he had been waiting for a while when Zandra came back.

"Where's the woman?" asked Zandra.

Phineas carefully pulled the tiny body out of his pocket.

"Good. It's going to be a couple hours before dark. Let's walk back into the woods so we can talk to her."

When they felt that they were sufficiently away from everyone, Zandra pulled the baby out of her flight bag. She cradled it in her arms as Phineas pulled the woman out, setting her on the ground.

"Okay, let's wake them at the same time," said Zandra.

Pointing their wands at the woman and baby, they said, "Aversa pars!"

The woman began to grow back to her normal size. She was very thin, as if she had not eaten well in a while; but she was beautiful, with high cheekbones and a strong, yet delicate chin.

The baby started crying, and the woman looked startled. Jumping up to grab her baby, she looked around with a disbelieving expression.

"How did I get here?" she asked confusedly, "and who are you?"

"I'm Zandra, and this is Phineas. What's your name?"

"Elizabeth," the woman replied. "How did I get here? What has happened?"

"I rescued your baby from the man, while Phineas took you away from your master."

"How?"

Zandra and Phineas looked at each other. Zandra clearly hadn't thought about how she was going to explain what had happened. Elizabeth looked at the two of them as she hugged her baby.

Zandra finally spoke, and told the woman the whole story of their rescue.

"You're witches!" the woman whispered, with a scared look on her face.

"No, I'm a wizard," said Phineas.

Elizabeth looked at Phineas for a moment.

"Don't be scared. We're not what you think; we're not evil. I've been helping people here for years. I use my magic for good, and most of my kind don't do harm to anyone."

Elizabeth hesitated for a moment, then nodded, though she still looked slightly wary.

"What's her name?" asked Zandra, gesturing at the baby, who had calmed down now that she was with her mother.

"Her name is Hope. Because she gives me hope. Hope that we could find a better life."

"She's beautiful," said Zandra. "Where is her father? We could free him also."

"You rescued me from her father. I hope to never see him again."

After a long silence, Zandra spoke softly. "Sorry."

"Where are we?" asked Elizabeth.

"Just outside of New York City," replied Phineas.

"Are you hungry?" asked Zandra as she started a fire.

"Yes!" Elizabeth watched in astonishment as Zandra pulled all the supplies to prepare a meal out of her flight bag.

"I've had dreams of running away to Canada and freedom," Elizabeth said with excitement.

"We could take you there. Do you know anyone up there?"

"No."

"Well, we have friends that might be able to help."

"Are they far?"

"Not far, but a little ways away. We would have to put you to sleep to transport you two."

"Why do you have to put us to sleep?"

"We have to shrink you down so that we can carry you when we fly."

"You really do fly?"

"Yes, we do," replied Phineas.

"We can leave after dark. But we need to get some sleep before tonight. We have been up for a long time." After they ate, Zandra and Phineas curled up together and took a nap as Elizabeth and Hope waited.

Waking at sunset, they put Elizabeth and Hope to sleep, shrinking them down. Phineas placed them in his pocket. Breaking camp, they flew off towards Boston and the O'Malley inn.

"Zandra, you have got to stop trying to rescue people all the time. You're going to expose us," said Finnghuala.

"I couldn't let her lose her baby," replied Zandra. "Besides, we can just keep them in a room with the windows blacked out until Gregor gets here to connect us with people in Canada."

Once Zandra finally had Finnghuala convinced, she, Phineas, and Finnghuala walked up to a room. Finnghuala blacked out the window, then left the room so that she wouldn't be seen. Phineas pulled the two little bodies out of his pocket and placed them on the bed.

"Aversa pars!"

Both of the spells reversed. Elizabeth cuddled Hope.

"Elizabeth, we will be staying here for a day or so until we find a safe place for you to live," said Zandra. "But we'll have to keep you in this room so you don't see any others of our kind."

"Okay," said Elizabeth. "Do you have any idea where we might go?"

"I have a friend that knows people near Montreal, Canada. I've contacted him, and he's on his way here now."

"Thank you for your help."

"It's no trouble. You just relax and spend time with Hope. I'll bring you food," Zandra said, handing Elizabeth a bell with no clapper.

She looked at Zandra, confused.

"Just ring the bell if you need anything," said Zandra.

"But it's broken," replied Elizabeth.

"Just wave it. I will hear it."

Over the next couple of days, Zandra and Elizabeth got to know each other. Phineas and Zandra had time to spend together, and Phineas treasured the time they had, hoping that Gregor would never show up. But finally, on the third day, Gregor walked through the door of the inn.

"Zandra!" he said, with a big smile on his face. "I see you're still getting yourself into trouble." He looked around. "Where's Finn? I'm sure she's missed me."

"You haven't changed a bit," said Zandra.

"Well, I don't know; I think I have a few gray hairs to disprove that," Gregor said as they sat down at the table. Leaning out of his chair, he called out, "Finn, dear! I'm back!"

Finnghuala came out of the kitchen. "It's not mealtime yet."

"Aw, now. I've been traveling; take pity on me, I'm wasting away."

"I think I have a while before I have to worry about you wasting away." Finnghuala went back into the kitchen.

Gregor turned to Zandra. "Zandra, my Ordie friends have agreed to help get your friends set up in their new life. We can head out tomorrow night."

As night neared, Zandra and Phineas went up to Elizabeth's room.

"We're about ready to leave. Some of my friends have gathered clothes and supplies for the two of you."

"That is very nice of them. Why would they do this for us?"

Zandra smiled kindly. "My people are not put into slavery, but we're often killed when found. So we understand your plight. Just like your people, not all of us are good, and not all are bad. Now we have planted a seed with you. Hopefully, you will teach your family, and if this happens enough, maybe we can someday come out of the shadows."

"Can you thank the people who helped me?" Elizabeth asked.

"Yes, I will," said Zandra, as she brushed Hope's cheek. "She did bring you a better life."

"I guess she did," replied Elizabeth.

"Lay on the bed, so we can start our journey."

Zandra put them to sleep and shrunk them, placing them in a padded box she had made to carry them in. Coming down to meet Gregor, they all headed to the streets of Boston and out into the country. From there, they mounted their brooms and took off.

They flew for most of the night, eventually stopping in the woods out of sight of Gregor's friends' home.

"My friends are named John and Martha," Gregor said. "I've told them your names. Just walk up to the house and knock. I'll meet you back here after you're done."

Gregor walked off. Zandra pulled the box out of her wand bag and set the tiny bodies on the ground. She reversed the spells.

"Are we there?" asked Elizabeth.

"Yes," replied Zandra.

She reached into her bag once more and pulled out a small bundle. She placed it on the ground.

"Aversa pars!"

The bundle grew to its normal size.

"These are your supplies to get started. The bell that I gave you is in there. If you or Hope ever need help, you can ring it five times. I'll hear it and I'll come as fast as I can." Zandra paused. "My friend has told these people that you had run away from your master. They have no idea that he is a wizard, and he would like to keep it that way."

"I won't say anything to them." Elizabeth wrapped one arm around Zandra in a tight hug. "Thank you, Zandra. You too, Phineas; I wouldn't be free if you hadn't done what Zandra asked of you." She looked down at the baby in her arms. "And I would have lost Hope."

She gave Phineas a peck on the cheek. Then they all walked up to the house and knocked on the door. Martha opened it.

"I'm Zandra," said Zandra. "This is Phineas."

"Hello, I'm Martha. John is not here. Where's your friend?"

Zandra motioned to Elizabeth. She moved towards the door.

Martha smiled. "Come in."

They all entered the house.

"Have a seat," said Martha. "Would you like something to eat?"

"Yes, please," replied Elizabeth.

"What is your baby's name?"

"Hope."

"A fitting name," replied Martha.

She got bowls of porridge for everyone. As they ate, Elizabeth and Martha got acquainted with each other.

After they were done eating, Martha took Elizabeth to the small room that she and Hope would share. Phineas took her new belongings to the room for her.

Late in the afternoon, they said their goodbyes, knowing that Elizabeth and Hope were in good hands. Zandra and Phineas headed off to meet Gregor.

It was their last night in Boston. Finnghuala made a special meal. They all ate and had a little too much to drink. Gregor's ribbing of Finnghuala only increased the more cider he drank.

Phineas tried to be happy, but the thought that Zandra would soon be leaving–and he didn't know when she would be back–kept creeping into his head.

Gregor got up, and, wobbling a little, walked carefully up the stairs. Everyone had turned in for the night. Just Zandra, Phineas, Cormac, and Finnghuala were left sitting around the fireplace.

The night had become slightly cool. Cormac stood up.

"Zandra, Finn and I have something for you."

He placed a silk bag in Zandra's hand. Zandra looked at him and Finnghuala for a moment. As she pulled the drawstring open, a small rectangle of pewter with a long thin strap of leather tied to the end fell out. Zandra looked back up at Cormac and Finnghuala questioningly.

"It's an ogham," said Finnghuala. "The marks on each side are an ancient Irish Gaelic written language."

Taking it from Zandra's hand, Finnghuala pointed at the longest of the markings.

"This one says perseverance." Rolling to the next side, she said, "this is strength." Rolling it again, she said, "life." She rolled it over once more. "And the last side says love. It brings luck to the wearer."

"Thank you," said Zandra. "You two have always been so kind to me. And Cormac, you saved my life. I owe you."

"No," replied Cormac. "You do the right thing. We need more people like you."

Finnghuala gave her a hug.

"Well, we had better turn in." Finnghuala headed for her room.

Cormac came over and patted Zandra on her shoulder. "See you in the morning," he said, following Finnghuala out of the room.

Zandra curled up beside Phineas and they sat there looking at the fire for a while longer, not saying a word until they fell asleep.

Zandra placed the last of the wand infusion materials in her bag. Evening was upon them as they walked out the back of the house. The three of them stood there in the fading light. Phineas' stomach turned as he looked at Zandra.

"Broken Arrow, you be careful, whatever you decide to do. I want to see you the next time I come back." She placed her hand on his shoulder.

"We will meet again," replied Broken Arrow.

Zandra walked over to Phineas, giving him a hug. He squeezed her tight, breathing hard. He tried not to let her know how sick he felt inside. He could feel the loneliness fading in already.

"When will you be back?" he asked.

"I don't know," she replied. "I have a feeling that I need to head west. I'll come back sometime soon."

"Are you going with Omar?"

"No," she said. "Something tells me that I need to go alone."

Phineas squeezed her one more time.

Then she picked up her broom and kicked off.

Broken Arrow walked back to his longhouse as Phineas stood there and watched Zandra disappear from view.

Slowly, the loneliness crept back upon him as the light of happiness drained from his eyes.

CHAPTER 13

West With the Night

Early Summer, 1789

It had been two weeks since Zandra had returned to her home among the hoodoos. Omar had had a hot meal ready for her when she had returned, which puzzled her–had he somehow known when she would arrive? Xavier had been happily drinking his barrel of rum that she had brought back from Epbaris' spring, and Zandra had been working on wands while Omar came and went. Their relationship had grown, and Omar was spending most of his time at Zandra's.

One evening, Zandra, Omar, and Xavier sat on Zandra's front porch and watched the sunset.

"I know," said Omar.

"I haven't said anything yet," said Zandra.

Omar looked at her and grinned.

"What else do you know about me that you haven't said?" asked Zandra.

"I know that you're being called to make this journey, and that you need to make it alone," replied Omar.

"Is that all you know?"

"For now," he said cryptically. "The future is hard to see."

Where are you off to? asked Xavier.

"All I know is that I'm heading west. I have some wands to finish and send off to Phineas, then I will leave."

A few days later, Zandra woke before sunset to prepare to head out. Omar and Xavier joined her on the porch. Zandra and Omar held hands and said little as they waited for the night to set in.

Eventually, Zandra got up to finish putting her supplies in her flight bag and put on her cloak.

"Don't drink all your rum up too fast," she said, looking at Xavier.

Be careful, he replied. *How long will you be gone?*

"I have no idea. Omar always seems to know. Ask him."

Xavier looked to Omar. Omar just shrugged.

Zandra patted Xavier's neck. Leaning against him, she gave him a hug.

Walking over to Omar, she said, "I will come back."

"That I know," he replied. "There are a lot of things out there that you have yet to encounter. Tread lightly and respect all you see."

Zandra looked up at Omar, leaned in, and hugged him.

"I love you," he said.

Zandra smiled. "I love you too."

They lingered there a while longer. Then she mounted her broom and flew off into the western sky.

She had been flying for three nights when she decided that she was far enough away from the Ordies to change to daytime flights. She was glad to get a rest. Flying by broom was much faster, but not as comfortable as horse or wagon.

The terrain had changed to grasslands, not much different than she had encountered when she had made her way to Ghost Mountain; a gently undulating sea of green.

After she had made a camp beside a creek bed, she sat in a chair that she had pulled out of her flight bag and watched as the grass came at her in waves. The sun was intense, so she pulled out her wand. “Umbraculum!” Shade appeared around her.

As she sat there, the gentle sound of the grass swaying in the wind was broken by a low rumble. Standing up, she could see a cloud of dust on the horizon. Puzzled, she stood there watching. Soon she could see a dark mass approaching her.

Before she could do anything, the beasts were upon her. Quickly, she pointed her wand in the air. “Integumentum!”

The green ribbon shot from her wand, forming a shield just as the first of the beasts came near, its voluminous head bouncing off of the shield. The others followed, until a fair quantity of them had knocked themselves out. The rest of the massive herd went around them.

Zandra had seen these creatures before, but not in such numbers. They were bison. Taking the opportunity to look at them up close, she walked up to the bison that were lying next to the shield, unconscious, and stuck her hand slowly through the magical barrier, a slight zap tingling up her arm as she did. She felt the coarse, curly hair that covered their head and neck. They had horns that curved up along the tuft of hair that topped their heads, and the front shoulders were set higher than the rear quarters, where shorter hair was found. After a bit, they recovered from their blows, stood up, and headed off with the herd that was finally thinning.

It took a while for the dust to settle enough that Zandra could drop the shield charm. It was hot, and she struggled to stay awake in the heat of the day. She always hated the fact that she had to switch back and forth from night to day flights so as not to be seen. But she wanted to see the land, and it wasn’t always easy to do that in the dark.

By early evening, she had lost her battle with sleep.

When she woke before dawn, she had something to eat and broke camp. As the sun rose, mist gathered in the low areas of the vast sea of grass, leaving only the top of the swells visible. As the morning grew warmer, the mist faded and a great storm appeared on the horizon. Zandra thought of the last time she was caught in a storm. There was no shelter to be had behind her, so she increased her speed, hoping to find some before the gap between her and the coming storm closed. The storm seemed to go north and south as far as she could see.

As the storm grew closer, she began to realize that it wasn't a storm she was seeing. It was a range of mountains, like she had never seen before.

It took until mid-afternoon to make it to the front range of the mountains. Landing in the foothills to set up camp, she pondered where she would penetrate the range. She could see that the mountains were so tall that they still had snow at their tops even though it was summer.

Getting a fire started, she cooked herself something to eat as the shadow of the great range crept across the grass lands to the east.

As night fell, Zandra sat beside the fire. The stars went off to the east into what seemed like infinity and disappeared behind the wall of the range to the west.

The next morning, she decided to travel straight up the mountains. She rose out of the foothills and through the pine and aspen, up past the tree line, soaring over the rocky tops of the mountains. On the other side, she found a river to follow. As it wound its way to the west, it passed through wide valleys, with great mounds of greyish gravel dotted with low trees.

It seemed that around every turn, the color and consistency of the rock changed. She dove down into canyons, some very narrow and so deep that she would not have been able to see if someone was standing at the top. There were giant mountains of greyish-white layered rock, with great piles of loose rock at their base.

As she traveled on, the rocks changed to tan, then back to gray, then light pink. They became flat on the top: mesas. The land to the sides of the river became arid, then just the tiniest bit of green lined its banks. The land was the palest of tan, with scant sage brush and just the slightest undulation. In the distance, she could see separate ranges of mesas.

As she continued to follow the river, the land began to rise once more; mounds of the pale tan rock began to form into hills. The rock once again changed to a rust color, mesas with layers of horizontal rock eroded by wind at the bottom rising to sheer vertical slabs of smooth stone, before leveling off into a huge flat plane at the top. The mesas appeared maroon in the afternoon sun as the river flowed green through the narrow canyon. It was an unreal world.

The mesas started to lose their flat vertical surfaces, becoming more undulated, then their tops began to smooth and soften. Zandra climbed out of the canyon to fly above the mesas. Monoliths of red rock rose to great heights on the tops of the already-high mesas, great stone arches were all around, and boulders that appeared to have faces were dotted around among the hoodoos. It was as if the flesh had been ripped away and she could see the very bones of the earth. Snow-capped mountains in the distance gave stark contrast to the scene before her eyes.

It had been a very long day. Setting up camp under an arch, she sat there as the night sky filled with stars over this magical land.

Zandra had spent the last two days exploring the high desert. Its beautiful isolation had sunken into her bones. She could sit on the edge of a cliff all day, watching the sun change the color of the land as it crossed the sky.

She had spent most of her time that afternoon on a point of land over a massive valley, which dropped to a lower canyon that looked as if a humongous dragon had stepped through, making a five hundred foot deep footprint.[1]

A glint of light caught her eye. Looking closer, she saw it again, then lost track of it.

Suddenly, a large silver bird popped up out of the dragon's footprint, gliding across the upper canyon's floor. Zandra stepped closer to the edge of the cliff as the Thunderbird flew straight up, just inches in front of her, looped out over the canyon, and headed back to Zandra.

As it landed next to her, she stood there for a moment, stunned at its presence. The great bird squinted its eyes at her, lowering its head. Zandra walked up to it, slowly raising her hand to its giant head. She stroked the side of its face.

"Thank you for saving me from the Mishipizheu all those years ago," she said.

The Thunderbird nodded its head noncommittally. Zandra continued to stroke it.

"Why are you here?" she asked.

The Thunderbird lowered its head until its neck lay on the ground.

"Do you want me to get on you?"

The Thunderbird slowly blinked its eyes. Zandra climbed onto the base of the Thunderbird's neck. Pointing her wand at her bag and broom, she said, "Revoco!"

They came flying over to her. She draped the strap of the bag over her head so it crossed her chest and strapped the broom to her back.

"I need a name for you," she said to the Thunderbird. She thought for a moment, then was struck by an idea. "Donder! That's the word for thunder in Dutch." She patted Donder's head. "I'm ready to take off."

---

[1] Island In The Sky, Canyonlands National Park.

Walking to the edge of the cliff, Donder dove off. The tips of his wings were parallel with his body. Zandra leaned back as they dove down the cliff face. Leveling out, they sped across the valley floor and dove down into the lower canyon. They came upon a river and followed its winding course. A thin green belt clung to the edges of the river at the base of the mountains.

Twilight had come when Donder landed in a water-sculpted, light tan stone canyon, striped in horizontal rust-colored bars and fingers of dark gray streaking toward the valley floor.[I] A stream had cut a hole through a stone mountain over the centuries, making a mammoth bridge. Zandra jumped off Donder's back. Stroking his neck, she looked out over the canyon as it glowed in the moonlight.

"That was a beautiful flight," she said quietly. "Are we going somewhere?"

Donder nodded his head slightly.

"You're quite a powerful and handsome creature."

Donder rubbed his beak against Zandra, and she stroked him some more.

"This land is very special," she said. "I can feel that there are many powerful spirits here."

Walking away, she gathered some wood and started a fire. When she had finished eating, she took her bed roll out of her flight bag. Spreading it out on the ground, she laid down.

"Goodnight, Donder."

He walked over to her and bedded down beside her, covering her with his wing.

She woke the next morning to the bright sun reflecting off the canyon walls. In the twilight, she hadn't been able to see the beauty of the place, but now it was there, in all its glory.

[I] Natural Bridges National Monument.

She walked up to the rim, looking to the north. A ribbon of green lay in front of a range of deep maroon mountains speckled with green. Beautiful twisted dead trees, dark gray in color, jutted into the deep blue sky.

Zandra sat there for a long while, just taking it all in.

Late that afternoon, Donder returned from his hunt. She stood up and waved at him. Landing next to her, he lowered his neck and Zandra climbed on. They flew off to the southeast, over low trees, breaking out into a broad valley of medium and light green.[I] Hooking back to the southwest, they passed over a deep canyon only the width of the river at the bottom. The river turned back on itself so sharply that it almost touched before turning again. The land changed to a rusty brown, dotted with sagebrush. Tall sandstone buttes speckled the valley.[II]

Landing in a large crevasse near the top of one of the buttes, Zandra climbed off Donder's neck. She looked over the large space. Sagebrush and bark covered the floor, which had been trampled until it was somewhat soft.

Zandra looked at Donder. "Your home?"

Donder nodded.

Setting her bag down, she walked to the edge of the precipice. She could see a steep trail that led to the top of the butte. As she walked up to the top, Donder flew up to meet her. The clouds streaked the deep blue sky with bright orange, reflecting the setting sun, hovering there until the stars came out.

Flying over the valley, Donder dived toward a small round building. When they landed in front of it, an old native man walked out, his long white hair flowing in the breeze. He was wearing a red and black wool tunic and sheepskin paints. He walked up to Donder.

[I] Valley of the Gods.

[II] Monument Valley.

"Ii'ni' ak'is ni jo."[I]

Donder bowed his head. The man pointed at himself. "Hastiin álííl yééhósinígíí bee."

Flicking her wrist, Zandra said, "Transferendum." The translation spell took effect.

"I'm Zandra Voorhies."

"Zandra, welcome." The man motioned for Zandra to come over. "Here, have a seat in the shade of my hogan. Would you like something to eat?"

"Yes, thank you," she replied. "You're not going to ask me about my spells?"

"No need."

He entered his hogan, coming out with two pots, two cups, and some flat bread. He set the pots next to a small pile of wood, waved his hand over it, and the wood crackled with flames.

Walking over to look in the pots, Zandra saw stems of a flowering plant bound together, floating in the water of one pot, and a chunk of meat in the other.

"What kind of tea is this?" she asked, gesturing to the pot with the plants.

"Greenthread,"[29] he replied. "It's a plant that is abundant here."

"Do you live here alone?" asked Zandra.

"Yes."

"Doesn't it get lonely?"

"No, I have the spirits to keep me company," he replied.

"Do you know why Donder has called me here?"

"I would imagine that he has things to show you."

"How does he know of me and the things that are going to happen to me?"

"There's a lot I don't know about the powers of the Thunderbirds," he replied. Pouring the tea from the boiling pot, he handed her a cup.

[I] Translation: "Thunder friend you have."

She took a sip and raised her eyebrows. "This is good! What was your name? I hadn't cast the translation spell yet when you introduced yourself."

"Man With Great Magic."

"You're a wizard?"

"I don't know what that is, but I can do things like you. You call your kind wizards?"

"No, I'm a witch. The males of my kind are called wizards, warlocks, or sorcerers."

"Why do the men have so many names and the women only one?"

"I don't know," replied Zandra. "What do your people call you and what tribe are you from?"

"My tribe are the Diné.[1] I'm a medicine man."

"Well then, maybe you'll be able to tell me about this land. It's so beautiful and I feel there's a sacredness in it, but it seems like a very hard place to live."

"Our gods gave us this land," said Man With Great Magic. "My people passed through three worlds to get here."

Zandra looked at him. "Three worlds?"

He nodded. "The first world was small and black, with four seas. On a small island was one pine tree. Beetles, dragonflies, and locusts lived there. Each of the seas were ruled by different supernatural entities: Big Water Creature, Blue Heron, Frog, and White Thunder. Each sea had a cloud—one of black, one of white, another of blue, and the last of yellow.

"When the blue and yellow clouds came together, First Woman was born. Then the black and white came together, and First Man was born. Great Coyote was created from the water, and he came to First Man and First Woman and told them that he knew all the secrets of sky and water. Then the second coyote appeared. His name was First Angry. He brought magic into the world.

---

[1] Navajo

"First Man, First Woman, Great Coyote and First Angry climbed to the second world, and all the others followed. The second world was inhabited with birds and other creatures. A swallow welcomed them. They lived there for twenty-three days, until they were banished to the third world.

"The third world was the Yellow World. Four gods lived there: Talking God, Black God, Water Sprinkler and House God. First Woman gave birth to twins which had no gender. In the next twenty days, five pairs of twins were born. The four gods took the twins and taught them. Then they returned them to First Man and First Woman.

"By eight winters on, many people had been born. First Man and First Woman came to the fourth world. The four gods created four mountains: White Mountain,[I] Turquoise Mountain,[II] Yellow Mountain,[III] and Dark Mountain.[IV] As long as my people stay between these peaks, they will endure."[30]

Taking the chunk of meat out of the boiling water, Man With Great Magic divided it into two pieces, laying them on flatbread, and handed one to Zandra.

"This land holds dangers also. There are many things here that should not be messed with. The Hopituh Shi-nu-mu[V] do not trust the magical kind. You need to be careful."

Just as Zandra finished her food, Donder came over to them.

"It appears that it is time for you to leave," said Man With Great Magic.

"Seems so," she replied. "Thank you for the food and the story of your people."

Man With Great Magic smiled. "I'm sure we'll meet again."

Zandra mounted Donder, and they flew off to the southeast.

[I] In original language: 'Sisnaajiní'. Currently called Blanca Peak, CO.

[II] In original language: 'Tsoodził'. Currently called Mt. Taylor, NM.

[III] In original language: 'Dook'o'oosłííd'. Currently called Mt. Humphreys, AZ.

[IV] In original language: 'Dibé Nitsaa'. Currently called Hesperus Mt., CO.

[V] Hopi tribe.

Soon the land rose, and they passed over mountains covered in trees, then back to a dry land of the lightest tan, dotted with sage brush. Coming to a long canyon,[31] Donder flew low over the floor. Zandra could see ruins of buildings strewn all over the canyon floor. She had seen small buildings like these in recesses of canyon walls since she had met Donder.

Donder landed next to a half-moon shaped ruin. Rectangle rooms lined the outside, and two courtyards lay in the center, divided by more rectangle rooms with large, round sunken rooms[I] dotting the outside edge of the courtyards. Some of the ruins had multiple floors, with wood beams still in place. Some rooms were still fully enclosed, with shards of pottery strewn about, and corn cobs still in the granaries.

Zandra felt uneasy. Something was amiss here.

Walking back out, she passed along the outside of the complex, coming upon a massive footprint on the ground–human-like, but much larger even than a Stonish Giants', and with only four toes.

She took a deep breath and tried to calm the feeling of unease rapidly climbing to the top of her senses.

Night had now fallen.

[I] Kivas.

CHAPTER 14

YE'IITSOH

Summer, 1789

A bright full moon had risen, casting a silvery light over the canyon. She placed her left foot at the heel of the print, then stepped off. The print was four and a half times the length of her foot. The creature that had made it must have been massive.

Kneeling, Zandra checked the print. It was a day or so old. Continuing on around the complex, she came across no more tracks.

As she arrived back to the front, something still felt wrong. Pulling out her wand, she raised it over her head and pointed it at the sky. "Quid hic!"

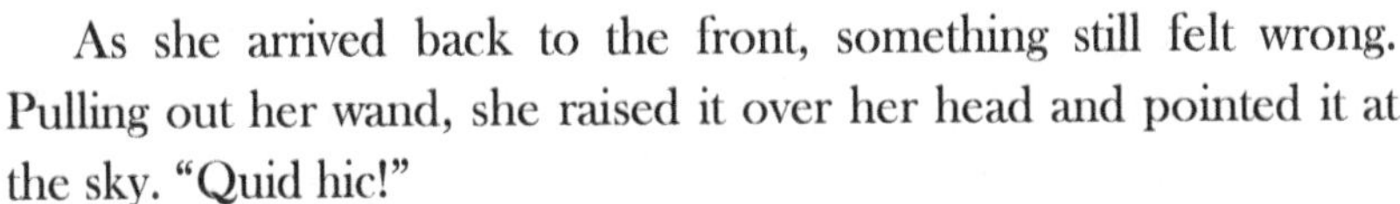

Purple veins of light spidered out in all directions, spreading to the width of the canyon. A purple fog hovered, forming into objects from long ago, displaying the place as it once was through a violet screen. Logs and stone materialized out of the violet haze, falling into the structures until they were back the way they would have been before the place went to ruins. Smoke rose from holes in the roof as it would have when people still lived there.

Zandra walked back into the compound. There was no one in the courtyard. She walked to the closest of the round buildings.

What appeared to be shamans sat in a circle murmuring, lighted only by the low fire.

Zandra puzzled over what she was seeing. She walked to another of the round buildings and saw the same thing. After looking around a bit more, she came back out into the courtyard. No one was moving about. All the rest of the natives were in their rooms.

Walking out to the front, she looked around the canyon. All seemed quiet.

Donder glided over the canyon, landing beside Zandra as a cool breeze drifted in. They began to hear commotion from inside the compound. The sounds of loud booms started drifting down the canyon. The round building to the south trembled as an intense pale blue light shattered the smooth coat of mud that covered it, emitting shards of light through the cracks in the stone into the night sky just before it exploded. Streaks of blue light shot straight into the air. The shafts of light could be seen all over the valley. The shamans must have been doing a mass ceremony that had gone terribly wrong.

Zandra walked to the closest of the circular buildings. Purple, ghost-like visages of people from long ago ran through her as they tried to escape. As she got closer, the light began to flicker until only thin beams escaped from the outer edges. A large figure began rising up out of the light, followed by several more otherworldly creatures. All over the canyon, the same thing was happening. Mass panic ensued as the shamans that survived fought the beings, but they were being overwhelmed.

Some of the beings were quite large, others more human-sized. They varied in appearance: some had horns, some even had what appeared to be antennae. The large ones were kicking down the buildings and eating anything they could get their hands on.

The young and old were running off toward the cliffs as warriors and shamans tried to slow the invaders. They had very powerful magic, but there were just too many of the beasts.

Then Zandra saw dots in the western sky. She turned to get a better look. Streams of light shot from the specks. *Wizards,* she thought.

Soon they came in view. They weren't on brooms; they were on staffs: Egyptian witches and wizards. Then she saw some of them were flying on carpets and wearing turbans. *Genies,* she thought.

Some of the new arrivals landed and fought alongside the shamans and warriors. An Egyptian witch raised her staff over her head. Holding the bottom of it, she twisted her wrist so that the top moved in a circle as a stream of green light twisted out of the eyes of the falcon head that topped her staff. Twisting like a tornado, it engulfed one of the giant figures. The figure now trapped, she lifted it and moved it toward one of the now-destroyed circular buildings. As she did so, a horned, humanoid creature ran up behind her. A genie flew in overhead, spells flying from his hands, hitting the creature. The Egyptian witch flicked her staff groundward and the giant fell back to where it came from as the horned creature at her back fell dead on the ground.

To Zandra's left, a mixed group of genies, witches, and wizards were battling a massive skeletal being. Its skin clung tightly to its huge body. It appeared to have a bubble over its head, and it was holding one of the native shamans in its hand. Their spells seemed to bounce off its emaciated frame. The light from their spells was intense, and the air crackled with the velocity of the attack.

Then a genie finally hit the bubble over its head with the right spell, rupturing it. Letting out a shattering scream, the creature dropped the shaman. One of the other genies caught the shaman mid-fall with a spell.

As the being hit the ground, it exploded into dust. Immediately, the group was charged by five of the giant creatures. They were close to twenty feet tall, covered in hair almost like a Stonish Giant, but much taller, without the extreme girth.

One turned, looking Zandra's way. It was ugly; great tusks protruded from its lower jaw, adding further hideousness to its face.

Another passed over her. Looking up, she could see the underside of its foot. It had four toes! The print she had found earlier must have been made by one of these.

All of the wizards, witches, and genies flew into the air except one. Raising his staff, the lone Egyptian wizard slammed the end down into the ground. A ripple of blue emanated out from it like a drop into a pool of water. As it hit the creatures, blue fingers of lightning raced up their legs, climbing to their heads. Smoke began to emit from them, then they burst into blue flames.

Shortly after there was just a pile of ashes. The battle had been going on for an hour or more. A large genie flew up, landing next to the Egyptian wizard, and started speaking to him.

Not knowing if the translation spell would work on top of the Quid hic spell, Zandra pulled out her wand, deciding to try. "Transferendum," she said. The voices came wafting over to her through the curtain of purple mist.

"Parth is chasing down the last of the creatures on the west end, and Ipy has finished on the east."

"Good. How many have we lost?"

"Don't know. At least eleven of our own. Don't know how many natives were lost; we're still trying to get a count. A lot of them may be under rubble."

"Well, it could have been worse. Let's all comb the area as we head down to help Parth."

Mounting their staffs and carpets, they spread out over the canyon, heading back west.

Zandra had never seen a battle like this. It seemed that the shamans had opened a portal to a different world or dimension. The building fell back into ruin as her spell faded.

Zandra looked at Donder. "Well, that was pretty unnerving. It seems that all of the unwanted guests were not sent back. The giant that passed over me had four toes, same as the print I found in back of this compound."

Donder brought his head down to hers and nudged her.

"I'll have to be careful," she said. "Omar hadn't told me of his people's involvement out here. I'll have to talk with him about this. I wonder where those wizards and genies came from?"

As she got camp set up, she set a shield spell in case some of the beings that did not get caught on that night long ago showed up.

The next morning, she mounted Donder, and they flew toward the north over sagebrush. The land became more speckled with foliage, with more mesas. Donder hooked back toward a green-topped mesa, circling around before landing on it. The air was sweet, with the smell of juniper and pinyon pine.[1]

They had landed on the side of a cliff. Zandra climbed off Donder and breathed deep, trying to get all the sweet air she could into her lungs. Walking to the edge of the cliff, she looked across the canyon—and there, clinging to the cliff face, was a multistory building much like the buildings in the canyon the night before.

Taking her broom in hand, she flew across the canyon to investigate. Upon landing, she couldn't tell if it was abandoned at around the same time as the canyon from the night before, or if the inhabitants from there had settled here after that night. But it was clear they had left in a hurry: food stores had been abandoned, clay pots, and rotting bits of clothing. Every room of every building told the same story.

After a while, she came back out, walking along a path that went up the side of the cliff.

Coming to a bend in the path, she could hear branches breaking, someone coming down the path. Zandra stood there, looking up to see who was coming.

After a moment, she saw a giant hairy leg through the trees—and it was close. Turning to look behind her, she ran to a crevasse in the rock, pulling out her wand. "Commuta Habitum!"

---

[1] Mesa Verde National Park.

A veneer of rock closed over her just as the thing came around the corner. Zandra was able to see out of the sheet of stone, but no one could look in. The beast was unbelievably tall; close to twenty feet. It didn't have the unreal girth of a Stonish Giant; it was built like a man, only way taller. Its huge feet had four large toes.

Then it turned. She could see its face for the first time in real life, without the purple, hazy visage of her revealing charm. It was very ugly: dark gray, wrinkled skin shone on its face and two great tusks protruded from its lower jaw. Zandra gasped, realizing it was the same creature she had seen the night before.

It had just passed her by when it stopped, turning its head from side to side, sniffing intensely. Stepping back, it took a swipe at the cliff face. Rocks fell down around Zandra as she ran out. Heading up the trail, she immediately realized there was no way to outrun the beast's huge strides. She started throwing spells back as she ran, but she never hit her mark. The trees were too dense to fly out.

Thunder started booming and a deluge ensued as Zandra reached a clearing near the top of the mesa. Mounting her broom, she kicked off hurriedly.

She was about twenty-five feet off the ground when the giant grabbed the tail of her broom.

In shock, Zandra turned to look at the beast as it pulled her back towards it. The storm was dropping torrents of rain, and it was hard for her to see.

Then lighting bolts shot from Donder's eyes, striking the giant in his arm. The giant let go of her broom, and she bolted off as Donder followed.

After a bit, Donder's storm faded as they flew beside each other, heading west. Some time later, they landed on a river bank.

"Thank you, Donder," Zandra said. "That's twice now you've saved me." She looked out at the river. "Do those beasts have any magical powers?"

Donder shook his head.

"Well, I guess that's good. Their size is enough to deal with."

Zandra sat down on the riverbank, taking some flatbread that Man With Great Magic had given her out of her pack. Turning back to Donder, she asked, "Do you know where those wizards came from?"

Donder nodded his head.

"Could you take me there?"

Donder nodded again.

Finishing her bread, Zandra mounted him, and they flew off to the southwest.

Coming to a valley where two rivers came together,[I] they dove down into it. Soon they came to an opening in the canyon wall.

Zandra climbed off of Donder and walked up to the opening. Passing through the rough entrance that appeared just like the rest of the canyon wall, she entered a room partially lit from outside. The room was about twenty feet deep and fifty feet high. A statue of Amun-Ra was carved on one side of a massive double door, and a multi-armed woman on the other.[32] The statues jutted out from the rest of the wall as though the stone had been carved away to reveal them. Walking through the doors, Zandra raised her wand.

"Lumino," she whispered. The room was too big to light. Pointing her wand up again, she said, "Eum Lux de Caelo!" The light shot out of her wand and bounced off the ceiling. She could see a vast room, with carved walls, adorned with Egyptian and Himalayan ornamentation. Massive doors lined the walls.

In the center was a monument. Stairs rose from all four sides. Hieroglyphs and Sanskrit were carved in the riser of the stairs. Zandra pointed her wand at the writing and muttered, "Transferendum."

The writing blurred and changed so she could read:

TO OUR FRIENDS WHO GAVE THEIR LIVES IN BATTLE.

[I] Northern Grand Canyon, AZ.

At the top of the stairs she found a large terrace with a stupa on top. Also on top of the terrace was a pyramid about the size of the ship she had taken to the New World all those years ago. Walking around the terrace, she found statues of wizards, witches, and genies placed on the large platform around the pyramid and stupa.

This must be the resting place of the ones that died that night, Zandra thought to herself. They would have to have had knowledge of what was to come to have been there so quickly after the portals were opened. *Must have been some of that Egyptian magic that Omar's not telling me about.*

She looked at all the statues, then descended. Looking around the room, she chose a door that had been knocked off its hinges, and entered.

She found herself in another large room, much smaller than the first.

"Lumino," she muttered softly.

This room only had Egyptian adornment. As she passed through the room, she found nothing of any consequence. This place had not been left in a hurry. The inhabitants had packed up and moved away.

I wonder why they left, she thought.

Walking back out into the bright light of the canyon, she saw that Donder had flown off. She sat on a rock and pulled some more flatbread out of her pack.

A crow flew up to her, flapping its wings, making dust billow into her face. She shooed it off, coughing, as she wondered what was up with the bird.

Soon after, she began to feel ill and light-headed. She threw up violently, coughing and sputtering. The world seemed to get darker and darker.

Before she knew it, her mind went blank and everything was black.

CHAPTER 15

SKINWALKER

Summer, 1789

Zandra's vision was blurry; there was no form in anything she saw. She still felt slightly nauseous. Man With Great Magic knelt down beside her, placing a hand on her head as he chanted.

Breathing deeply, she fell back to sleep.

When next she woke, it was a day later, and she felt a lot better. Man With Great Magic handed her her wand.

"Transferendum," she said. "How did I get here?"

"You've been very sick," he replied. "Donder brought you to me. What's the last thing that you remember?"

Zandra thought back to the day before. "I had exited a cave that appeared to have been home to Egyptian and Himalayan wizards and genies. I was sitting on a rock, eating some of the flatbread that you had given me, when a crow flew up and flapped its wings in my face. It was incredibly dusty. I shooed it off, then shortly after, I became ill."

Man With Great Magic nodded sagely. "I believe that crow was what we call a skinwalker.[33] It is very rare for them to take the form of a crow, but it has been known to happen from time to time."

"Skinwalker?" repeated Zandra.

"They're shamans that can change form into animals," he replied.

Zandra thought for a minute. "The dust that billowed when it flapped in front of my face must have been what made me sick. But why would one of these skinwalkers come after me?"

"What have you been doing since you left me?" Man With Great Magic asked.

Zandra told him of the night in the canyon, the cliff dwellings, and the beast she barely got away from.

Man With Great Magic took in her story with a grave expression. "I don't think all of the people that you saw running around that night were just images of the past. There are things some don't want others to know."

"I suppose you could be right. What was that creature that I encountered at the cliff dwellings? It was the same as the creatures that traveled through the portals in that valley."

"Ye'iitsoh," he said. "They're not magical, but they're not to be messed with. Not many live here. Our people encountered great numbers of them in the north land." Man With Great Magic placed a hand on her shoulder. "But you should rest for now. Get your strength."

After a couple of days, Zandra was doing much better. She was sitting outside of Man With Great Magic's hogan.

"This skinwalker," said Man With Great Magic, "he will continue to come after you if he knows that you're still alive."

"What can I do?" asked Zandra. "I have no idea who it is."

"You will have to find out," he replied. "If you confront him or her, the skinwalker will die within three days."

"Die?" she repeated nervously. "I don't want to kill anyone."

"Sometimes you're not given a choice."

Zandra frowned as Man With Great Magic turned to look at another of the incredible sunsets.

The next morning, Donder returned. Zandra walked up and stroked his face.

"Thank you for bringing me here," she said. "You saved my life."

Donder slowly closed his eyes as she talked.

"I need go back to that valley and find out who this skinwalker is."

Donder nodded. Zandra gathered up her things, threw her flight bag over her shoulder, and grabbed her broom. Donder bowed to let Zandra on.

"I'm not asking you to go," she said.

Donder continued to bow, so she climbed on and they flew off.

They arrived at dusk. The place was just as deserted as the last time they were there. Standing near the spot she had been on that night, she pointed her wand up. "Quid hic!"

Once again, veins of purple light spread across the valley. The fog spread as the buildings came back together. The round building exploded, and the creatures began to crawl out of the portals. Zandra walked around, scanning the valley as she rounded the west side of the half-moon structure. The natives were running to the cliffs.

Then she saw him. He was there in the flesh, not another visage among the hordes of purple ghosts, and he was dressed differently than the rest, wearing sheepskin pants and tunic. One eye was blinded.

She took off after him. Noticing her, he started running, trying to mix in with the crowd that was heading toward the crevasse in the cliff. Zandra threw spells at the man, but they passed through the crowd and never hit him. He ducked out of sight, but Donder followed.

Zandra mounted her broom and flew a search pattern. Further up the crevasse, a single crow flew off to the west. Donder saw the bird and headed off after it. Noticing this, Zandra followed behind him. Donder's vision enabled them to follow at a great distance.

They were coming up on the green mountains that separated the arid lands. Zandra was skimming the tops of the pines. The crow turned and headed south over the top of the ridge, and after a while, there appeared a dry valley. The mountains hooked to the west, where the range closed to form a mouth for the valley. The crow headed for the base of a large mountain.[I]

Donder landed a mile or so back. As Zandra flew past him, she saw the crow land. Zandra did the same. Pulling out her wand and pointing it at herself, she said, "Commuta Habitum!"

A wave of green and beige washed over her as she walked toward the crow, camouflaged, stopping a good distance from it, but close enough to keep an eye on him. The crow had landed at a small camp. Now that she was close, she could see that the crow didn't look quite right. Something about its movement was wrong.

Slowly, it began to morph back into a human form, until a naked figure stood where the crow had been. It was the man with the blinded eye. He looked around, then disappeared into the crude shelter.

Zandra tried to think of what to do. She didn't want to be responsible for his death, but if it was the only way to stop him from attacking her again, did she really have a choice? She watched for a while as he came out after he had put on some clothes and had started a fire in preparation to fix something to eat.

She decided to reveal herself to him, as she could think of nothing else. Taking her wand in hand, she said, "Transferendum!"

Then she walked up to him, not dropping her cloaking spell. The man looked toward her, confused, as Zandra dropped her

---

[I] Zilditloi Mountain.

cover. The man was shocked as he realized what was happening. He turned to run, but Zandra yelled out, "Wait! I want to talk with you!"

Zandra gave chase, losing him in a deep crevasse. She searched for a long while, but could not find him. *I guess I will never find out what he was hiding,* she thought to herself. She wished there had been a different way. She hated the thought that she had caused this man's death, but she couldn't let him kill her, either.

"You didn't kill him. He made the choice when he started down that path."

"What do you think he was hiding?" asked Zandra.

"Hiding his contact with the creatures that traveled here that night long ago," replied Man With Great Magic. "Maybe he found a way to communicate with them. It's hard to say. Maybe he found you to be a threat to what he was doing."

Man With Great Magic turned and walked into his hogan. Zandra sat there, contemplating his words for a bit, then she turned back to the letter she was writing to Omar.

Dear Omar,

Sorry that I haven't written. It has been an amazing journey so far. The land is incredibly beautiful, especially on the other side of the great range of mountains. This dry, red land seems to hold many secrets.

I've met my Thunderbird protector. I've named him Donder, which means thunder in my native Dutch. He has directed me to some interesting things, one of which has led to me having a hand in someone's death, which bothers me greatly. You have not told me of all that your people have been a part of in this land. Wish you weren't so secretive.

Don't know when I'll be returning. I feel that there is more that Donder has to show me. Tell Xavier hi. I miss you so much, and hope to be with you again soon.

Love, Zandra

Placing the letter on the ground, she tapped it with her wand. "Missito," she said. As usual, the paper folded and flew off.

Twilight had come as she climbed under her blankets, with Donder at her side.

The next morning, Donder indicated he was ready for them to head off again.

"It is time for me to leave," Zandra told Man With Great Magic. "Thank you again for saving me, and for all you have taught me."

Man With Great Magic nodded, handing her some more of his flatbread. "Donder will take care of you. Hopefully we will cross paths again."

Zandra said goodbye, hopped on Donder, and they flew off to the west.

As they passed near the cave where she had found the ruins, the river canyon grew to the point where it was miles across. It seemed to go on forever: another unbelievably beautiful sight.[I]

After a couple days' flight over the great western desert, the land rose abruptly as they flew north over the gray mountains covered with pine. Donder landed one evening among the evergreens. As Zandra pulled her things out of her bag, she noticed some incredibly large trees.[II] Their trunks were unbelievably broad—they must have been over twenty feet wide, and a couple of hundred feet high. *These trees must be very old,* Zandra thought.

[I] Grand Canyon National Park.

[II] The sequoias at Mariposa Grove, California

Walking over to them, she felt uneasy at their size, but was also in awe of them. Finding some branches that had fallen, she placed them in her flight bag.

As she slept that night, she could hear the chatter of Stonish Giants in the distance.

She was woken in the early morning by the sound of a deer in distress. She got up to investigate. After stumbling through the trees for a while, she came upon a clearing. The moon was bright, and she could see that a small deer lay on the ground. A wolverine stood beside it.

What an impressive animal, she thought. This short-legged, thirty pound bundle of muscle and large paws had brought the deer down on its own. As she watched, she heard rustling off to her left. Soon, a young Stonish Giant emerged from the trees, walking up to the wolverine, hoping to take its kill.

Growling fiercely, the wolverine leaped at the Stonish Giant, slashing at it as it passed. The Stonish Giant pulled back, grasping the arm that had been cut by the wolverine's sharp claws. Then the Stonish Giant moved forward.

Again, the wolverine leaped at it, this time biting at the Stonish Giant's chest and holding on, as it used all four feet to slash at its belly. Letting out a yell, the Stonish Giant turned and hurried back into the woods as the wolverine let go and returned to its kill.

What a tenacious little animal, to stand there and fight off a Stonish Giant, she thought. *Even if it was a young one, it was still a hundred times the wolverine's size.*

Later that day, they ascended over the giant trees heading to the north. Climbing the range, they hugged a mountain top. As they rounded it, a magnificent valley laid out before them.[I] Cliffs soared above the valley floor; waterfalls cascaded off the nearly three-thousand-foot cliffs. One of the cliffs gave the appearance of being half a dome. As the noon sun bounced off the light gray, granite cliffs, it was blinding. The waterfalls glistened in the sun.

Exiting the east end of the valley, they headed north over the high peaks. They flew over a brilliant cobalt blue mountain lake.[II] Turning to the west, they flew down out of the range and over a broad valley, then back over a lower range and out over the ocean.

Two days later, they landed on a large island that protected a huge bay.[III] Setting up camp on the inland side of the island, Zandra turned in early. She was tired; it had been a very long few days, although she found the country to be very beautiful.

Early in the morning, she was awoken. Large numbers of Stonish Giants had encircled her camp, chattering and breaking trees, but at a distance. They were agitated at Zandra being in their territory, but Donder's presence was making them keep their distance, and he wasn't bothered with them.

Later that day, Donder left to hunt. Zandra sat on the shore, looking across the bay, when a native came out of the tree line. Walking up to Zandra slowly, she gestured what Zandra thought to be a hello. Zandra pulled out her wand slowly. The woman started to turn to run, thinking that she had a weapon. Quickly, Zandra said, "Transferendum!" She called out to the woman. "I'm not going to hurt you!"

[I] Yosemite Valley.

[II] Lake Tahoe.

[III] Vancouver Island.

Turning to look at Zandra, the woman stood there for a moment. Finally, she spoke. "You're a friend of the Thunderbird, and you have magic."

"Yes," replied Zandra.

"I came to see why the Sasq'ets[34] were excited."

"Sasq'ets," said Zandra. "Do you mean the Stonish Giants?"

The woman looked at her, confused.

"The big hairy ones," Zandra added.

The woman nodded in recognition. "Yes."

"I heard them last night, but they never came close," said Zandra.

"The Sasq'ets know the power the Thunderbird poses, and they respect them."

"Sasq'ets," said Zandra. "I like that. It's easier to say than Stonish Giant. I think I'll start using that."

Donder came flying along with a large snake in his talons.

"What has he caught?" asked Zandra.

"He hasn't caught anything," replied the woman. "It's the Thunderbird's friend, the Haietlik."

Just then, lighting shot from the serpent's mouth and struck the water. Donder released the snake and dove toward the waves. Hitting the surface, he rose with an orca, flying back toward the shore as the woman disappeared into the forest.

Landing on a spot down the beach from Zandra, Donder begin to eat the orca as the Haietlik slid up on the beach beside him. The two of them ate until they had gotten their fill. Then Donder grabbed the orca carcass, flew off over the forest, and dropped it deeper in the island. Returning, he drug his talons in the water to clean them, and landed once again by the Haietlik.

Zandra walked over to the two of them. The Haietlik raised to a few feet above Zandra's head, its dagger-like head glistening in the sun. Iridescent scales of aqua, emerald green, and cobalt formed beautiful patterns along its body.

"Hello," said Zandra.

The Haietlik looked down at her. Donder walked near.

"Your friend?" Zandra asked.

Donder nodded his head, looking back at the Haietlik.

"You're incredible," said Zandra, looking at the Haietlik. She thought for a moment. "Bliksemslang," she said. "That's what I will give you for a name—it means 'lightning serpent' in my native tongue." Zandra stroked its side. "You two work good together. I saw you shoot lightning from your tongue. Neat trick. You're obviously a magical creature also. Do you live near here?"

Bliksemslang slid off to the north, entering a cove. They headed to the opening to a cave. Pulling out her wand, Zandra said, "Lumino." The tunnel burst with light as they descended into a room lined with Thunderbird feathers. Bliksemslang curled in among them.

"Nice place," said Zandra. "Did Donder bring me here to get a sample for my wands from you?"

Bliksemslang nodded his head.

"Could I get a section of your tongue?" she asked. "I can do it without causing you any pain. I think it might work good in my wands."

Bliksemslang looked at Zandra, then laid his head down among the feathers. Zandra pulled out her wand.

"Pulso," she said.

Bliksemslang fell asleep. Struggling to open his mouth, Zandra pulled out his tongue. "Segmentum," she said. A sliver of tongue fell into Zandra's hand. Placing it into a special bag that would dry and preserve it, she turned back to Bliksemslang. "Percuro!" The tongue healed. "Excito!"

Bliksemslang woke. Stroking his head, Zandra thanked him.

The next morning, Zandra woke to the sight of Donder diving down at the water, tapping Bliksemslang's head as he broke the surface. Zandra watched them play for a while, then walked back to her camp to get something to eat.

As she sat there and enjoyed the morning, she could hear the Sasq'ets chatter, as they must have found the remnants of the orca.

Late that morning, Zandra climbed onto Donder. Finding a thermal, Donder climbed to a great height and entered a strong tailwind. Riding the wind, they flew off to the east at a great speed.

As evening came, Donder descended. They were at Ghost Mountain.

Zandra set up camp a few miles to the west of the magical mountain. A storm had passed before their arrival, giving a dark blue backdrop as the setting sun illuminated Ghost Mountain.

"This is where you came to me in a dream." Looking at Donder, she smiled.

Zandra decided to check in with some old friends the next day.

"Donder," she said, "can you take me to the Arikara? I would like to check in with them while I'm near."

It didn't take long to find them. Zandra and Donder landed near the camp. The tribe hid from them, but an old man walked out to greet them. It was Spotted Pony.

"Zandra!" he said. "It's been a long time. You have befriended a Thunderbird?"

"No, he befriended me. I've given him the name Donder."

Spotted Pony smiled. "Welcome, Donder."

Donder lowered his head.

"How have your people been doing?" asked Zandra. "Did my potion help slow the smallpox?"

Slowly, heads began to peek at Donder and Zandra.

"Yes, we have been doing much better. We thank you for your help."

"You're welcome," she replied. "It's hard to fight something that you have never encountered."

Donder was getting restless, and Spotted Pony's people were not getting any more comfortable with their presence.

"Well, it looks like I should be leaving," said Zandra.

"Yes," replied Spotted Pony. "My people have never seen a Thunderbird this close. I think they're uncomfortable."

Climbing up on Donder, she took off, rising in a thermal once more. Flying into the velvet sky, they crossed the Mississippi river, and she was home once again.

CHAPTER 16

Lonely Way to Go

Fall, 1789

Dear Phineas,

Here is my latest batch of wands. I'm glad to hear that the Haietlik wands are selling good. Sounds like Safferon is becoming quite the rebellious little witch.

Got a letter from Cormac and Finnghuala recently. They're well. Don't know when I will be back east, but I have big news: Omar and I are getting married! We're not having a big party, as our friends are so scattered. I've sent letters announcing this to everyone. Wish us luck.

Thanks for all the work you do selling my wands. Hopefully I can get back there sometime soon.

Miss you,
Zandra

Sitting at the table, Phineas had not touched his food. He didn't eat much anymore.

It had been a month since the letter had arrived. By now, Zandra and Omar were married. Looking out the dirty window onto the overgrown pasture, tears welled in his eyes once more. He had thought that he had no more tears to shed, but he had thought that before.

Broken Arrow had returned to his people to help with their fight. Phineas had been all alone when the letter arrived. He was lonely to the point of insanity. His mother, Zipporah, was of no help. All she ever did was make him feel worse about himself. The only thing that gave him relief was flying. Every night, he would fly as fast and as far as he could, and sometimes even that wasn't enough; he couldn't outrun the sadness that consumed his waking hours and disturbed his sleep.

Eventually, he collected himself and grabbed his broom. Disguising it as a walking stick, he headed to the Chalice.

He sat down in his usual corner. Thalia walked over to him, a big smile on her face, batting the one beautiful eye that was not covered by her long, silky, jet black hair in a unnoticed attempt to flirt with Phineas.

"Hi, Phineas," she said. "How are you?"

In a low voice, he struggled to hide his sadness. "All right."

"It was a lovely day today," Thalia replied.

"I guess."

Thalia swayed her head to expose her other eye. "What can I get you?"

Phineas still did not look at her. "A rum, please."

Clearly disappointed at his lack of attention, Thalia turned and walked back to the bar to get the rum. Strozor walked to the end of the bar.

"I can't get hardly any response out of him," said Thalia.

"He's hurt," replied Strozor. "Give him time. He'll come out of it someday."

"Some never really heal," Thalia said, as she gave Strozor a look. Gathering up all her courage as she approached Phineas, she placed the rum on the table.

"It's going to be a great night. How about you and I go for a flight after I get off?"

"I don't know, maybe," replied Phineas.

Thalia gave a shy grin. "Okay. See you then."

After an hour, Phineas felt so out of place, the sadness was overtaking him. Trying to melt into the walls, he got up and headed for the door. Thalia looked up in time to see him walk out. Her hair fell over her face as she bowed her head.

You're not the only one who hurts, she thought.

CHAPTER 17

New Arrivals and the Pukwudgie

Late Summer, 1790 - 1794

Donder had shown up just moments earlier. Zandra's toes curled over the edge of the birthing bricks,[35] turning white as a strong contraction came. Omar had made the bricks by hand, carving images into their sides to ask the magic of the gods for the health and happiness of the children and mother. He had insisted that Zandra squat on them as she gave birth to their children—it was an Egyptian tradition.

Soon she began to push. A head emerged. Two more pushes, and the girl fell into Omar's hands. Panting at the effort, Zandra thought that between the pain of labor and the burning of her thighs from squatting so long that she would fall off these bricks and just die. But after a while, the second baby emerged, and it was over.

She collapsed on the ground as Omar wrapped the boy up in a cloth and placed them both in Zandra's arms. Xavier sniffed at the new family members, then stepped aside to let Donder do the same.

Looking down at Zandra, Omar asked, "How are you doing?"

"Alright now."

"What names are we giving them?" Omar asked.

Looking at the baby girl, Zandra said, "Lavinia." Turning to the boy in her other arm, she smiled at him. "Ansel."

Omar nodded his head.

Dawn had just broken as they all looked out over the forest; golden in the morning light. Donder nuzzled Zandra's hair with the tip of his beak, walked to the edge of the cliff, and flew off to the west.

Exhausted, Zandra fell asleep. Omar floated the three of them into the house and placed them on the bed.

Although magic made child-rearing much easier, the next days and months were a radical adjustment for them. Soiled diapers were taken care of with the swipe of a wand, and the extra laundry was likewise dealt with. Zandra's strength came back over the following weeks, and she started turning wands again, although at a slower rate than before. She had turned some extra wands prior to the births. Magic had helped give her more stamina by supporting her back to help her stand for a longer amount of time, although her belly had still interfered with her ability to get close enough to the lathe.

Now that the kids were here, Omar helped to gather materials for her wands while she turned. Lavinia and Ansel would play on the floor, and Zandra would entertain them by making items float above them. She turned toy wands and staffs for them to play with, and Omar had gotten them training brooms once they were old enough.

Ansel favored Zandra, with his blond hair and brown eyes, and he was always on the go. Zandra found him hard to keep out of trouble. Lavinia, on the other hand, was dark-complected, with raven-black hair and dark eyes. Her features were a mix of Zandra and Omar, not favoring either of her parents. She was always at Zandra's side.

Both of them showed the quickness to learn that had helped Zandra in all of her endeavors, and signs of magical powers revealed themselves early in their childhood. As they grew, Zandra started to take them out into the forest with her as she swept for Sasq'ets hairs.

One evening, when the twins were about four, Zandra, Lavinia, and Ansel were taking a walk through the forest when Ansel got separated. Noticing this, Zandra started panicking. Grabbing Lavinia up, she ran back through the woods, calling out for Ansel and getting no answer.

Hoping that she was close enough for Xavier to hear, she called out with her mind as forcefully as she could. *Xavier, Ansel is missing! Get Omar.*

Xavier replied, *Right away.*

Racing down the hill, Xavier found Omar running up to him, clearly already aware that something was wrong.

Ansel has gone missing, said Xavier hurriedly.

"Where's Zandra?"

The clearing below the house on the south side, Xavier replied.

Grabbing his staff, Omar flew off to meet her as Xavier raced around the base of the hill.

When he landed next to Zandra, Omar asked, "What happened?"

Panicked, Zandra yelled, "I don't know! I just turned around and he wasn't there!"

Lavinia stood there, shaking, near tears.

"Stay here with Lavinia. Xavier is on his way."

Ansel walked deeper into the woods. He kept getting glimpses of the little man. Ansel laughed at the Pukwudgie as it peeked out at him from behind the trees. The Pukwudgie produced a fireball and made it hover above its hands, juggling it back and forth.

Ansel found it fascinating, and he followed deeper into the woods.

The blue light of twilight was creeping in as Xavier arrived.

Have you found him yet?

"No," said Zandra. "Xavier, watch over Lavinia. I'm heading out to search for Ansel."

Omar followed the trampled plants, until he came to a clearing. It had not rained in a while, so no footprints could be found. Raising his staff, he said, "Tisynive edu!"

Zandra ran up behind him. Turning to look at her, he said, "We have a magical creature involved. My revealing spell didn't work."

"He must be being lured by a Pukwudgie," replied Zandra. "You fan out that way." She gestured to the left. "I'll go to the right. Maybe we can find some physical clue that will tell us where they're heading."

After a few minutes, Omar found a broken stem. "He must have gone this way!" he called out to Zandra, who came running over to see.

As he ran off into the forest, Zandra followed.

The Pukwudgie began to disappear and reappear, luring Ansel deeper into the woods. As he came to another clearing, the Pukwudgie appeared on the far side. Ansel walked out into the clearing. When he was halfway across, the Pukwudgie pulled an arrow from his quiver and drew back on his bow—just as Omar hit the edge of the clearing.

Omar raised his staff to cast a deflecting spell, but before he could, a huge dark figure emerged from the trees on four legs. Moving at amazing speed, it came between Ansel and the Pukwudgie, batting the arrow to the ground. Skidding to a stop, it stood on its hind legs as Zandra emerged into the clearing next to Omar.

Facing the Pukwudgie, the dark figure let out a scream that seemed to suck the air from Ansel's lungs and shook him to the bone. The creature charged the Pukwudgie, which was standing there, frozen. Gathering its senses just in time, the Pukwudgie vanished.

Ansel stood still, immobilized with fear.

Turning to face Ansel, Zandra, and Omar, the dark figure stood there, looking at them.

"A Sasq'ets," Zandra said. She raised her wand. "Transferendum. Thank you for saving my son."

The Sasq'ets didn't say a word.

"I've heard your troop around here for years. I'm glad to finally meet one of you. I'm Zandra," she said, pointing to herself, "and this is Omar." Gesturing at Ansel as she walked up to stand with him, she said, "This is my son, Ansel." She put her hands on his shoulders and pressed him against her.

After a typical long silence, the Sasq'ets spoke. "I'm Taug," he said. "That Pukwudgie will not bother you anymore."

"Is there anything that I can do for you and your troop?" asked Zandra.

"Leave us alone as you have." Turning, Taug disappeared into the woods.

Zandra stood there, Ansel still pressed against her. Taug had frightened Ansel so much that he had wet himself. He had heard the chatter of them many nights as he fell asleep, but had never gotten a glimpse of one, and it had overwhelmed him.

"What were you thinking?" asked Zandra. "We've both told you about the Pukwudgie; you know how dangerous they can be. You could have been killed!"

Omar had joined them, but said nothing.

"I'm sorry!" cried Ansel. "It seemed nice enough."

"Well, I hope that you'll listen to our warnings and follow our advice more readily from now on," said Omar.

Ansel nodded his head.

Lavinia was in tears as they emerged from the woods with Ansel at their side. Xavier lowered himself down to the ground, and Lavinia hopped off, running up to hug Ansel.

Well, I think it's time to head back to the house for some rum, now that we're all safe, said Xavier.

"Everything with you is about rum," said Omar. "It's a good thing that we don't keep too much of it on hand, or you'd be drunk all the time."

It keeps the blood thin.

"You're a horse," Zandra pointed out. "I don't think you're at risk of your blood thickening."

As they walked back up to the house, the chatter of the Sasq'ets reached a fever pitch.

"It appears that your little adventure has caused a dispute among Taug's troop," Omar said to Ansel.

After the sounds had gone on for a good while, a huge roar rang out over the forest. Then there was silence.

Soon, the forest noises rose again.

CHAPTER 18

NAHANNI VALLEY

Summer, 1799

As the wagon rocked on the crude road through the Ohio River bottoms, Ansel and Lavinia were getting restless. They had been to the Egyptian settlement of Memphis to sell some wands, and were growing weary of the road.

The mosquitoes are terrible here. I'll be so glad to get out of these bottoms, said Xavier.

"Well, then, move along and stop complaining," replied Omar.

Lavinia and Ansel chuckled in the back of the wagon. The woods began to clear slightly as a road converged with the one they were on from the right.

"Shh, everyone." Zandra cocked her head toward the merging road, hearing the sounds of baying and barking in the distance as Xavier came to a halt. "Dogs coming this way."

Just then a man burst from the trees and ran in front of them, covered in mud. His ripped clothes hung sloppily off his thin frame as he ran into the standing water on the other side of the road. He collapsed beside a tree, exhausted.

"Stay still," Zandra said as she pulled out her wand. "Commuta Habitum!" she said, then added one more spell. "Delens Odos!"

The man melted with the tree that he had collapsed against, and his scent trail disappeared.

Just then, the dogs that Zandra had heard earlier came running from the woods. They ran in front of Zandra, Omar, and the rest of the family, turning back on themselves and sniffing the ground intently. They circled, trying to find the scent.

Zandra stuck her wand back in the pocket under her thin cloak as three men rode up on horseback. The man closest to them spoke.

"Pardon me, ma'am; sir," he said in a gruff voice, nodding at Zandra and Omar in turn. "Did a nigger pass by here?"

Zandra winced at the word, and her anger spiked. Omar blocked her hand in the process of reaching for her wand. Zandra gave Omar a look that said everything, but she knew he was right–it was not a good time to teach these men a lesson, not with the kids in the wagon behind them.

Omar spoke. "No," he replied. "We heard your dogs and had stopped to see what was going on, then you showed up."

As Omar spoke, one of the men got off his horse. Walking over, he kicked one of the dogs. Yelping, the dog moved away from him, its tail between its legs. The man moved to the next dog. "Stupid, no-good dogs," he growled, rearing back to kick another. But, inexplicably, this dog slid to the side as though some invisible force had moved it, and, failing to make contact with the dog, the man landed on his butt in the road.

Zandra quickly turned to look at Lavinia and Ansel sternly as they attempted to wipe the smiles off their faces. She knew one of them had moved the dog with magic, but she couldn't scold them now.

Frowning, the man still on horseback looked at the other man lying in the road. "The dogs must have lost his trail," he said. "Gather them up. Let's double back and see if they can pick up the trail again."

The man on the ground climbed back on his horse angrily, and they turned and headed back down the road.

Once the men were out of sight, Zandra dropped the spell. The man she had hidden in the tree became visible again. He was still lying there, too tired to move.

"Atollo," Zandra said. The man floated off the ground and into the wagon. "Ansel, cover him with that tarp," she said. "Xavier, get us out of here."

They got on a ferry to cross the Ohio river, and rolled off on the north side. Traveling for a while, they eventually pulled off the side of the road and set up camp. When he woke up, their guest said nothing, just watching them, almost fearfully.

Once everything was in order, Zandra turned to the man. "We will have some warm food soon." She pulled out her wand, and he jumped. "I'm not going to hurt you," she said. "I'm going to get you some clothes." She waved her wand, and clothes appeared in her hand. She held them out, and the man took them.

"I'm Zandra," she said.

"Name's Emem," he responded, as he turned and took off his shirt, revealing a back covered in slashing scars.

Zandra gasped. "What has happened to your back?"

"I'z run away. Masser punishez me."

Zandra didn't know what to say. Finally, the words came together. "I can help you," she said softly. "I have a friend that lives in a place where you could be safe. Where is your family?"

"I haz no family."

"You had to have a mother."

"I'z never knowed my mother."

Zandra blinked the tears out of her eyes. "I'll let you get dressed. Come join us to eat when you're ready."

She returned to Omar to help with the meal. Omar could see that she was upset.

"How's our new friend?"

"His name is Emem." Zandra tried to collect herself. "I've been so busy with my wand business and helping the natives that I've been neglecting others who need help. Emem has been whipped horribly, and he has no family. He has no idea who his mother is."

"There's always a slave and a master class," replied Omar.

"There shouldn't be. I'm going to take him up to Elizabeth."

185

They had been home a few days when Zandra readied herself for the trip. Letters had been sent to Elizabeth and Phineas, as she had decided to make a quick stop in Danvers to drop off some wands. She would head up north from there to a place called the Nahanni Valley.[36] Zandra had heard tales of strange goings-on, and figured there must be some kind of magical creature responsible for the stories. She had already explained to Emem that she would have to shrink him down for the flight to his new home, so he was prepared when she came for him.

Placing him in her special box, she then put the box in her flight bag. She grabbed her broom and stepped out of the house.

"I don't want you to go, Mommy!" begged Lavinia.

"I'll be alright," Zandra said. "I haven't been away for a long time, and I need to help Emem, and find new magical creatures for my wands. You know my dream is to make a wand to rival the best of the old world wands, and I haven't achieved that yet."

"But, Mommy," said Ansel, "you make great wands! You sell a lot of them!"

Lavinia nodded.

"I have to try to do even better," said Zandra. "This is my goal. You and your dad and Xavier will do fine without me."

"Doing fine and having what we need are two different things," said Lavinia.

Omar said nothing, but his look told Zandra that he agreed with the kids, though he knew better than to contradict her.

Xavier walked up. *Say hi to Phineas. And be careful.*

"I will." Zandra patted him on the neck, then turned and hugged Ansel and Lavinia.

"Be good for your father. No sliding dogs." She embraced Omar, and they kissed. Then she walked to the top of one of the hoodoos and flew off into the night sky.

"They're a handful sometimes. When we came across Emem, one of them moved a dog sideways, making the man miss it and land on his butt in the road. It was funny, but I worry that they might expose themselves some time."

"I'm sure it'll be alright. At least they care about how people and animals are treated," replied Phineas.

"Yes, you're right," she said. "I just worry. Being a magical mother has its own stresses."

"Would you like to go the Chalice tonight?" asked Phineas.

"I have to leave tonight," she said, shaking her head. "The kids didn't want me to go, so I can't stay long. After I leave Emem with Elizabeth, I'm heading up north to the Nahanni Valley to see what magical creature might be up there, and maybe get some new infusion materials for my wands."

Phineas's face dropped. It was clear he had hoped to have more time with her than just a couple hours.

"I need to get some rest so I can fly tonight," said Zandra. "Will you wake me toward evening?"

"Yes," he said glumly.

"Thanks," she said. "See you this evening."

Phineas walked into the bedroom. He had prepared a meal for Zandra, and it was time to wake her. He stood there for a minute, watching her sleep, wishing that she had never left.

She had only become prettier with age, at least in his mind. Her blond hair draped over her cheek. He had not seen her natural hair color in a long time. He stood there for a while, just dreaming of what could have been. Despite his sadness, Phineas was glad

Zandra was happy, and that Omar was a good man, although he did seem a little mysterious.

Finally facing the inevitable, he gently grabbed her shoulder and gave her a shake. Slowly, her beautiful brown eyes opened to little slits and she stretched.

"Already?" she yawned.

"I have food ready," he said. "And it's coming on evening."

"Thanks. I'll be there in a minute."

Phineas walked out of the room as Zandra got dressed.

"Have you heard from Broken Arrow?" Zandra asked when she came out.

"No," Phineas replied. "Last I heard, he was camped near Montreal."

"Get me some paper. I'll send him a letter and tell him to meet me."

"How is he going to know where to meet you?" asked Phineas.

"Hmm..." Zandra thought. "I'll have to send him a second letter when I find Elizabeth. She probably doesn't live in the same place anymore."

Eating her food as she wrote the letter, Zandra finished both, and tapped her wand on the letter. It folded up and flew off.

"Hope he can meet me. It's been so long. I'd like to find out what has been going on with him."

"Let me know what you find out," said Phineas. "Tell him that his longhouse is still in one piece."

"I'll do that." Zandra stood up. "Well, I had better get going. Tell everyone at the Chalice hi for me, and tell them I'm sorry I didn't have time to stop in."

"I'll do that."

Pulling her stuff together, she gave Phineas a hug. It felt so good to hold her again.

Then she walked out the door, and she was gone into the purple dusk sky.

Phineas stood there in the doorway, his stomach sinking. Grabbing his broom, he flew off—in no particular direction, only speed and the long night.

Zandra hugged Elizabeth, looking down at Hope. "You've grown into a striking young lady like your mother."

Elizabeth introduced her. "This is Zandra. She is the woman that saved you all those years ago."

Hope just smiled.

"She doesn't talk much until she gets to know someone," said Elizabeth.

"How have things been for you here?" asked Zandra.

"We're doing all right. The work is hard, but the boss is good, and we're free. As you can see, we've been able to move into this small house."

"I'm happy for you," replied Zandra.

"You said you had someone needing my help."

"Yes, but before I introduce you, I have a business proposition for you," said Zandra. "I want to help more slaves to get their freedom like you. I need someplace for them to come and start a new life. I was hoping that if I was to get you a place that was a little more off the beaten path, I could pay you to take care of setting them up with a new life. Do you think you could help me?"

Elizabeth thought for a moment, then turned and looked at Hope. "What do you think, Hope? Do you want to help?"

Hope thought for a while, then said, "I think we should."

"Great!" said Zandra. "I'll go out tomorrow and find a place. I thought we could get a small farmstead started, and the escapees could help you run it so you can grow your own food and raise some livestock."

Zandra pulled the little box out of her pack that contained Emem's body. Hope walked up as Zandra opened it, looking in amazement at the little man.

"This is how I got you here, all those years ago," said Zandra. "I shrunk you and your mom and flew you here on my broom." She pulled out her wand. "Aversa pars!"

Emem gradually began to grow. Once he was back to his normal size, he woke. Hope watched, fascinated.

"Emem, this is my friend Elizabeth, and her daughter Hope. She has agreed to help us get you set up in a new life."

Looking at them, Emem said, "Thanks, ma'am."

"I'll get something cooking. You two must be hungry," said Elizabeth.

"Can I help?" asked Emem.

"Sure," replied Elizabeth.

Zandra did tricks for Hope with her wand while they prepared the food.

As they ate, Zandra told of her adventures and her new family, as well as her plans to have people help between her home in the southern Illinois country and Elizabeth's place in Montreal, so that Zandra would hopefully not have to deliver the escaping slaves herself all the time. She was thinking about having a series of safe houses, and she could put a protection charm on them without them knowing.

After they had finished eating, Zandra turned in for the rest of the morning as Emem, Elizabeth, and Hope got to know each other.

Waking in the afternoon, she sent Broken Arrow the second letter to let him know where she was. She told Elizabeth that she had an old friend that she hoped to see, and that he might be stopping by. Then she went out searching for a farm.

It took her until the next morning to find one. She found a carpenter who would add on to the house to make it what they needed.

As she walked back up to Elizabeth's small house, a figure was sitting on the front stoop.

"Broken Arrow!" She ran up and hugged him. She pulled out her wand to cast the translation spell, but Broken Arrow stopped her.

"My English has gotten much better," he said.

Zandra smiled. "I'm so glad you came. I've been worried about you. How have you been?"

"I've been alright," said Broken Arrow heavily. "It has been a very bitter time. I've fought many battles, lost some friends. I have no more use for war than I did before. We have lost our homeland, but at least the crown gave us *some* land, which is better than I thought we would get."

"I'm glad that you survived. Are you happy that you joined with your people?"

"Yes," he said, limping over to stand under a tree.

Zandra frowned. "What's wrong with your leg?"

"I took a musket ball in one of the battles. It still pains me."

Zandra pulled out her wand. "Auxilium," she said.

Broken Arrow's expression changed as the pain disappeared. He looked down at his leg, then back up at her. "Thanks."

"No problem," Zandra replied.

Broken Arrow leaned back against the tree. "But enough about me. What about you? How has your life been going?"

Zandra thought for a moment. A lot had happened since she had last talked to Broken Arrow. A lot had changed. "I'm married to an Egyptian wizard named Omar, and we have twins—a boy named Ansel, and a girl named Lavinia. They're nine now. I've met and become friends with the Thunderbird that saved us that night from the Mishipizheu. I've explored some of the western lands, and I've been befriended by a Diné shaman. And I've learned some dark secrets about this land. I had an encounter with a skinwalker that almost killed me, and unfortunately ended in the dark shaman's death."

Broken Arrow took in her words for a moment, before saying, "You have experienced much."

Elizabeth came out of the front door. "I have some food ready. Would you like something to eat?"

They spent the rest of the day catching up with each other. As Broken Arrow was leaving, Zandra stopped him.

"Elizabeth," she said, "do you have the bell I gave you?"

"Yes, I do."

Zandra pulled out her wand and produced another bell. Although slightly different than the first, it was still missing its clapper.

"If you ever need me," said Zandra to Broken Arrow, "swing it three times, and I will hear it wherever I am, and I'll come as soon as I can."

Broken Arrow took the bell from Zandra and looked at it, perplexed. He swung it, but no sound came from it. He looked at her, confused. "A magic bell?"

"Yes," replied Zandra. "Take care of yourself."

Broken Arrow turned and walked off down the road.

Zandra turned to Elizabeth. "I need to take you out to the farm in the morning. I've arranged for a carpenter to meet me there so that we can discuss the work to be done. I plan to put an addition on to the house that is already there. You will be the one he will be dealing with, so you need to be introduced to him. Emem, do you have any carpentry skill?"

"I'z can do some."

"Good. You can help the carpenter, then."

The next morning, they all headed out to the farm. Walking up the long lane, Hope ran up to the house and dashed around it, meeting them back in front.

"Mom, it's great!" she said, excited. She took off to the barn and explored the pasture.

After a short while, the carpenter showed up. Introducing them, Zandra described what she was wanting done, and they came to an agreement on price. Zandra told the carpenter that he would be dealing with Elizabeth from here forward.

After everything was squared away, they headed back to Elizabeth's.

"I will send you money from time to time, and letters to give you updates on my progress on getting the chain of safe houses set up," Zandra told Elizabeth. Pulling out a bag, she held the open end toward Elizabeth and Hope. "Reach in the bag, both of you, and grab the wand inside."

Looking confused as she did what Zandra told her, Elizabeth said, "What is this for? I'm not a witch. This won't do me any good."

"You're right, but this is a special wand. Now that you both have touched it, it will allow you to write on the backside of any letter that you receive from me, and when either of you touches it with this wand, it will fold up and fly back to me. Be sure that no one sees you do this." Zandra handed the bag to Elizabeth. "Well, it's getting dark. I had better get on with my journeys."

After giving Elizabeth and Hope a hug, she turned to Emem. "I hope this is the beginning of a good life for you. Good luck."

With a quavering voice, Emem spoke. "Thanks fo' everything, miz Zandra."

Zandra had been flying over the great northern forest for three days. The land was so sparsely inhabited, and the forest so thick, it made day flights safe. The forest was dotted with many lakes, and the mosquitoes had been horrible.

Landing on the edge of a lake for the night, she set up camp and cast a shield charm to keep the mosquitoes at bay. After eating, she sat on the bank and watched the sun set.

She had turned in for the night when there was a big splash in the water. She ignored it at first, thinking it was probably Sasq'ets that were unhappy with her presence.

Then came another big, hissing splash.

She looked up as a giant, dark head emerged from the water, steam rising around it. It looked like a spiky serpent's head, made of jagged volcanic rock, with veins of lava coursing up the underside of its neck, illuminating its craggy scales. The surface of the water glowed red as the creature dove back into the water.

Then, suddenly, it shot out of the water toward the center of the lake, riding a ribbon of fire.

"Gaasyendietha," Zandra breathed, fascinated.

Grabbing her broom, she flew off into the night sky after it. Trailing up behind the water dragon, the smell of molten rock and sulfur was intense. Once she was close enough, she pulled her wand out and pointed it at one of the spikes on its back.

"Segmentum!" she shouted.

A sliver of the spike flew off. The Gaasyendietha turned, and a chunk of molten rock shot from its mouth, coming so close to Zandra that it singed her hair, making her miss the sliver.

The molten rock hit the ground, igniting the trees. Zandra was now the chased, and the massive dragon was the chaser. Jets of red-hot lava streaked by her as she did evasive maneuvers and threw spells back at it.

"Ambiguus!" she shouted, weaving to the right, almost slipping off the broom. "Pulso!" Pulling herself back on her broom, she climbed steeply, rolling as she streaked upward. "Resisto!"

Nothing was slowing it down. Zandra stalled out and dived back down at the Gaasyendietha. Throwing multiple spells in quick succession, she finally stunned it as she passed so near that she scraped some flesh off her leg. Quickly, she pointed her wand at the Gaasyendietha's back.

"Segmentum!" she yelled. A sliver blew off one of the Gaasyendietha's back spines, cutting her hand as she caught it.

She pulled out of the dive just before hitting the ground. Flying fast at treetop level, she could see the Gaasyendietha slide into the forest in the distance as the trees burst into flames.

Quickly returning to her camp, she threw all her things in her flight bag and took off, hoping to get as much distance between her and the Gaasyendietha as possible.

It had been a couple days since Zandra had left Phineas when he finally headed to the Chalice for a drink. He sat far in the back. Thalia was taking care of the bar as Strozor sat at the table with Phineas.

"You have to move on," Strozor said gently. "She has a husband and children now. You can't just waste away over her. You have people that care about you. You just need to open your eyes."

Phineas sat there with his head down.

After a long silence, Strozor asked, "Where was she off to?"

"Montreal," Phineas replied quietly. "Then to a place called Nahanni Valley."

"Nahanni Valley?" blurted Strozor, alarmed. "Was she going by herself?"

Phineas looked confused. "Yes...I think."

"How many days ago did she leave?"

Phineas shrugged. "A couple days."

Strozor jumped up. Walking to the door, he looked back at Thalia. "Take care of the place until I get back," he said hurriedly as he rushed out the door.

Finally, Zandra had arrived at the south Nahanni River. She had set up camp where the Nahanni joined the Liard River. The night was alive with the sounds of the forest, including a troop of Sasq'ets that had not missed her arrival.

The next morning, she headed upriver. Flying low along the shore, she saw what she thought to be Dire Wolves.[37] As she flew further up the river, she came across a man lying near the edge of the forest.

That seems strange, she thought, so she circled around to investigate. Coming in behind the man, she landed and walked up to where she had seen him.

The man was still lying there. Slowly, she walked up to him.

"Hello?" she called. No answer.

As she got closer, she saw that his head had been ripped from his body—not cut, nor chopped, but ripped. Searching around, she could not find the head.

Feeling uneasy, she hopped on her broom and distanced herself from what she had found.

As she traveled, the river dug deep into whitish-gray cliffs, and the pines grew right up to the edge of the stone. Some of the limestone cliffs rose two thousand feet above the river.

Coming upon a waterfall divided in half by a pillar of limestone,[I] she decided to land on the south cliff, as evening was fast approaching. She stood there for a moment. The thundering of the water and the mist rising off the base of the fall was amazing.

Dropping her flight bag and broom, she turned and walked into the forest.

As Zandra distanced herself from the waterfall, she realized that the forest was eerily quiet. She stopped for a moment. For the second time that day, she felt uneasy. As she scanned the forest, her heart began to beat faster.

[I] Virginia Falls in Nahanni Valley.

Then they came.

The forest exploded with the sound of trees breaking all around. Zandra turned and ran back to the cliff. Just as she got to the clearing where she had landed, she tripped, twisting her ankle on a root. As she looked back, she could see the trees crashing down behind her.

She could see them—hoards of Ye'iitsoh, racing toward her. Zandra threw a spell in a feeble attempt to hold them off while trying to get to her feet, but her ankle was too painful.

"Revoco!" She tried to summon her broom, but it did not come.

Turning, she threw more spells at the Ye'iitsoh, trying to slow them. "Revoco!" she shouted again, and once again, her broom did not come.

Finally, she threw a shield spell between her and the hoard. It stopped their forward movement, but she was putting all she had into the shield, and it was showing signs of imminent failure.

Then she heard a thump come from behind her.

Great, she thought. *They've gone around the shield.*

Turning to see the new threat, she shouted with surprise. "Strozor!"

Strozor jutted his large hands out in front of him, and a wave of distortion emanated from them. The shock wave hit the Ye'iitsoh, tossing them back into the forest that they had just devastated.

Strozor reached down, picked up Zandra, and ran back to her flight bag. Her broom had fallen and gotten jammed into a crevasse, which must have been why she couldn't summon it.

"Can you fly?" asked Strozor.

She tested her ankle. "Yes, I think so."

Then the thundering sound of the Ye'iitsoh's stampede began again.

"They're coming!" yelled Strozor. "Get in the air!"

Throwing her flight bag over her shoulder, she freed her broom and gently kicked off. As soon as she was in the air, Strozor leaped off the cliff, flying without a broom.

They soared back down the river, passing out of the valley. As she flew, Zandra cast an Auxilium charm on her ankle to heal it enough so she would be able to land. They flew southeast for an hour or so before landing near midnight.

Zandra turned to Strozor. She didn't know where to start. "Thanks for saving me. Why are you here?" She took her flight bag off her shoulder and dropped it on the moss-covered ground.

"Phineas told me of your plan to visit the Nahanni Valley. My family has spent much time in the north. I knew the danger that you were in."

"This wasn't my first encounter with the Ye'iitsoh. But the first time I saw them, I only encountered one, and luckily I had the help of a Thunderbird," she admitted. "This must be the land to the north that Man With Great Magic talked about. He said his people encountered great numbers of them here." Zandra started setting up camp. "You're a very powerful wizard. I've never seen anyone with powers like yours."

Pulling a log over, Strozor sat down. "The Ye'iitsoh are called mountain giants up here."

Throwing sticks into a pile, Zandra pointed her wand at it, and flames rose up from the wood. She started cooking, hoping that Strozor would offer up some insight into his past, but nothing came. Finally, when she handed him a plate of fresh johnnycakes, he spoke, but his words came as a shock to her.

"You know, Phineas is having a hard time," he said.

Zandra looked at him in confusion.

"Your marriage caught him by surprise. You were the one positive thing in his life. He feels all alone. He looks at you as another failure that he has made. He was too scared of losing you to tell you how he felt, and in the end, that caused him to lose you anyway."

Zandra picked at her food. She had thought that Phineas seemed hurt, but had no idea that he was still distraught.

"Phineas is very important to me," she finally said. "I never intended to hurt him."

"I'm sure you didn't. He needs to move on. There is someone who has been trying to get his attention, but he's too overrun with grief to see it."

Swiping his plate clean with a stroke of his hand, he gave it back to Zandra. Then, stretching out on the ground, he fell asleep.

Zandra had never talked this much with Strozor, and now that she had, she didn't know what to do with what he had said. She was physically and mentally exhausted. She sat there for a bit, mulling everything over in her head. She would have to do something to help Phineas move on.

But for now, she needed to sleep.

Zandra broke off from Strozor as he flew on to the Chalice. Walking up to the door of Phineas's house, she knocked and walked in.

Phineas looked up, obviously surprised to see her. He tried to hide his face.

Zandra sat down beside him.

"I didn't know you were coming back," he said softly.

"You've been crying," she noticed. "What's the matter?"

"Nothing," he said quickly.

Zandra moved close by him, putting her arm around him. Phineas said nothing, trying to turn away from her. Zandra could feel his breath come in short, sharp bursts that he couldn't keep back.

Still trying to look away from her, he broke down. Zandra sat there patiently waiting.

It took a long while before he could talk. Finally, he spoke.

"I love you," he said.

She laid her head on his shoulder. "I love you too," she said. "You're very special to me. I don't like seeing you this way."

Phineas tried to get his breathing under control.

"Our friendship means so much to me," she went on. "I need you to move on. Don't throw away your life over me. I will always be there for you. The rest of our life as friends can be great. Let's make the best of it."

They sat there for a long time, hugging. Evening came, and Phineas finally calmed down.

"Let's go to the Chalice for something to eat," Zandra suggested.

As they walked into the tavern, she noticed Thalia look at Phineas with a slight smile.

Zandra looked over at Strozor and winked.

CHAPTER 19

Goodbye, Old Friend

Winter, 1809

Sharif had been knocked out of the sky by the Piasa Bird's long tail. It was just Zandra and Omar now.

In hindsight, Zandra thought, maybe it hadn't been a good idea to jump the Piasa Bird as it passed over their home, but they had thought it wouldn't expect an attack this far away from its lair.

Diving in and out of valleys and around hills, flames shot from the bird's eyes and barely missed Omar. Flying in under its belly, Zandra pointed her wand. "Uro!"

She could see a spot on the beast's underside scorching as the spell hit it. The bird curled slightly as it lashed at her with its large talons, just barely missing her.

Then two bolts came from in front of them. Spells kept coming, distracting the Piasa Bird. Zandra rushed up beside its ugly face. "Segmentum!" A sliver flew off its fang. Snarling at Zandra, the bird shot flames toward her as a shield charm materialized in between them.

Whirling around, Zandra saw that Lavinia had thrown the shield charm. Ansel had joined Omar in the battle.

Zandra headed for the forest floor, flying among the trees as Omar, Ansel, and Lavinia followed. The Piasa Bird flew overhead, shooting fire into the treetops. Flying through Taug's camp, the Piasa Bird ignited the trees, enraging the Sasq'ets. Picking up large stones, they began to hurl them at the bird.

Finally, the bird had had enough. It gave up and flew off to the west.

They found Sharif lying on the ground, safe, but unconscious. They floated him back to the house, and he finally came around.

"That thing is stronger every time we fight it," Sharif said as he lay there, gathering his senses.

When everyone was safe, Zandra let Ansel and Lavinia have it. "I told you not to come!" she said. "The Piasa Bird is very dangerous. You could have been killed!"

"You could have been killed, too," Ansel and Lavinia said in unison.

Zandra waved the words aside. "I don't worry about myself. But if something happened to the two of you—"

"And what would we do without you?" Lavinia interrupted.

Zandra stood there and didn't know what to say.

"Did you at least get your wand infusion material?" asked Ansel.

"Yes," she said. "Your attack distracted the bird long enough for me to get it."

"See?" said Ansel. "We did help you!"

Omar returned from putting out the fires that the Piasa Bird had set, just as a letter fluttered up to Zandra.

"It's from Phineas!" said Zandra.

Opening the letter, tears welled in her eyes.

Everyone stood there silently, waiting to hear what Phineas had to say. Turning, Zandra walked over and picked up her flight bag and broom, tears streaming down her face. "I'm off to Boston," she said shortly.

"What is it? What's happened?" asked Lavinia.

"Cormac is dying."

Grabbing their flight bags and brooms, Ansel and Lavinia hurried over to Zandra. "We're going with you," said Ansel firmly.

Zandra nodded.

Xavier came to the window, nudging it open. *I would like to see him one more time.*

Omar turned to Sharif. "Could you watch over things here?"

Sharif nodded silently.

"It's going to be a cold flight," Zandra said. "And we'll have to push hard. I don't know how long he has left."

Omar got his flight bag and went outside to shrink Xavier down so they could bring him along. Sharif followed.

"Are you sure you'll be alright?" Omar asked Sharif.

"That bird almost got the better of me," said Sharif. "But I'm fine."

"Thanks for taking care of the place. Cormac is an old friend of Zandra's. He means a lot to her."

Zandra, Ansel, and Lavinia stepped out of the house.

"We're ready," Zandra said.

Xavier walked up.

"Are you ready?" Omar asked.

Yes.

"Lie down. I don't want you falling on me."

Xavier did so.

"Ni Geni Mykro." Xavier shrunk, and Omar bent down and picked him up, placing him in the travel box and then in his flight bag.

Then they all walked to the edge of the hill and flew off to Boston.

Thalia greeted them at the door of the inn. She had a grim look on her face. "We didn't know if you were going to come."

"We left the night we got the letter," replied Zandra.

"Phineas is downtown. He's been working with Cormac's nephew. He's going to collect the newcomers to the inn from now on. Now that Cormac...can't."

"How are you and Phineas doing?"

"It's been a long road, but he's coming around," replied Thalia. "Thank you for all the nudging over the years. It's helped him a lot."

"It was nothing," said Zandra. "Can we see Cormac?"

"Yes," Thalia led the way. "Finnghuala is with him. I'll have something for you to eat when you're ready."

When they got to the bedroom, Zandra knocked on the door. Finnghuala's voice came from inside. "Come in."

When they opened the door, Finnghuala's eyes brightened a little. "Zandra! You came."

Cormac opened his eyes, smiling. Zandra walked up to the bed, kneeling beside him. She grabbed his hand, looking into his eyes.

In a weak voice, Cormac spoke. "Look at your family. They have grown so much since the last time."

"Well, it's been a long time since we've been here," said Zandra. "Too long," she added with a sigh.

"Omar," wheezed Cormac. "Are you keeping these two in line?"

"They have too much of their mother in them."

Cormac gave a low, weak chuckle. "Ansel, you still favor your mother. What is the latest trouble you two have been in?"

"Well, we helped Mom with the Piasa Bird. She wasn't too happy."

Cormac coughed slightly as he laughed. "Yes, I'm sure she let you know how she felt about that." He turned slowly to Lavinia. "Lavinia, you have become a striking young witch."

"Thanks," Lavinia replied shyly. "I've never thanked you for saving my mom."

Cormac took a shallow breath. "No need."

Zandra stood up. "We have someone special who wanted to see you. Could everyone clear out this side of the room?"

Omar pulled the box out of his bag. Taking Xavier out, he placed him on the floor. "Epanyri."

The floorboards creaked under his weight as Xavier grew back to his normal size.

Cormac grinned broadly. "Xavier! I thought I'd never see you again. How have you been?"

Well, the rum's not up to snuff back home.

"Don't think we have any rum around here. We'll have to see if we can get you some."

Zandra turned back to Cormac. "You were the first wizard I met in this country," she said quietly. "You and Finnghuala were always so kind to me. You two made my first days here so much easier. You have helped so many people, with your years of standing out there on Salem Street in the heat and cold, helping people get started on their new lives. I'm glad for the life I've been given, but I'm sorry that my life took me away from here. Away from you both."

Zandra squeezed Cormac's hand as she looked over at Finnghuala with tears in her eyes. She could feel him slipping away.

"I'm tired. The banshee is screaming," Cormac said, closing his eyes.

As he faded away, the last thing Cormac heard was Xavier.

Goodbye, old friend.

CHAPTER 20

Wendigo

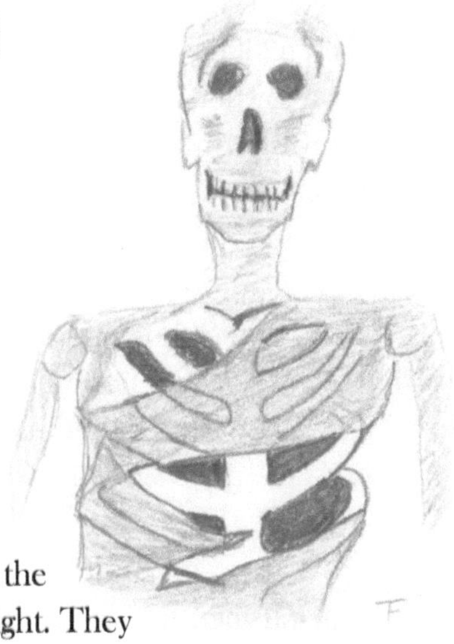

1809 - 1810

The storm was intensifying; they could barely see through the snow in the darkness of the night. They had been blown off course by the nor'easter on their way back from Boston, and they were having a hard time holding on to their brooms in the cold. Seeing a cabin below, Omar gestured for them to land. Snow flew up into the air as they hit the drifts that had formed in the clearing.

The cabin's door had been ripped off its hinges. They entered cautiously. No one was inside, but a fire was still going in the fireplace. Waving her wand, Zandra said, "Exsarcio." The door flew back into place, its leather hinges repaired.

Looking around, they could see that there had been a struggle. A table was knocked over, and various things had been tossed about. As they inspected the place, trying to ascertain what had happened, they heard a man scream from the forest.

"That must be the owner of the cabin," said Lavinia.

The storm was subsiding, so Omar headed out to see what was going on. As he came out of the cabin, another scream came from the trees. He headed in the direction the sound had come from, tramping through the deep snow. He walked over a small rise. The snow helped to give light and dimension to the dark forest.

Then he saw it—a tall, emaciated figure; the monster's rotting skin was pulled tight over its skeletal body, no muscle visible. Omar was too late: the owner of the cabin was already dead. The creature was feasting on the man. As it ate, it increased in size, but always stayed the same disgustingly thin and rotten entity. The smell of rotting flesh wafted through the air, even though it was well below freezing.

A Wendigo, Omar thought. It had not seen him, so he turned to head back to the cabin, not wanting to endanger the family—not to mention the fact that he didn't want to fight it in this weather.

Back at the abandoned house, Zandra suddenly realized someone was missing.

"Where's Lavinia?" she asked.

"I don't know," Ansel replied.

Looking out the door, Zandra could see nothing. The snow had drifted over any footprints that might have been there. She called out and got no response. Pulling the box that contained Xavier out of Omar's flight bag, she stepped outside.

"Aversa pars!"

Xavier woke and grew back to his normal size. *Jeez, you could have left me asleep in my box. It's horrible out here!*

"Omar went after some cries in the forest, and Lavinia has disappeared," said Zandra hurriedly. "I need you to help me find her."

Xavier sighed. *Those two! Always getting themselves into trouble. Hop on.*

Ansel came out of the house, and he and Zandra climbed up on Xavier's back.

Which way do you think they went? Xavier asked.

"It sounded like the scream came from behind the cabin, so they probably tried to follow it."

Xavier took off around the cabin, rushing through the cold night air.

Omar had taken a few steps when he heard a branch break to his right.

The Wendigo straightened, sniffing the air. It had finished the meal at hand and took off toward the sound. Omar stopped and walked back to see the Wendigo disappear into the forest.

He stood there for a moment, confused at what had just happened, but glad that the thing had moved on.

Lavinia had not been able to find Omar's tracks, and was aimlessly wandering, trying to find Omar or the source of the screams. It was very cold; the blowing snow blurred her vision.

As she stepped into a small stream, the ice gave way.

Reaching for a branch that gave under her weight, Lavinia fell up to her knees in the water as the Wendigo appeared. She had never seen one before, but she had heard them described. The descriptions didn't do this thing justice; it was more horrible than she had ever imagined.

She frantically pulled her wand out, trying to stand up, but the Wendigo knocked it out of her hand. Lavinia scrambled up and took off through the forest, weaving in and out of the trees, plowing through the deep snow. She was not going to be able to outrun it.

She tried to find the thickest part of the woods, hoping the monster wouldn't fit between the trunks of the trees. The Wendigo swiped at her; she could feel its fingers brush through her long hair.

Coming to a frozen stream, she fell, sliding across to the other bank. Exposed tree roots stuck out from the dirt.

She climbed under the roots as the Wendigo approached. It reached in, trying to pull her out.

Just then, Xavier blasted through a snow drift. Rearing up, he struck at the Wendigo. It backed away momentarily. Zandra and Ansel slid off Xavier, hitting the Wendigo with spells. It continued to back away, letting out a ghastly howl. Wandless, Lavinia could do nothing but cower underneath the roots and hope her mother and Ansel could hold the monster off.

Zandra and Ansel had moved the Wendigo away from Lavinia, trying to give her a chance to get away.

Crawling out from underneath the roots in the bank of the stream, Lavinia saw that Xavier had moved away from the Wendigo to stay out of the line of fire. Seeing her, he galloped up beside Lavinia.

"I've lost my wand," she said.

Get on me, replied Xavier.

Moving away from the fight, they watched as Omar flew into the fray. He charged, pointing his staff at the Wendigo. "Prystet!"

Bouncing off the invisible shield Omar had summoned, the Wendigo hit the ground, screaming an ear-piercing, ghastly screech once more.

Looking at Zandra and Ansel, Omar said, "On three."

Standing back up, the Wendigo's disgusting frame lurched toward them.

"One," said Omar.

The Wendigo stumbled forward.

"Two..."

It reached out a bony, withered hand.

"Three!"

Red streams of light erupted from their wands and Omar's staff, striking the Wendigo in the chest. It hit the ground, writhing, and burst into flames.

They lowered their wands, and Omar his staff.

"That was a nasty one," Ansel said.

"Yes, it was," Omar panted. "How did you end up out here?"

"Your daughter went out after you," Zandra replied, glancing over at Lavinia sternly.

"How come they're always *my* kids when they get in trouble?" asked Omar, looking over at Lavinia as he spoke. "Where is your wand, Lavinia?"

"The Wendigo knocked it out of my hand."

"Let's head over and retrieve it," said Omar. "Xavier, come with us."

The snow began falling again as Zandra walked over to the remains of the Wendigo, kicking at the pile of ash. Coming across a long, white shard of bone, she picked it up.

Stopping and looking at Zandra warningly, Omar said, "Nothing good can come from that thing."

Zandra looked at the bone, thinking. "But it would make such a powerful wand!"

Omar shook his head ominously. "Don't say I didn't warn you."

Omar turned, and he, Lavinia, and Xavier continued off to retrieve Lavinia's wand as Zandra and Ansel walked back to the house, with the Wendigo bone in hand.

Spring had finally come. Zandra had been busy over the winter making wands, and her training of Ansel and Lavinia on wandmaking was coming to a close. Her business had expanded; with the growth of the new nation came more witches and wizards, as well as places to sell her wands.

She had taken a brief break from wandmaking during the winter, however, to attend Phineas and Thalia's wedding. Phineas had finally warmed up to Thalia, and the two were now happily living in Zandra's old house back in Danvers.

She had been spending more time traveling to the new shops. They had just walked out of the new magical shop, called Maalik's

Wands, Cauldrons and Magical Artifacts, in Nashville, Tennessee. She had sold a batch of her newest wands, one of which was infused with a sliver of the bone from the Wendigo that they had battled during that storm back in the winter. The wand had not been as powerful as she had expected it to be, despite Omar's warnings.

Zandra, Ansel, and Lavinia noticed a commotion down the street. Upon arriving at the scene, Zandra saw that a tall, thin man with a sharp, narrow face topped with strawberry-blond hair was berating another man. A crowd had developed around the two as the tall man's anger intensified.

Zandra turned to a man standing next to her. "What's going on?"

"Don't know." The man shrugged. "It doesn't take much to rile Mr. Jackson."[38]

"Who is this Mr. Jackson?" Zandra asked.

"He's a businessman, lawyer, military man, politician, and a judge. He owns the Hermitage."

"What's that?"

"It's a plantation off to the east."

As the tall man—Mr. Jackson—continued his ranting, Zandra noticed the man standing with him—a tall man with piercing eyes and graying, curly brown hair.

"Bazel!"

"What?" asked Lavinia.

"That man standing with Mr Jackson!" she said heatedly. "That's Bazel! Bazel Blackbone."

"The man that threatened to out you during the rebellion?" asked Ansel.

"That's the one," Zandra replied grimly. Trying to hide herself in the crowd, she moved closer to see what he was up to.

"Looks like your old friend has an apprentice," said Lavinia.

A young man in his early twenties, of medium build, with dark, curly hair stood with Bazel. As the argument subsided, Bazel turned to Mr. Jackson.

"If you'll excuse me for a moment," he said. "We need to stop and get some things before we head back to the Hermitage."

In a voice that was still agitated, Jackson replied, "Fine. I'll meet you here in thirty minutes."

Zandra turned to hide her face as they walked with the crowd, keeping Bazel in sight.

Glancing around to make sure nobody was watching, Bazel and the younger man who was with him ducked into Maalik's Wands, Cauldrons and Magical Artifacts. The Ordies walking by outside seemed not to be able to see the shop; their eyes slid over it like it didn't exist.

Zandra turned around. "Lavinia, he won't recognize you. Go in and see if you can find out what he's doing here."

Entering the shop, Lavinia started to look over some of the wares as the shopkeep talked with Bazel.

"Did you forget something, miss?" the shopkeep called out.

"Yes," she replied, thankful that the shopkeep hadn't used her name.

"I'll be with you in a minute."

"That's fine." She bent down and pretended to look under one of the shelves.

The shopkeep turned back to Bazel. "Anyway, you were saying, Mr Blackbone?"

"Do you have any wands?" Bazel leaned against the counter. "I'm looking to buy a new one for my son here." He gestured at the young man next to him.

"Yes, I just received some new ones today," replied the shopkeep, pulling Zandra's wands out from behind the counter. "I haven't even gotten them marked for sale yet."

Running his hands over the wands, Bazel picked one up slowly, handing it to his son. "Kern, I think this will work nicely," he said, handing it to the boy.

"Devil's backbone, with a Wendigo bone shard infusion. Nine and a half inches," said the shopkeeper.

The wand vibrated in the boy's hand. Nodding, Bazel said, "How much?"

After paying, Bazel and his son left the shop and headed off down the street to meet Mr. Jackson.

"What can I get you, Miss Voorhies?" asked the shopkeep.

"Oh, nothing," replied Lavinia. "I've changed my mind." She left the shop.

Following Bazel, she reached for her wand under her cloak. "Subausculto," she whispered. The eavesdropping spell took effect.

"I don't like Mr. Jackson. He's a nasty man," Kern said.

"He will become an asset if we play our cards right," said Bazel. "I see great things in his future."

Bazel turned to look Lavinia's way. Quickly, she spun and walked down a side street.

Zandra and Ansel had been following at a distance and now walked up to her.

"What did you find out?" Zandra asked.

"Bazel thinks this Mr. Jackson is going to be in a position to help in his quest."

"His quest for power," Zandra said darkly.

"The apprentice is his son."

"Some witch had a kid with him?" said Zandra incredulously.

"Mom, not all witches are like you," Ansel said.

Zandra said nothing.

Lavinia shifted her feet nervously. "And, Mom....he bought your Wendigo wand for his son."

"I told you that nothing good could come from that thing," Omar said.

"We don't know that Bazel's son is a bad wizard," replied Zandra. "And the wand was nothing out of the ordinary."

"Maybe not in your hand."

Zandra gave Omar a look. "Don't you have to meet Sharif or something?"

Omar walked off.

Zandra watched him go, apprehension building up inside her. She knew he was right. That Wendigo wand might behave differently in someone else's hands, and if it responded well to Kern....

I hope he's wrong about Bazel's son, she thought.

But she couldn't shake the feeling of dread rising in the pit of her stomach.

CHAPTER 21

Quake

1811 - 1812

Zandra had been busy following a native chief named Tecumseh[39] on his recruiting mission. He had been trying to get the native tribes to unite against the ones who were kicking them out of their homelands, making them move west. Zandra had been keeping a close eye on Tecumseh, for fear of the Blackbone family's interference.

Back at home, exhausted from her travels, she was dead asleep when the room started shaking violently.[40]

Omar jumped from the bed, grabbing his staff. "Enyscyo!" A wave of energy passed over the house, making it more resilient to the shaking.

In the other rooms, Ansel and Lavinia cast reinforcing spells too.

Eventually, the shaking subsided. Outside, the roar of the Sasq'ets echoed through the air.

"Ansel, Lavinia, are you all right?" Zandra yelled.

"Yes," replied Ansel.

"I'm okay," replied Lavinia. "What was that?"

"Xavier, are you alright?" asked Zandra.

I'm fine. Have to stop eating clover with my rum.

"It was an earthquake, Xavier," said Omar.

Oh, good. Thought it was me. I do enjoy clover with my rum.

Omar rolled his eyes as he walked around the house, looking for damage. Some plates had been broken, but the house had survived the shaking with the help of their spells.

After a while, they all headed back to bed. Gradually, the Sasq'ets quieted down.

The next morning, a second quake shook the land. Omar took off on his staff to the nearby town of Karnak to check on Sharif and to see if he could be of any help.

Rumbles shook the forest throughout the day, and there was a general unease on the land. As night fell, the Sasq'ets were restless. There was lots of chatter, and occasionally a loud scream.

As the night darkened, the forest erupted. Clearly, the Sasq'ets were fighting. Zandra, Ansel, and Lavinia grabbed their heavy cloaks and headed out into the forest to find out what was happening.

The woods were very quiet except for the Sasq'ets.

Off to their right, a Sasq'ets howled, "Whoorp! Whoorp!"

Then, in the distance off to the left came, "AAAAAARRRRCH! AAAAAARRRRCH!"

The forest exploded. Trees splintered as a group of Sasq'ets passed far in front of them in a big hurry.

As Zandra, Ansel, and Lavinia continued through the cold, dark forest, their breaths rising in mist, they came upon a crack in the ground.

"This fissure must have opened in the quake last night," said Zandra in a whisper.

"Wow," said Lavinia. "It's big enough to climb into!"

A short distance later, they came across the body of a Sasq'ets blocking the path.

"It looks like he was hit by a spell," Ansel said.

Zandra frowned. The cold was creeping in on them. Something moved through the trees behind them, but she couldn't get a glimpse of what it was.

"AAAAAARRRRCH! AAAAAARRRRCH! AARRRCH!"

The cry was shattering. Coming to the edge of a clearing, they could make out a large group of Sasq'ets. Taug stood tall above them, holding a head from some hideous creature.

"Goblins!" Zandra exclaimed.

Just then, a group of the creatures ran up behind them, spells flying.

They pointed their wands at the newcomers, throwing spells at them. Some bounced off the goblins, other spells knocked them down.

Pointing his wand at one, Ansel said, "Capto!" A ribbon of red light shot from his wand, wrapping around the goblin. Ansel raised his wand skyward, rotated his wrist, and quickly brought his arm back down, slamming the goblin's head into the ground and knocking it out cold.

The Sasq'ets ran past them, and, grabbing the fallen goblins, ripped them to shreds. Zandra, Ansel, and Lavinia fought to bring the other goblins down. One came at Lavinia, and before she noticed it, a Sasq'ets ran up from behind her, grabbing it by the head. The Sasq'ets twirled the goblin through the air until its body separated, flinging off into the trees. Zandra cast a spell, tossing a group of goblins against the trees. Some of the Sasq'ets rushed them, tearing them to shreds.

The goblins were now in retreat. The Sasq'ets and the Voorhies gave chase. Soon they were back at the fissure. The goblins scampered down into the dark crevasse, and the Sasq'ets were too large to continue the chase. Grabbing large boulders, the giant creatures filled up the crevasse.

Taug walked back to Zandra as she cast the translation spell.

"Are you alright?" asked Zandra.

"I'm not hurt," replied Taug.

Zandra looked over at the dark fissure in the ground. "It looks like those goblins arrived here after the quakes."

"They came up tonight through this crevasse." Turning to his troop, Taug motioned for them to retreat back into the forest.

His troop started walking, passing by Zandra and her kids.

"We work good together," Zandra said.

Taug looked down at them, nodding his head. Then he disappeared into the darkness.

On the walk back to their house, Lavinia asked, "Do you think the goblins were here because of the quakes, or did they cause the quakes to get to the surface?"

"I guess time will tell," replied Zandra.

Omar flew back in a day later. Zandra, Ansel, and Lavinia ran out to meet him. There had been many more small tremors since the first big shock.

"How are things going out there?" Zandra asked.

"There's been a lot of damage," said Omar, "but Sharif is safe, and the magical community has fared well. The Ordies have not been as fortunate, but luckily there aren't many of them yet in this area."

"We had a battle with some goblins the night of the first quake," said Ansel.

Omar nodded. "Goblins are at the heart of these quakes. We're gathering an army to counter them. They've been pushing up through the crust of the earth, and they're wreaking havoc. We're going to have to push them back down into their holes."

"I haven't seen goblins since the old country. I was unaware they lived here, too," said Zandra. "Until I saw them the other night, that is."

"This is the first time in a long while that we've had to deal with them here," replied Omar.

"What can we do?" asked Lavinia.

"Well, at this point, we're still formulating a plan," replied Omar. "I'm supposed to meet Sharif at Karnak and fly on to Cairo to meet with Aharon and the rest of the local magical community. There we'll determine our plan of attack. I suppose you could come."

"I think we should all go," said Zandra.

"If the goblins are here as well, we would have to set a charm to protect the house, and we'd have to bring Xavier with us, if we're all going to go," replied Omar. "Let's pull things together and get out of here tonight."

A diverse group of witches and wizards filled the room. A small aftershock shook the meeting as a tall, dark Egyptian wizard in flowing gold robes called the meeting to order.

"I think you all know me," he said, "but for those who don't, I'm Aharon. As we all know, we have a major problem. Goblins have been popping up all over Little Egypt since the quakes started. We've managed to contain them, but I'm sure more will come. We need to have a cohesive plan to deal with the threat. I'm open to any suggestions on how to combat this intrusion."

A short, heavy-set witch stood up.

"Yes, Belladonna?" said Aharon.

"We need a way to call everyone to a conflict when the goblins arise," said the witch, Belladonna. "I suggest we place charms on amulets that people can wear, so we can call everyone together and gather as quickly as possible. We can put a directional charm on them so they will lead us to the appropriate places."

"Great idea," said Aharon. "Let's take a vote on that. Everyone in favor, say yea."

Most everyone in the crowd answered 'yea.'

Looking around, Aharon said, "Well, Belladonna, could you take care of the amulets and the charms? Sabine, could you help? You're good at those things."

Sabine nodded.

"We also need everyone who is going to be fighting to be able to see in the dark. We will have to be in the goblins' tunnels. This is a very dangerous place to be, so we need all the advantages we can get. Who can help with this?"

A wizard shouted out, "I've already started creating some goggles to help with that. I'll have enough in a day or so."

"Good. Now we'll have a way to rally everyone at a particular place, and we'll be able to see in the dark. Historically, we've tried to negotiate with the goblins, to no avail. And this time, they seem to be even more aggressive. We've never seen this level of earthquakes caused by them, and many more have made it to the surface. It seems that our only choice is to drive them back into the holes from which they came and seal them back in. So, that being the case, we need a swift and decisive response to this threat, with which the amulets and goggles will help."

Omar stood up.

"Yes, Omar?"

"We've had goblins at our house also. The Sasq'ets and my family have battled them."

Aharon furrowed his brow in concern. "We weren't aware that they'd been that far north. We'll have to have your family be our northern lookout."

"We can do that," said Zandra. "Between us and the Sasq'ets, I think we can keep everything at bay, except maybe a big push by the goblins."

"Good," said Aharon. "I'm sure Zandra will be a sufficient guard for our northern gate." He paused. "Now, we need to have our forces located in a good place to respond to all calls. There seems to be more activity south of here, near the town of New

Madrid.[41] If we place our forces here in Cairo, we could respond quickly to all areas. Is everyone in agreement?"

The crowd indicated their consensus.

"Remember, the goblins have hundreds of miles of tunnels throughout this part of the country. Going down to their world is incredibly dangerous, so if it comes to that, be very careful. We'll set up a command center and expand it tonight to house all who will fight. Thank you all. With luck, we will prevail and keep the Ordies oblivious of our endeavors."

As the crowd dispersed, Omar turned to the family. "I'm staying here to help with the fight. You're both old enough to make your own decisions on this," he said, nodding at Ansel and Lavinia, "but one of you should go back with your mother. I don't want anyone to be at home alone." Omar turned to Xavier. "Xavier, you watch over Zandra. These goblins are dangerous. And stay away from the rum."

Xavier huffed. *I will. All of us need to be careful.*

Ansel and Lavinia came to an agreement: they would switch off every week while Zandra kept watch on the northern front.

Zandra shrank Xavier and placed him in her flight bag. She hugged Omar for a long while. "You be careful," she said. "Watch over the kids when they're here."

"I will."

"I never wanted them to have to see this kind of fight." Giving Omar a kiss, she turned to Lavinia. "You've never fought anything like this. This won't be like any of the battles with the creatures we've gathered wand supplies from. I don't like the idea of you fighting these goblins."

"I'll be careful." Lavinia hugged her mother and Ansel, then watched as they flew off into the sky.

The amulet started vibrating. Lavinia jumped up, and the hall came to life. Throwing her heavy cloak on, she made sure she had her night sight goggles. Grabbing her wand and broom, Lavinia walked into the crowd.

They headed out the door. She hoped that the alarm had not come from her father's amulet. If it had, that meant he was in danger.

Turning to the south, they kicked off their brooms into the night and the coming battle.

Omar was the first to arrive. Belvon, who was supposed to be on duty, was nowhere to be found. The back of Omar's neck tingled with apprehension. Using the amulet to guide him to Belvon, Omar felt that eyes were upon him the whole time. He could hear faint whispers throughout the forest.

Stepping over a tree root, his foot came down on something soft. Bending down, he realized he had found Belvon. He could see the scorch marks and axe cuts on his body. Searching for a pulse, he felt nothing. Belvon's amulet was not on him. Knowing the goblins' affinity for gold, it was clear they had taken it. The fact that the goblins had taken the amulet could work to their advantage, as they could now track them without the goblins' knowledge.

Standing up, Omar sent up a marker so they could find Belvon's body later.

Sensing something, Omar quickly hit the ground as a spell hit the tree in front of him. Raising his staff, he sent off a spell that shot out in all directions, crackling through the trees. Hearing some screams, he knew that he had hit some of them. Lots of spells began flying back.

Hoping that help was near at hand, Omar hunkered down.

It was after midnight when they arrived. Flying over the forest, Aharon could see spells shooting up through the branches. A sparkling charm caught his eye, flying up through the trees.

They started sending spells down into the woods, catching the goblins by surprise. The first volley felled a lot of them. As they pushed the goblins farther away, they slowly descended. Aharon could see Omar throwing spells at the goblins through the trees.

As soon as they landed, Aharon walked up to Omar. "Where is Belvon?"

Omar pointed to the body. "I had hoped that we could contain this without loss of life. He was a good wizard."

"It looks like he stumbled upon a major emergence of the goblins," said Aharon.

"Yes, it appears so," replied Omar. "His amulet is missing."

"Really?" Aharon said. "That's great! The goblins will have no idea that we can track it. This will give us the upper hand."

"Do you know if Lavinia is here?"

Aharon glanced around. "She left with us, but I haven't seen her since we landed."

The ax hit the tree as Lavinia ducked: the second time she had almost lost her head tonight. The goblins were on the run finally. They had been putting up a good fight. She threw a spell at her attacker, and he fell dead.

As if the goblins' magic wasn't dangerous enough, the craftsmanship of their weapons combined with their skill made them very formidable. Their ability to see in the dark also gave them a distinct advantage. Even with her night sight goggles on, it was still hard to keep track of all the attackers.

The battle had been at a fever pitch for most of the night. As daybreak approached, the goblins were losing their advantage, and they were in retreat. Lavinia raced ahead, hoping to find the source of the amulet's call and rescue the witch or wizard that must have been taken prisoner before they entered the underground tunnels.

All the while, she kept hoping it wasn't her father that had been taken prisoner.

The last of the goblins disappeared into the large fissure. Taking a deep breath, she followed.

The goblins had retreated to the underground all over the forest. Most of the wizards were regrouping around the openings.

Omar had not found Lavinia throughout the night. He decided to follow the signal of Belvon's stolen amulet, thinking that being her mother's daughter, Lavinia might be trying to save an already-dead wizard.

Omar walked up on the group of witches and wizards standing at the mouth of the fissure.

One of the witches recognized him. "Omar, your daughter! She went down after the goblins!"

Zandra will kill me if anything happens to her, he thought.

A letter flapped up to them. A witch opened it and read it, then shouted out, "Everyone is to enter the fissures and bring the battle to the goblins!"

The tunnel was damp and cool. Lavinia could hear shuffling in front of her. Picking up her pace, she rushed by a side tunnel without noticing. A group of goblins fell in behind her.

As she closed in on the group in front of her, she began throwing spells, leaping over a couple of goblins. They turned, and some threw spells, while others charged her. Lavinia shot several spells at them, knocking most of them down.

Catching Lavinia by surprise, the goblins that were behind her started their attack. Fighting on two fronts, she held her ground for a bit, taking care of almost all of them.

Suddenly, a spell thrown by one of the goblins hit the ceiling above Lavinia. Rocks fell on her, knocking her out.

Coming up on Lavinia, Omar and a few of the others moved the rocks off of her. Most of the group moved on past them to bring the battle to the goblins once more. Hoping she was still alive, Omar bent down to check and saw that she was just knocked out. Slowly, she opened her eyes.

"Dad," she said. "You're safe."

"Seems I should be the one saying that," Omar replied. "Are you alright?"

"Yes, I'm fine. Let's go get those goblins." She slowly got to her feet and found she was not able to stand. "One of the rocks must have fractured my leg."

Omar pointed his staff. "Nyrthekas!" A splint formed on her leg.

Separating his wand from the staff, Omar gave it to her so she could use it to walk. They could hear the battle raging down the tunnel.

"I can't leave you here, but I will be needed in the coming battle," said Omar. "Can you follow?"

"I think I can." As she struggled to take her first step, she looked down. "Dad, my amulet is missing."

"Belvon's was also," Omar replied.

Walking was hard for Lavinia. When they arrived at the battle, they found that the goblins had made their stand in a cavern. Many tunnels had lead the witches and wizards to this place. Lavinia thought it was odd that the goblins had chosen this cavern over ambushing them in the tunnels.

Spells were flying from both sides. A wizard raised his wand to cast a spell, but a goblin threw its ax, chopping the wand in half.

Omar and Lavinia joined in the battle. The energy from the spells made Lavinia's hair stand on end. Looking up, she saw the goblins' king as he stood over the rest of the creatures. He had two of their amulets hanging from his neck.

Word came from Aharon for the Egyptian wizards to target the ceiling, and for the others to put up a shield charm to protect everyone on his mark. Aharon's spell hit the ceiling, and the others joined in as the shield spells went up.

At first, nothing happened. Seeing what was about to occur, the goblin king retreated into a tunnel as the spell was increased by the witches and wizards.

The ground at the surface rippled out from the center of the battle like waves on the ocean, and sand erupted into the air like water from a geyser. River banks slid into the water, and trees toppled. The spell was felt all over the countryside for many miles.

In the process of bringing the roof down, they had cracked the floor. Sulfurous gases leaked into the room. Some of the Egyptian wizards hit the ceiling with spells again and broke through to the surface, letting the gases escape.

When at last the cavern cleared, the witches and wizards were safe under their shields, and most of the goblins lay under the rubble. All was quiet. The goblins that had managed to escape had been sealed into the lower tunnels.

Gradually, the witches and wizards returned to the surface. The destruction of the battle was readily visible. Aharon sent scouts to the nearest villages to assess the damage to the Ordies and to find out what they had thought had happened.

As they waited, assessment of the wounded took place, and the most badly injured were sent back to Cairo for further treatment. Several witches and wizards recovered the bodies of the goblins that were above the surface, so the Ordies wouldn't stumble across them.

When the scouts returned, they reported that the few Ordies who lived in the area had sustained damage to their homes, but most seemed to be safe. The goblins had not been seen.

"We were lucky," Aharon said to the gathered witches and wizards, "but I doubt that we've heard the last from the goblins."

"The goblin king was wearing two of our amulets," said Lavinia.

"That could be to our advantage," said Aharon. "When they get close to the surface, we could track them. The next battle could be on our terms. We will have to intensify our patrols in this part of the country and be prepared for the next offensive."

They had returned to their house on the hill so Lavinia could recuperate in comfort, and so they could rotate Ansel back to Cairo. Zandra was berating Lavinia for charging after the goblins, while Ansel grinned behind her.

"Goblins are dangerous enough above ground, but in their element...." Zandra trailed off, shaking her head. "You're lucky you only received a broken leg."

"What would you have done?" Lavinia asked.

This always sent Zandra through the roof, because she couldn't respond to it in a way that would support her rant.

Xavier laughed.

"You stay out of this!" Zandra yelled.

She gets you every time with that, he said.

"You know I took care of most of the goblins on my own before I was knocked out," said Lavinia. "You could praise me for that."

Zandra sighed. "Okay, you're right. That was impressive." Zandra turned around. "Finnghuala sent a letter asking if the ground had shaken here. I guess bells have been ringing in Boston from our quakes. I sent her a letter back explaining what was happening."

"Wow, all the way to Boston...," Lavinia said.

"Have you had any more goblins here since we left?" Omar asked.

"No," Zandra replied. "Except for the quakes, it's been calm." Zandra walked over to the stove. "You must be hungry. Ansel, help me get some food ready for them."

The quakes had been continuing. Obviously, the goblins were not giving up. Many more people had shown up for the coming battle. Witches and wizards had been crossing the skies at night, searching for a sign from the amulets that the goblin king had stolen. It seemed that the next emergence would be somewhere around New Madrid, an Ordie town about thirty-five miles downriver of Cairo. Aharon had set up a camp near the town so they could have a fast response when the goblins moved. Donder was staying with Zandra, Lavinia, and Ansel to help with any trouble they might have.

Early on the morning of February seventh, Ansel flew off to the south. Omar had sent notice that the battle was at hand.

"I've been able to penetrate the ground with the goggles that I modified," said Aharon. "I now know where the main cavern is, and they seem to be slowly gathering there. I propose that we divide our forces. I want thirty Egyptians to go with me into the cavern. My plan is for us to use a cloaking spell and a silencing spell, then we all spread out around the goblins. When I drop my cloaking spell, the rest will follow, and then we'll do an incinerating spell in unison. Hopefully, we'll be able to wipe them out right then and there. I would like to have the rest of you fly over the area and look for any that come above ground. Who's willing to go in with me?"

Many raised their hands, including Omar and Sharif.

"Good," said Aharon. "That should do. Gather what you'll need, and be sure to bring your night sight goggles. We'll meet back here in half an hour. This is a very dangerous endeavor. Everyone, be as careful as possible. I want to see you all here after we've rid ourselves of the goblins."

It was a dark night. The moon had passed the last quarter a couple of days ago, and the night sight goggles were a great asset.

They landed at the mouth of the tunnel that lead to the goblins' cavern. They placed a silencing charm over themselves, and a wave of gray flowed over them as they cast cloaking charms. Then they entered the tunnel.

Weaving their way silently through the underground space, they quickly dispatched the goblin sentries as they came upon them. Carefully, they sealed all the side tunnels as they passed, until they came upon the cavern where the war party was gathered.

As they entered the cavern, their cloaking spells changed to match the low light that filled the space. The goblin king was giving a speech that Omar could not understand. Slowly, the witches and wizards circled them. As Omar passed close by a goblin, it turned and sniffed intently. He stopped as it stared in his general direction.

Eventually, the goblin looked away, and within a few moments, the witches and wizards had circled all of them. Omar could see that the cloaking spells were dropping.

As the goblins became aware of their presence, the witches and wizards lifted their staffs in unison. "Epotyfro!" they all shouted at once.

Waves of blue rippled from the base of their staffs, traveling into the gathered goblins. The blue veins of light traveled up their bodies like lighted spider's webs, and the screams were deafening. When the blue light finally reached the tops of the goblin's heads, smoke began to rise, and they burst into blue flames.

Ten miles north, Ansel flew along the river, heading towards the battle. Lights shot up in the distance. He could see trees falling in the forest, and sand was shooting up in the air.

The battle has started, he thought. Then he saw the Mississippi River. It had reversed direction, and was coming back at him. The trees were falling in front of the wave of water that was floating up the river in the wrong direction. The river continued to travel back at him until he reached a waterfall that had never been there before. Water was flowing into what was now lowlands to the east.

Something big has happened, he thought. *I hope Dad is alright.*

"ARHOOOOOOOOOOOOOOOOOOO!" Taug's voice boomed across the treetops, and Donder leaped into the air just before the quake hit.

Xavier raced around the perimeter of the property, watching for goblins. Zandra and Lavinia doubled the strengthening charm on the house. Donder circled over the forest for a time, watching as he flew. Not finding any goblins, he returned to Zandra and Lavinia.

"Did you see anything?" Zandra asked.

Donder shook his head.

"Good," Zandra sighed, looking out on the horizon. "I hope Ansel and Omar are all right."

Back in the cavern, things had deteriorated. When they had cast their spells, the force of it had released pressure on a fault that traveled through the area, and a tremendous earthquake ensued. The cavern roof had fallen in from the shaking. Most of the witches and wizards had thrown up shield charms in time to protect themselves.

As things subsided, Omar threw up a repulsing charm to cast off the dirt that had fallen on him. A short time later, Sharif emerged from the ground. Slowly, most of them emerged, and after some searching, the bodies of the rest were recovered.

Aharon stood in front of them. "We got a great number of the goblins. I would like for us to fan out and search for any goblins that might have made it to the surface. Help the Ordies where you can as well, without revealing yourselves, of course. There must have been great damage in the surrounding areas. We unknowingly caused this destruction, so we need to do all we can to right this."

Ansel arrived at the scene shortly. The sun was just coming up in the east as Omar and Ansel cast cloaking spells over themselves so they could fly up to check on Zandra and Lavinia in the light of day. They flew back to the north. The destruction was everywhere. The town of New Madrid was totally destroyed, and they could see some of their brethren helping the people who lived there. To the north, trees had been toppled from the shaking and the power of the waters that had run backwards on the Mississippi River for a while. New sand bars had formed in the river, and the water now flowed along a slightly different path than before.

As they arrived over their home forest, Donder flew up beside them, escorting them in. Xavier met them first.

You're all right! he said. *It shook violently here, but no goblins ever appeared.*

"Good," said Omar. "We trapped the main force and got the king. Hopefully, we've cut the head off the beast."

Zandra came out to greet them. After exchanging hugs, they entered the house so Lavinia could hear Omar and Ansel's stories.

After a few days, Donder flew back off to the west. No goblins had been seen for a while, and he obviously felt it safe enough to leave.

The whole family stood out on the pasture, watching as Donder spread his wings and flew off into the darkening western sky.

CHAPTER 22

Tecumseh

May - October, 1813

Since the war of 1812 had broken out, Zandra had been doing all she could to make sure nothing bad befell Tecumseh. His confederation of tribes were fighting on the side of the British in this war, hoping, once again, that if the war went in favor of the British, that the crown would grant them their homelands. Tecumseh had formed an agreement with General Brock,[42] and the general would support an independent native nation, if Tecumseh helped in the war. Bazel and his son had not been spotted in the conflict as of yet. But Zandra could see their hands in things.

She had followed Tecumseh down to the southern lands as he tried to strengthen his confederation. In Tecumseh's absence, the American forces had been preparing to attack Tecumseh's brother Tenskwatawa[43] in the settlement of Prophetstown.[44] Tecumseh had told Tenskwatawa not to engage the Americans, but Tenskwatawa had had a vision that the Americans' bullets would not be able to harm his braves, so he attacked. The braves were not bulletproof, however, and Prophetstown was burned to the ground.

Upon her arrival at Prophetstown, Zandra cast a Quid hic spell to see precisely what had happened. Playing the battle over and over again, she finally saw Bazel among the trees.

So he *had* interfered. She had assumed that he and his son were still hanging off Jackson's coattails. But they were obviously working all over this war.

Zandra's next stop was Fort Detroit,[45] and she marveled at what she saw. The joint British and native warriors were outnumbered by the Americans in the fort, but they marched by a clearing within sight of the fort, looping around to pass by the opening over and over, to give the appearance that there were way more of them than there were. The Americans in the fort, fearing the coming battle, surrendered.

The next battle was at Frenchtown[46] in the Michigan territory. The joint British and native forces destroyed the Americans. There was no evidence of intervention from Bazel.

As winter came, all hostilities ceased. The Americans spent the winter building a huge wooden fort just down the Maumee river[47] from the abandoned Fort Miamis.[48]

Zandra had returned home over the winter. When she finally returned around May first, the British were bombarding the newly-built Fort Meigs[49] from across the river. Cloaking herself, she flew over the battle, looking for signs of Bazel or his son. They appeared not to be anywhere around.

Zandra stayed out of the fight, as things seemed to be going fine for the British and Tecumseh's forces.

Then she noticed movement downriver. The Americans had brought in reinforcements. As they approached, some broke off and circled around behind Fort Meigs, while the bulk of the force assaulted the British and native forces that were bombarding the fort. The new American arrivals caught them by surprise and quickly had them in retreat.

The Americans chased Tecumseh's forces into the woods. The carnage was great, and many were taken prisoner. Tecumseh and the British retreated to the abandoned Fort Miamis.

When the battle was over, Zandra landed near the British and native forces and offered her help with the wounded.

She had been working in the abandoned Fort Miamis for a couple of days, helping Tecumseh's troops, when she heard a commotion among the prisoners that had been taken in the battle. Coming out the door of the makeshift hospital, she could see that the natives were killing the American prisoners. Tecumseh ran over to the warriors.

"This is not how a warrior behaves," he told them.

The killing stopped.

What a great man Tecumseh is, Zandra thought. She had seen how different men behaved in war, and he was not one of the dishonorable.

Tecumseh gathered more warriors for a second attack on Fort Meigs. Zandra had never seen so many natives in one place; thousands of warriors had converged on the fort.

Kern flew in over the British lines. The sounds of gunshots rang out over the land, but there was no opponent in sight.

They're staging a mock battle, Kern thought. *They must be trying to lure the Americans out.*

He flew in to the American camp and, wasting no time, disguised himself as an American soldier. He crept into General Green Clay's[50] office and shot a Pulso spell, knocking the general out immediately. Then, hearing footsteps outside, he quickly shrank the general down, stuffed him in his pocket, and cast a Transverto spell to disguise himself.

The door opened, and a captain stepped in. "Everything okay in here, General?" he asked.

Kern nodded. "What is it, Captain?"

"We're hearing the sounds of a skirmish off in the distance. Should we go investigate?"

"Order all men to their stations," said Kern. "We'll sit tight for now."

The captain nodded. "Yes, sir." He left, closing the door behind him.

Kern flicked his wand, and a storm began to build up outside. Before long, the sounds of the mock battle subsided.

Kern grinned. He had outsmarted Tecumseh and the British once again.

By the time fall came, the war had not gone well for Tecumseh and the British, and they had been in retreat. The Americans had taken control of Lake Erie in a naval battle that Zandra assumed Kern had manipulated in her absence. He must have changed the wind's direction, giving the Americans the advantage. Then, later, Kern had forced two of the British ships together and entangled them, making them sitting ducks for the American ships.

Zandra was continuing to just observe, although it was getting increasingly hard for her to keep out of the battle. She wanted the natives to achieve the security of their homeland. But she had her doubts that the British would keep their bargain, even if the war took a turn for the better.

Finally, as they reached the Thames River,[51] Tecumseh had shamed the British commander into making a stand. So, there in the Thames River Valley, they turned to face their enemies.

When the battle finally came to them, Zandra was watching from behind the lines. She could tell that something was wrong. The battle was being manipulated.

Placing a shield charm on herself, she wove her way through the trees, watching for signs of Bazel's presence. The flash of the guns filled her eyes as the musket balls whizzed through the air, ending far too often in a thud as it penetrated its victim. The battle was clearly going poorly for Tecumseh and the British, and they continued to get mowed down.

Zandra spotted a group of American soldiers standing in the midst of the battle. No bullets hitting them, moving almost mechanically, they fired their guns, hitting their targets every time.

Then, looking closer, she saw him.

It was Kern. There was so much going on that she felt she could pull her wand out without being noticed. Pointing her wand at him, she said, "Pulso!"

But just as she did so, Kern saw her and deflected the spell. Zandra ducked behind a tree as the battle fell silent.

Looking around from behind the tree, she could see that everyone was frozen in place. Her shield spell must have protected her from whatever magic Kern had done.

I've never seen anyone stop this many people, she thought.

Then Kern spoke. "You must be Zandra Voorhies," he called out. "My father has told me of you. You still haven't learned to keep your nose out of our family's business, have you?"

"It would be much easier to do that if your family business didn't involve beating people down, or stripping them off their land or off the earth," Zandra said.

She stepped out from behind the tree and threw a spell at him. He ducked, and it hit the tree behind him, leaving the bark smoking.

Kern snickered. "Dad said you were always trying to help the common people. They're there for us, magical and non-magical alike, to manipulate for our advancement. We're meant to dominate those people," he said, walking around as he talked, seemingly not worried about Zandra being a threat to him.

"You're even more arrogant than your father," Zandra said as she threw another spell at him, which he deflected. "Is your father still hanging around that nasty Mr. Jackson?"

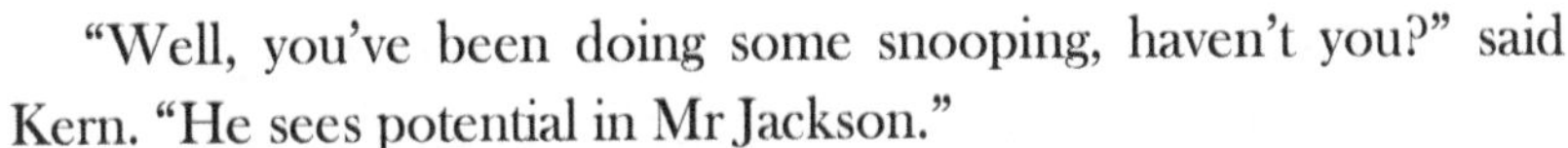

"Well, you've been doing some snooping, haven't you?" said Kern. "He sees potential in Mr Jackson."

Zandra threw another spell at Kern. "Well, birds of a feather."

Kern blocked her spell unconcernedly as he continued to stroll around.

Someone needs to knock some of the stuffing out of this one, Zandra thought.

She had slowly made her way near Tecumseh as she talked to Kern. Reaching around the trees, she prepared to throw another spell, but she was too slow. Kern shot his spell first, and Zandra's shield charm failed as he threw a second spell.

She stumbled backwards as Kern threw another spell, making her stumble and fall awkwardly on her arm. She heard a crack and felt a jolt of pain–it was broken.

Then Kern walked up to her and said, "Resisto."

Frozen, all she could do was move her eyes.

Walking up to her, Kern knelt beside her. In a low voice, he said, "I should rid us of you right now, but my father has other plans for you." Standing up, he pointed his wand at Tecumseh.

"Neco!"

Tecumseh fell dead. Zandra's eyes opened wide as they welled up in tears.

Kern grinned harshly. "This is the second time you have meddled in our business. The third time will not be a charm."

Walking off into the woods, he dropped the freezing spell when he was out of sight, and the fighting continued.

Zandra sat there; cradling her broken arm, crying over the broken body of Tecumseh, thinking of words that she had heard him say once:

The way, and the only way, to check and stop this evil, is for all the Redmen to unite in claiming a common and equal right in the land, as it was at first and should be yet; for it was never divided, but belongs to all for the use of each. That no part has the right to sell, even to each other, much less to strangers—those who want all and will not do with less.[52]

CHAPTER 23

The Battle of New Orleans

Winter 1814 - 1818

"Stop your whining," said Zandra. "I'll get you something for that hangover as soon as I can. If you could control yourself and stay away from the rum at Lafitte's[53] blacksmith shop when we're down here, it would help. You know you're getting a little old for this."

Well, that dark Jamaican rum is so good. And anyway, you wouldn't have found out that Bazel had secured clemency for all of Lafitte's pirate friends in return for their help in the upcoming battle if I hadn't gone down there, replied Xavier.

Turning off Rue de L'Union[54] into a narrow alley, they came to a dark doorway.

Zandra climbed off Xavier. "I'll be back as soon as I can. Try not to get sick all over the alley."

She opened the door and entered a dark room. Voodoo and magical paraphernalia lined the walls. The man behind the counter spoke with a heavy French accent. "Ah, Miss Voorhies! It is good to see you again."

A young woman of mixed race looked up from the counter of voodoo wares as Zandra and the shopkeep talked.

"I always look forward to your visits. Do you 'ave wands to sell?"

"Yes," Zandra replied. Pulling them out of her flight bag, she placed them in front of the man. "Do you have any potion supplies for a hangover?" she asked.

"Yes, over on zat wall," said the shopkeep, gesturing over near the young woman. "I didn't know you drank."

"It's for my horse, the old fool," said Zandra.

The young woman laughed. After a few moments, she got her breath back. "Oh, I'm sorry," she said in a Creole accent. "Didn't mean to be rude."

"It's alright," said Zandra. "He just loves his rum a little too much. I wish he would lay off a little. I'm Zandra Voorhies."

"Marie Laveau,"[55] said the woman. "Your horse drinks?"

"Yes, he's quite a rummy at times," replied Zandra.

"How did he get started drinking rum?"

Zandra frowned. "Don't remember. I don't think he ever told me."

"He can tell you?" asked Marie.

"Yes, he can talk telepathically."

"He sounds like an incredible horse," said Marie. "I could help him. We can treat addiction with voodoo."

"Oh, no, thanks," said Zandra. "He's been this way for years. I wouldn't want to change him now."

"Just thought I'd offer," replied Marie.

"Miss Voorhies," said the shopkeep. "I'm ready for you when you're finished."

Grabbing the rest of the stuff for the hangover potion, she headed up to the shopkeep to buy them.

Marie walked up. "May I meet this horse of yours?"

"Sure," said Zandra. "He's outside."

When they walked out the door, Xavier didn't look good. He looked up at Zandra.

Did you get the ingredients?

"Yes," said Zandra. "And I have a friend who wants to meet you." She turned to Marie. "Marie, this is Xavier."

"Nice to meet you, Xavier," said Marie. "Seems like you're quite an interesting horse. Are you feeling any better?"

No, replied Xavier, as he wobbled slightly.

"How much rum does it take for a horse like you to get drunk?" Marie asked.

Well, those pirates will be surprised when they pull those barrels for delivery, that's for sure, Xavier said. *Could we get the potion going before I die?*

"My place is nearby. You're welcome to come over to brew the potion," offered Marie. "We could talk more over some chicory."[56]

"Thank you," said Zandra. "That would be great."

Then Zipporah came out onto the porch—and she slipped and fell in the gift that I left there! finished Xavier.

Marie burst out laughing. "You're something else, Xavier."

Zandra stood up. "It's getting late. We'd better get back before curfew. Thank you for the chicory," she said to Marie. "It was really great meeting you."

"It's been wonderful meeting the two of you," said Marie. "You're welcome here anytime. You'll have to tell me more stories next time, Xavier."

Zandra had been at the Chalmette plantation just south of New Orleans since before dawn. She had heard that a battle[57] was brewing, and since she was in the area, she had decided to watch to see what hand Bazel had in it.

Mr. Jackson's confidence was overflowing. He had just slaughtered the Creeks at the battle of Horseshoe Bend.[58] Narrowly escaping death during the battle, he was saved by Junaluska[59] of the Eastern Cherokee. He expected to dispatch the British today the same as he'd done with the Creeks.

Zandra could see where Jackson's army had dredged the Rodriguez canal, and along with the mud from the canal, logs and bales of cotton formed a parapet that ran from a cypress swamp all the way to the Mississippi River. Cannons had been placed along the line on both sides of the river. Every able-bodied man stood beside Jackson's army, including freed slaves, Choctaw, and even a few of the pirates Xavier had mentioned before; poised, waiting for the British to arrive.

Finally, a spot of red was visible through the morning fog. They had arrived.

As the British came into the clearing, Zandra could see that Jackson's army was greatly outnumbered. Nevertheless, they opened fire; laying waste to the advancing British.

As the smoke from the muzzle loaders and the cannons mingled with the fog, the sickening thud of lead hitting flesh rose from the air, along with the screams. The British army line began to fall apart. The commanding officer came riding up to rally the troops. Soon after he arrived at the front, he was hit by a slug, and his horse shot out from under him. Grabbing another horse, he tried to rally his troops once more.

Hit by cannon fire, he fell to the ground.

Zandra had cloaked herself and was flying over the battlefield. *Something is wrong here,* she thought. Pointing her wand, she said, "Tardo!"

The battle slowed enough that she could follow the cannon shot. As she watched, she could see the cannonballs leave the cannon, and then curve to meet their victims.

Bazel again, she thought. Scanning the area, she noticed a blur in the fog.

"Detego," she said.

The blur gradually cleared to reveal Kern, Bazel's son. He was so intent on what he was doing, he didn't notice that his cover had been compromised.

Zandra watched him direct the cannonballs to the end of their bloody mission, using the Wendigo wand she had made. The battle was so heated that no one noticed him before he raised the cloak once more.

Zandra had moved in behind some trees before Kern could find her. The British were being slaughtered, so she cast a shield spell in front of the soldiers that were standing there without a leader, being mowed down. She didn't have a side in this battle, but she couldn't stand seeing so many people die. And besides, if Kern was working on Jackson's side, it couldn't mean anything good. Anything she did to slow him down could only help.

Zandra could see the blur of Kern's cloaking spell moving around as he continued to direct the battle.

As she thought of what she was going to do, she saw another blur fly up in the fog.

Must be Bazel, she thought. She landed, standing against a tree and blending in with it. She watched as the blur crossed the sky. Bazel must have been searching for her.

Zandra noticed that a general retreat had been called by the British. Dropping the shield charm she had placed on the soldiers, she stood by the tree, waiting for Bazel and Kern to leave.

When she was in the clear, she pointed her wand at herself. "Commuta Habitum," she said. Taking the appearance of a soldier, she headed back to Xavier.

What did you see? Xavier asked.

"Bazel's son was interfering in the battle," she said. "And he was massacring the British with my Wendigo wand."

Omar warned of the possibility of this, replied Xavier.

"I couldn't fight them both, not after what happened last time I tried to take on Kern alone. He's too powerful." Thinking about what she had just witnessed, she blinked back tears. "The carnage was terrible. What have I done?" she said dejectedly. "I should have never made that wand."

You had no idea when you made it, said Xavier. *Everything can be used for good or evil. You did what you could to minimize the damage.*

Just then, Bazel and Kern came rushing down the line.

"He's still looking to see who interfered with his plans," said Zandra.

Bazel looked her way as General Jackson rode up. Zandra turned to put her back to him. She was still in disguise as a soldier, but she wanted to be doubly sure that Bazel wouldn't recognize her.

"Mr. Jackson," said Bazel. "You have been handed a great victory."

Mr. Jackson gazed down at Bazel from his horse. "It has been a great day for our nation, Mr. Blackbone."

"I think this will be good for your chances in your future political goals," replied Bazel.

Jackson grinned. "Maybe so."

The wounded started to stream past Zandra. The terrible sounds of groans and dying breaths filled her ears; blood and missing body parts attacked her eyes.

As Bazel and Jackson continued to talk, oblivious to the ghoulish parade passing them by, Zandra and Xavier walked off down the road toward New Orleans, following the wounded.

Gangrene had set into Zandra's patient's leg. She had hoped it wouldn't. She looked around, waiting for everyone to move away from him.

"Do you have a girl back in Tennessee, Bill?" she asked him.

"Yes," he said. "We're going to marry."

Marie Laveau was in the infirmary as well, helping to heal the wounded. Zandra gave her a look, indicating for her to come over.

Marie walked over to the opposite side of the bed. "What's her name?" Marie asked Bill.

"Sarah," he said wistfully. "She's a great lady. I can't wait to get back to her."

While Bill was distracted, Zandra sprinkled his wound with the powder she had pulled out of her pouch.

Looking back at Zandra, Bill asked, "How is my leg doing?"

Zandra winked at Marie. "It's going to be fine. You'll be back to Sarah in no time."

Zandra and Marie had been helping the wounded since the battle, sneaking in magical and voodoo remedies whenever they could. They had saved many from terrible fates.

Then the door opened and Jackson and Bazel walked in. Zandra had been changing her hair color and had done her best to disguise herself before she came to help the wounded, but she still worried that Bazel would recognize her. She kept her back to him as he passed.

"I think we'll be heading back to the Hermitage within the week," said Jackson.

"Good," said Bazel. "We have much to do now that the war is over."

Bazel stopped behind Zandra, looking at her for a long moment. "How is this man doing?" he asked her.

"He's fine, sir," Zandra said carefully. "He'll be up in no time."

Bazel gave her a long, deep look. "Have I met you before?" he asked.

"I've been working here since the end of the battle," said Zandra. "Maybe you've seen me on another day."

"No...," said Bazel slowly. "I don't think so, but...I can't place you."

Zandra shrugged. "Don't know, sir."

Jackson had moved on. Bazel frowned and left to catch up with him.

Zandra sighed with relief. "That was close."

"Yes, too close," said Marie. "You know, things are just about under control. Maybe you should be heading back home before it gets too dangerous for you here."

The kids were striking out on their own. In June of 1815, Lavinia married Dirk Rookwood, an Ordie from Shawneetown.[60] He worked the salt springs south of Shawneetown and southeast of the Voorhies home. Lavinia had met him one day when she had come to purchase salt, and they quickly fell in love. Dirk had readily accepted her status as a witch, and soon after they married, they had a child, Chione.

Loran Barbeck had been in Cairo during the goblin war of 1811 and 1812. Helping the wounded, she had seen Ansel coming and going as he headed out on patrols. They had met later, and she had determined to someday marry him. Eventually, she got her wish, and they were married in October of 1816. They had their first child, Zara, in September of 1817.

Phineas and Thalia's son, Gunnar, was reaching an age where he was able to help distribute Zandra's wands to the southern end of the East Coast, though Zandra had been on her own in making the wands, as both of her kids were tied up with their new families. All of her spare time had been devoted to her grandkids.

But by April of 1818, Zandra was back in the fray. General Jackson, with the assistance of Bazel and Kern, had been invading Spanish Florida to attack the Seminole tribe.

Zandra finally confronted Bazel and Kern at a swamp along the Econfina River.[61] Jackson had fifteen hundred troops, along with eighteen hundred Creeks fighting on his side. The Creeks were trying to force the Seminole out of the swamp and onto an open field, where they could do their deed.[62] Just the size of Jackson's forces alone was overwhelming to the Seminole.

Zandra had cast a camouflage spell and was off to the side of the battle. Melting into the trunk of a tree, she could watch the fighting and keep an eye on Bazel and Kern. She had been working on a partial shield charm, one that would divert the oncoming projectiles rather than blocking them completely, so it wouldn't be as noticeable. Casting the spell now, she gave the Seminole some breathing room.

Bazel and Kern had been watching the battle from above, hidden by their cloaking spells, but Zandra could still see the blur that the spell left behind. Bazel must have begun to notice something was amiss, because Zandra could see the two blurry distortions in the sky come together, then separate.

They were on to her.

The distortions started flying lower as they passed back and forth along the open field next to the swamp where the Seminole were holed up. Zandra watched nervously as they continued to search for her.

Then one of the blurs stopped near her and hovered. Suddenly, musket balls started hitting the trees next to her until they worked their way to the tree she was standing against. Bazel, or Kern, whichever one of them was inside the blurry distortion, was using a spell that mimicked musket fire so as not to give himself away.

Zandra suspected it was Kern inside the mirage. She could feel the strength of the shield charm waning as whatever spell he had cast pounded against it, and only the Wendigo wand could have been so powerful. Dropping her camouflaging charm and the shield charm, Zandra ran off deeper into the swamp. As the shield she had put up over the Seminole came down, they were quickly overwhelmed.

The blur tailing Zandra dropped away, revealing that it had been Kern who had discovered her. Once again, she was going to have to go up against that Wendigo wand.

Kern landed and followed her deeper into the swamp. Soon Bazel was on her tail as well. Spells whizzed by her head, hitting trees and splashing swamp water up all around her. Zandra stopped behind a tree and threw some spells back, but the only ones that hit their mark were either blocked or deflected by the two Blackbones.

Then she saw her broom lying next to a tree just a few feet behind her. She had finally made it back.

She tossed her flight bag over her shoulder and took off, hoping to outfly Bazel and Kern. She could see that the Seminole had surrendered as she flew off to the north. It looked like they had been driven out onto the open field, where Jackson's combined forces ultimately defeated them. Jackson had no mercy—she could see that he was capturing everyone, including the women and children from the Seminole settlement.

She had gotten a good head start on Bazel and Kern, as they had to retrieve their brooms. As she flew low over the trees, the first spells began to streak by her. She started maneuvering to avoid them, and shot her own spells back at the two Blackbones, to no more effect than she had had in the swamp.

The forest became less dense, so Zandra flew down into it, hoping to shake Bazel and Kern. As they wove in and out of the trees, she was at a disadvantage. Flying up behind her, Bazel and Kern could easily hit her in the back with spells, whereas she couldn't glance back to to cast even the tiniest charm. She rose out of the trees, circling back to catch them as they climbed out.

Bazel appeared first, and Zandra came up behind him. Her spell hit him in the bristles of his broom. As the fire consumed it, he fell from the sky.

Circling back around, she waited for Kern. When he finally appeared, it was apparent that he had had the misfortune of meeting a rather large tree branch, as a nasty black eye could already be seen, swelling up purple. He spotted her and weaved to the side just as she threw a spell, which missed. She had lost the element of surprise.

She quickly shot another spell at him, but it missed as well. As she flew past him, he circled around behind her.

Kern was now on the attack.

He shot a spell, and it hit near enough to her that she fell off her broom from the impact. She dropped fast, streaking down through the air so quickly that she could barely breathe.

Suddenly, a flash of silver came across her eyes as Donder rolled up underneath her, grabbing her in his talons. Righting himself, he brought the attack to Kern and began to build up a massive storm. The rain came down in sheets, making it hard for Kern to fly. Lightning started to streak the sky as Kern continued to throw spells.

Then a lighting bolt finally hit home, knocking Kern from the sky.

After a short while, Donder landed. Soaked and sore, Zandra lay there for a while, exhausted from the battle. Donder laid beside her, putting a wing over her as she gathered her strength.

After a bit, she stirred, and Donder stood.

"That was a close one, Donder," she panted. "You've saved me one more time." As she hugged his neck, she said, "Omar was right. That Wendigo wand has caused nothing but trouble for me."

Once they were ready, Donder flew Zandra back to southern Illinois. She felt miserable and drained, and she worried about what was yet to come.

She had lost yet another battle to the Blackbones.

CHAPTER 24

The Piasa Wand

Fall, 1836

Bazel had gotten Jackson into the White House. Zandra never minced words when talking about "that awful wannabe emperor." By 1830, Jackson had passed the Indian Removal Act.[63] The Cherokee had taken the state of Georgia to court to try and keep their home lands, but Jackson had ignored the court.

Ansel and Lavinia ran the wand business, while Zandra did what she could to help the Cherokee as they crossed to their new homes west of the Mississippi River. It seemed that no matter what Zandra did, she could never get the better of Bazel and Kern. She had barely gotten away a couple of times, and she had the battle scars to prove it.

Zandra and Lavinia had been back on the East Coast for the last week. Lavinia's daughter, Chione, was a father's girl and had no problem with Lavinia leaving. They had been successfully ferrying escaped slaves up to Elizabeth in Canada for some time now, and Zandra was working on setting up an East Coast branch of the ferrying system.

Lavinia had decided to travel around for a couple of days to give Zandra time to visit with Phineas and Thalia. She climbed onto Xavier gently, as his back was giving him trouble. He had lived extraordinarily long for a horse, and they could only surmise that his longevity was connected to his gift of communicating.

As Lavinia rode through Lowell, she came upon some women singing and marching.

Oh! isn't it a pity, such a pretty girl as I,
Should be sent to the factory to pine away and die?
Oh! I cannot be a slave,
I will not be a slave,
For I'm so fond of liberty
That I cannot be a slave![64]

I think they need to work on their song, Xavier said.

Smirking at him, Lavinia said, "And you think you can do better?"

Xavier snorted.

Turning, Lavinia stopped a man that was passing by. "Excuse me, sir," she said. "Do you know what these ladies are doing?"

"They're complaining about their pay being cut," said the man scathingly. "They should just get back to work and be happy that they have a job."

Lavinia gave him a stern look and walked away. It didn't surprise her that the people in the mills were treated poorly. Lavinia had seen how badly a lot of the factory owners treated those below them. She hoped that the marching women would prevail in their quest, but she didn't expect they would.

Back at Phineas's house, Zandra, Lavinia, Phineas, and Thalia were on the front porch.

A puff of smoke rose in front of Zandra, and as the smoke cleared, a letter floated down. Zandra raised her hand and grabbed the letter out of the air.

Phineas, Lavinia, and Thalia looked at Zandra inquiringly.

"It's from Marie," Zandra said as she read the letter.

"What did she have to say?" asked Lavinia, once Zandra was done reading.

Zandra hesitated. "A man who knows that she is friends with me has asked her...." She paused. "Well, she's been asked to inquire about the availability of a wand with...with a Piasa Bird infusion."

"We sold the last one a while ago," replied Lavinia.

"I thought you weren't going after that thing any more?" Phineas asked.

"I'm not," said Zandra. "I've gotten too old to tangle with that thing. We can make a living without dealing with the risk of confronting it." Zandra sighed. "I'll have to write Marie and tell her that we don't make them anymore."

It had been a month since Marie had sent Zandra the letter about a wand with a Piasa Bird infusion. Zandra had sent her a letter back to explain that she was not selling them anymore.

As the whole extended family—including Lavinia's daughter, Chione, Ansel's daughter, Zara, and Ansel's son, Magnus—sat down for a rowdy midday meal, a puff of smoke appeared over the table. As the smoke cleared, a letter floated in the air.

The grandkids had never seen a letter from Marie before, and were amazed at the mode of delivery that she used.

As the letter landed on the table in front of Zandra, she picked it up and read it:

Dear Zandra,

Hope this finds you all well. Monsieur Chaput, who had inquired about a Piasa Bird-infused wand, has contacted me again. He has asked me to offer you one hundred dollars[1] *for the same wand. I know that you are not interested in messing with the Piasa Bird anymore, but I thought that at that price, you might reconsider. Monsieur Chaput is a very prominent French aristocrat; tall and dark. No one knows his lineage, but he seems to have a lot of money, so I'm sure he can spend a lot on this wand. Let me know your decision as soon as you can.*

Hope as soon as spring comes, you can make a trip down to New Orleans. It would be good to see you.

Be careful in all your endeavors,

Marie

After Zandra was done reading, she placed the letter down on the table. Omar picked it up to look at it.

Before long, all the adults had read it.

"Wow," breathed Ansel. "A hundred dollars! I think we should visit the Piasa Bird one more time."

"That *is* a lot of money," said Lavinia. "I know it's risky, and you're both a lot older...but you have Ansel and I this time. I think if we came up with a totally new strategy, we could pull it off."

Zandra looked at Omar.

"It's not worth the danger," he said. "We don't need the money. There's no reason we should do it."

Ansel and Lavinia gave each other a look, but said no more.

Zandra once again sent a letter back to Marie, declining the offer.

[1] $2,000 in 2019 money

As winter passed, Zandra had been stretched thin trying to help save as many natives as she could, as the Indian Removal Act had wreaked havoc on them. On top of that, the influx of escaped slaves was ever increasing. Money was getting short in the family.

Then, one day, with another puff of smoke, the third letter floated down.

Dear Zandra,

Monsieur Chaput has asked me to write once more. He has upped his offer for a Piasa-infused wand to two hundred dollars. Sorry for the short letter, but I'm very busy.

Let me know what you decide, as I'm sure he will be back soon to ask about your reply.

Take care of yourself,

Marie

It had been a couple of days since the letter when Zandra finally brought it up over dinner.

"Marie has contacted me again," she began. "This man—this Monsieur Chaput—has raised his price to two hundred dollars." She paused while everyone around the table took in her words. "Money is getting tight, what with all that we're doing. I thought that maybe...maybe we should see if we can come up with a new strategy to get our samples from the Piasa Bird."

Ansel spoke up over the chaos of the kids at the table. "What if we cornered it in its lair? That's never been tried."

"With good reason," replied Omar. "How would we get out when things go bad?"

Ansel shrugged. "I think if the four of us and Sharif were working together on a Pulso spell, we could subdue it long enough to get what we needed."

Omar gave Ansel a look that clearly said *that's a crazy plan.* But he said nothing.

Zandra looked at Lavinia. "Do you have a better idea?" she asked her.

"No," replied Lavinia.

Zandra sighed. "I just keep thinking about what Shakock said that time I was visiting back east, when Phineas and I rescued Elizabeth and Hope."

Omar frowned. "What did he say?"

"He said I've been lucky with the Piasa Bird," Zandra said. "But...he said my luck was running out."

A couple of days had passed, and Zandra could not come up with another plan. They were in the wand workshop when Zandra brought up the subject again.

"Has anyone come up with a different plan?" she asked. "I'm out of ideas."

Everyone shook their heads.

Zandra hesitated. "If we don't get more money coming in, we'll have to stop our attempts to help all these people—the natives who are dying, being ousted from their homes; the slaves who have managed to escape and deserve to have the chance at starting a new life where they can live in safety." She paused. "I think...as much as I hate to do this, I think we need to take Monsieur Chaput's offer."

Ansel spoke up excitedly. "Well, then, let's go!"

Zandra looked at Lavinia.

"I'm not as excited as Ansel," said Lavinia, "but I think we should do it."

Zandra turned to Omar. "Do you have anything to add?" she asked. "Any of your Egyptian mysticism?"

Omar sat there for a long moment. When he finally spoke, it was with much hesitation. "I don't have any insight into the future of this endeavor," he said, "or a different plan of attack. We should be prepared for the worst, though, I think."

Zandra nodded. "Could you talk to Sharif and see if he would be willing to help? We're going to need all the assistance we can get. Tell him we could give him some of the profit."

"I'll talk to him," said Omar. "Then we'll see."

They had been on the west side of the Mississippi, opposite the Piasa Bird's lair, for most of the night. Sharif had shown up just before sunrise.

In the blue pre-dawn light, the Piasa Bird spread its terrifying wings and rose off of the island downriver of them. They watched it land on the bluff and enter its lair.

Around mid-morning, Zandra stood up, gazing across the river at the bluff.

Steeling herself, she turned to look at everyone. "Remember, Auris Silentium and Nubes charms *before* we enter the lair. We want to be silent and as hard to see as possible." She took a deep breath. "Please, everyone, be careful. I want to see you all back here after we're done." Looking back at Xavier, she added, "Hold down the fort. We *will* be back."

Xavier nodded, his mane fluttering in the wind. *Be very careful, all of you.*

As they mounted their brooms and staffs, Zandra took a deep breath, readying herself for what was about to come.

Then they kicked off.

Flying low over the water, they soared up the face of the bluff, landing at the opening. Zandra, Ansel, and Lavinia placed their brooms off to the side, while Omar and Sharif kept their staffs intact, as that would give them more power in the coming fight.

They all cast their spells. Then, one by one, they headed silently into the dark and ominous lair of the Piasa Bird.

The lair was spacious. The Piasa Bird stirred as soon as they entered. Lifting its head, but not opening its eyes, it sniffed the air suspiciously. Before Zandra could get too worried, however, it laid its head back on its front legs.

They carefully fanned out in front of it, preparing to cast their spells. Zandra took another deep but quiet breath, trying to calm her nerves. It was going good so far; her fear was going to mess things up.

Then she noticed something: though the bird had laid its head back down on its front legs, its nose still twitched, almost as though it was not really going back to sleep...as though it knew they were there, and was waiting for them to get closer....

Before Zandra could do anything, the massive, reptilian bird reared up in the air, letting out a deafening, howling, otherworldly roar. It was much bigger than the last time Zandra had encountered it, and the sight of the terrible creature rising high above her like some demon from the darkest depths of the earth was truly terrifying. It shot fire from its eyes, and sandstone rained down on them from the roof of the cavern.

Zandra jumped to the side to avoid being hit as a boulder crashed down from the ceiling. The Piasa Bird's scaly talons scraped the side of the boulder, just barely missing Zandra. She heard Omar across the room, shouting orders at the others as the creature's tail lashed about, knocking rocks off the side of the wall, where they tumbled down to the ground, shaking the cavern.

The others scattered as the Piasa Bird lashed out, its rage filling the cavern with echoed screeches.

"We have to fan out around it if we're going to knock it out!" shouted Omar.

"We can't!" yelled Lavinia.

The bird shot fire from its eyes again, almost catching Sharif, but he jumped back just in time. Ansel shot a spell at the bird, but it bounced right off its scales.

"I'm making a run for it!" Lavinia said. She ran to the mouth of the cave while the bird was distracted with Sharif and Ansel. Omar followed, and the two of them raised their wands.

"Now!" yelled Omar.

Omar struck first, then everyone else followed with their Pulso spells. The Piasa Bird let out a sickening yell as it struggled to fight them all, but the combined spells of three wizards and two witches were too much.

The massive, hideous bird fell back to the floor with a thundering *boom.*

Zandra rushed up, pointing her wand at the bird's fangs. "Segmentum!"

A large sliver fell off of one of the front fangs. Grabbing it off the floor, Zandra put it in her flight bag. She could see that the others were having a hard time holding the Pulso spell, as they were concentrating so hard that their cloaking spells had dropped.

Before Zandra could move away—as she stood beside the hideous face of the Piasa Bird—it broke the spells.

Fire shot out of its eyes, incinerating Zandra's wand. She felt the heat whoosh past her hand. The Piasa Bird turned to Sharif, and its long tail lashed at him. Sharif got a shield charm up just before it hit him, but the monster's tail still slapped him out the entrance of the lair.

Zandra watched, helpless, as he fell out of sight, but before she even had time to wonder about his fate, Omar ran toward her, grabbing her and ducking behind the creature to an alcove at the back of the lair. Ansel and Lavinia continued to throw spells at the beast, as did Omar. Zandra stood there helpless, without a wand.

The lair became swelteringly hot with the flames from the Piasa Bird's eyes. The room looked a lot smaller now that they had lost control of the situation, as the bird was thrashing about, filling up the space with its fury. Its great tail slammed into Ansel before he could react, throwing him against the wall of the lair. Blood ran down his face, and he sat there, dazed, as Lavinia stood over him, casting spells, trying her best to hold the Piasa Bird off.

Zandra was helpless without her wand. Searching for stones to throw, she found a stick instead. She found herself drawn to it, and the sounds of the raging battle seemed to fade out as she picked up the stick.

Covered with smooth gray bark, it had had a vine twisted around it like a strip of leather. The center of the stick was rusty red, as could be seen from the end, which looked like it had been broken off of some ancient tree long ago.

As Zandra gazed at the stick, an idea, perhaps more crazy than any she had had before, sprung into her head. She started frantically rubbing one end of the stick on the walls of the lair, trying to smooth it out.

Omar hit the Piasa Bird in the behind with a spell, and it rounded on him as it swatted at Lavinia with its tail. Zandra feverishly rubbed the stick until she had formed a crude point.

Fire baked the stone that separated Zandra and Omar from the Piasa Bird. Lavinia had gotten its attention again, and she was taking fire from it as she struggled to hold the shield charm over herself and Ansel. Zandra pulled the fang fragment she had just retrieved from the bird out of her flight bag and set it on the ground. Getting Omar's attention, she shouted over the roaring, hissing sound of the Piasa Bird's fire. "Get a sliver off this," she yelled, pointing to the fang, "and infuse it in the stick!"

Lavinia's shield charm was about to fail. She didn't know what to do. Ansel lay slumped against the wall beside her; Sharif had been thrown off the bluff and could be dead. Her mother and father were trapped on the other side of the room, barely protected by a large rock. On top of all that, her mother was *wandless.*

Or, at least, she had been.

Lavinia stared as Zandra rose into the air, her hair floating about her head as though underwater, her entire body levitating over the rock she and Omar had been hiding behind. In her outstretched hand, she held a mysterious, vine-entwined wand. The Piasa Bird turned, but it had no chance to react.

Lavinia watched the monster's expression change from anger to rage as Zandra raised the primitive wand high into the air and pointed it at the Piasa Bird.

"Pulso!" she screamed, with more power behind the words than Lavinia had ever heard before.

The lair fell silent.

The Piasa Bird lay motionless on the ground.

Slowly, Zandra descended down to the cavern floor, her hair laying back down on her shoulders. Omar came out from behind the rock, and Lavinia turned to tend to Ansel.

The Piasa Bird was out cold. Slowly, carefully, Zandra and Omar walked around the creature.

"How did you do that?" asked Omar. "You knocked it out. And you were floating."

Zandra looked up at him. "You don't know? I would have thought you of all people would."

"There are mysteries even I don't know the answer to," Omar said.

Zandra looked over at the Piasa Bird. "I don't really know either," she admitted. "I've never seen this thing knocked out like this." She turned the newly-made wand over in her hands. "I don't what type of wood this is, but...this wand saved us."

"That was a much bigger shard of Piasa Bird fang than you've ever used in a wand before," Omar said. "Could that be why it's so powerful?"

Zandra shook her head. "Usually when I use that much, it makes the wand unstable, uncontrollable. Whatever wood this is, it must be the perfect combination to make a stable, yet powerful wand."

Omar looked at it wonderingly. "We may never know."

Zandra looked over at Ansel as he came out of his daze. She walked over and knelt down, pointing the wand at the cut on his head.

"Percuro," she whispered. The cut healed up. "Auxilium," she said. Ansel sighed with relief as his pain disappeared.

Omar went out to find Sharif. Zandra turned to the Piasa Bird, took more samples, and placed them in her flight bag. She looked at Ansel. "Can you walk?"

"Yeah," Ansel replied shakily.

"Let's get out of here," Zandra said.

As they exited the lair, they saw Omar at the bottom of the bluff. Sharif had managed to cast a spell to slow his fall, but he had still been knocked out. Omar had revived him and retrieved his staff just before Zandra, Ansel, and Lavinia had come out of the lair.

They recovered their brooms as Omar and Sharif rose to meet them.

As they flew over the Mississippi River to the south, Zandra pointed her new wand at the lair and reversed the Pulso spell on the Piasa Bird. They flew as fast as they could toward home.

"You knocked it out on your own with that wand?" Sharif asked.

"Yes," Zandra said. "I've never seen the Piasa Bird so quiet in my life."

"Well, it seems that you have made another powerful wand...this one maybe greater than the Wendigo wand that you have been losing to," said Sharif.

"You may be right," Omar replied.

"Well...," said Zandra, "if that's the case...we might just stand a chance against Kern and Bazel."

As they flew off to the south, Zandra raised the wand high in the air.

It was her biggest accomplishment in wandmaking, perhaps the greatest wand ever made in the New World.

It was the Piasa Wand.

Monsieur Chaput knocked on Marie Laveau's door, with his Xolo[65] dog by his side. Its smooth black hairless body, pointed ears, and yellow eyes gave it a sinister look, though it was a very sweet dog.

Marie answered the door. "Monsieur Chaput!" she said. "Come in, please."

As he entered, she gestured for him to sit down. "Would you like some chicory?" she asked.

His dog sat beside the chair. "I would like to see my wand," he replied shortly.

Marie walked over to a buffet. Opening a drawer, she pulled out the wand. "Do you have the payment?" she asked.

Monsieur Chaput pulled the money out of his pocket and placed it on the table.

Marie put the wand in his hand. She reached for the payment, but Chaput placed his hand over the money, blocking her from picking it up.

She looked at him nervously. "What?"

Looking the wand over slowly, Chaput didn't say a word.

Then he pointed the new wand at his dog, muttering a dark, hideous incantation under his breath.

The dog fell dead.

Chaput got to his feet, turned, and walked out the door, leaving Marie standing there in shock.

As he passed down the street, he turned down a narrow alley, dropped the Transverto spell, and disappeared into New Orleans.

CHAPTER 25

The Battle at Potts Inn

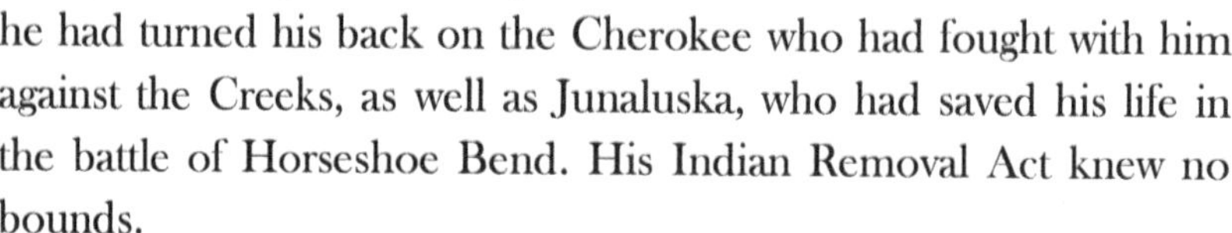

Winter, 1838

Jackson had been ignoring the ruling of the Supreme Court, and he had turned his back on the Cherokee who had fought with him against the Creeks, as well as Junaluska, who had saved his life in the battle of Horseshoe Bend. His Indian Removal Act knew no bounds.

The Cherokee had taken their plight to the Supreme Court and won the right to their ancestral land. But Jackson had ignored the court.

Struggling through the brutal winter of 1836, the Cherokee passed near Zandra's southern Illinois home on their way to their exile in the Oklahoma territory.[66]

Zandra had returned home the previous night to gather more supplies.

"Xavier, I'll be out to load the wagon in a little bit," she called out. "We'll be leaving soon."

There was no reply.

"Xavier?"

Still nothing.

"Xavier?" Zandra started out to the barn.

"Xavier, you better not have gotten into that rum. I told you not to." She swung the barn door open.

Xavier lay there on the floor, completely still. No sign of breath was visible.

Zandra walked over to him slowly. Standing there for a long moment, tears welled in her eyes as she knelt down and hugged his cold neck. He had lived much longer than a normal horse, but it still felt like the time she'd had with him had not been enough. She would never go on another adventure with him again; he would never complain about another hangover.

A tear dropped from her face onto Xavier's side as she whispered softly,

"Goodbye, old friend."

It had been a couple of days since Xavier had passed. Zandra was still having a hard time with it. He had been with her from the beginning, and his passing had left a huge hole in her life.

Ansel and Lavinia had kept the wand business in good shape. So when Zandra had hitched Omar's horse up to the wagon, they climbed on their horses as well to help her save the Cherokee who were dying on their forced migration.

Arriving along the trail, Zandra divided the supplies among the three of them. "You two head west," she told Ansel and Lavinia. "Help anyone you can. If you catch up to a group, watch for the weak. I will head back to the east and look for anyone who's been left behind to die. We'll meet back here in two days. Be very careful and stay together. Bazel and Kern keep an eye on these removals, as you know, and that Wendigo wand is nothing to mess with."

It didn't take long for Zandra to come across an elderly man curled next to a tree, waiting for death to come. Bending down, she brushed the hair from his sad eyes.

"I'm going to help you," she said.

A slight smile shone across his face. Putting a blanket around him, she pulled out her wand and cleared the snow. Piling some wood, she started a fire and made a crude lean-to. She moved the old man close to the fire and prepared some hot food for him. He was very weak and did not have the energy to talk.

She placed the food in front of him, then realized he wasn't able to feed himself. Taking the fork, she stabbed a small piece of the meat and placed it in his mouth. A tear trickled down his cheek as she fed him.

The man only took a couple of bites before he fell asleep, never to wake.

Zandra dug a grave there beside the trail for a man she never got to know, and whose family would never know what became of him.

Before long, Ansel and Lavinia had come up on the back of the column of Cherokee trekking across the snowy land. They both cast a Nubes charm so that they wouldn't be discovered.

The column's movement was slow, as the snow was deep and the Cherokee were frail from their long journey. When they stopped for the night, Ansel and Lavinia dropped their cloaking spells and walked up to the camp with some of their supplies.

For the most part, they had not witnessed the soldiers being aggressive to the Cherokee they were forcing across the frosted land. But then they heard a commotion up ahead of them. A soldier had grabbed a young girl and was dragging her off toward the woods.

Running in to intercept them, Lavinia found the soldier throwing the girl on the ground. Pulling her wand out, she stunned the soldier. The girl took the opportunity to run back to her family.

Then Lavinia was hit in the back by a spell and fell near the soldier.

Bazel stood there, gazing down at her with a distasteful expression. Before long, Kern arrived.

"We have troublemakers," Bazel said. "Go and search for any others."

"Yes, Father." Kern disappeared into the trees.

When Ansel woke, he was bound to Lavinia. Bazel and Kern were standing over them.

"It seems we have two meddlers," Bazel said as he walked around them.

Lavinia gave Bazel a dirty look.

Bazel spoke in a low, soft, menacing voice. "I don't know you two." He kicked Lavinia. "What is your name, girl?"

Saying nothing, she just glared at Bazel.

"You, boy!" Bazel spat, turning to Ansel. "Are there more of you out here helping these savages?"

Ansel said nothing.

"I would hate to force this out of you," said Bazel quietly. "But if you refuse, I will have no choice." He glared down at them for a moment. "I will let you think this over. But I will not tolerate your silence much longer."

Turning to Kern, Bazel said, "Gather some wood, and we'll start a fire while they think this over in the cold."

Once Kern had gathered enough wood, Bazel started a fire well away from Ansel and Lavinia, so as to not afford them any comfort. As evening closed in, the cold was seeping into Ansel and Lavinia's bones.

Once darkness fell, the fire had burned down to faintly glowing embers.

Slowly, Bazel got up and walked over to them. "Are you ready to tell me your names?"

"We don't talk to your kind," Ansel replied.

Bazel raised an eyebrow. "And just what type of man do you think I am?"

"Greedy," replied Lavinia. "And evil."

Bazel gave a sinister grin. "You seem to have an opinion of me, even though I've never seen you. Curious," he murmured. "I think I have an idea who you are."

Pointing his wand at Ansel, Bazel said, "Dice Mihi." Ansel's face clouded over. "What is your name?" Bazel asked.

Convulsively, as though his mouth were moving of its own accord, Ansel replied, "Ansel Voorhies."

Bazel's face darkened with a sinister grin. "Ah," he muttered. "My suspicions were correct. And you must be Zandra's daughter."

He pointed his wand at Lavinia. "Dice Mihi. Your name, please."

"Lavinia Voorhies," she said, before she could stop her mouth from moving.

Bazel nodded. "As I thought. Well, I think it's time for your mother and I to have a talk."

Bazel pulled supplies from his bag and wrote a letter. As he tapped the paper with his wand, it flew off into the approaching night.

Turning, he pointed his wand at Ansel and Lavinia. "Emarcesco!"

They both shrunk down, and Bazel picked them up, placing them in a padded box. He called for his broom, and he and Kern flew off.

Arriving in the forest behind Potts Inn,[67] Bazel pulled Ansel and Lavinia out of the box. "Atollo," he said.

Their tiny bodies floated up in the air to a height of eight feet. "Aversa Pars," he said.

The two of them grew back to their normal size, still trapped up in the air. Looking down on Bazel and Kern, Ansel asked, "What are you up to?"

"I've invited your mother here," Bazel said. "We need to finish this infuriating exchange."

Kern started a fire and flew logs over to set on it while they waited for Zandra to arrive.

The letter fluttered up to Zandra as she left the man she had tried to save. Opening it, she read:

Ms. Voorhies,

It is time for us to discuss our differences of opinion. Your son and daughter are in my care. Meet me in the woods behind Potts Inn.

Bazel Blackbone

Letting Omar's horse go, she grabbed her broom and flew off toward Potts Inn, thinking as she flew.

What am I heading into? Potts Inn and Cave-In-Rock had a reputation for harboring nefarious people, and she didn't know what kind of lowlifes she might run into there. Especially if Bazel had recruited some of them.

She shivered in the cold and held tight to her broom as she sped off into the dark night.

A light freezing rain had started as Zandra landed in the woods out of sight of Bazel's fire. As she walked into the camp, she could see Ansel and Lavinia suspended in the air.

The dark silhouette of Bazel stepped in front of them. "Ms. Voorhies," he whispered spitefully. "I see that the bitter taste of defeat has not become strong enough to deter you."

He pulled his wand out, and with a slight gasp, Zandra realized she recognized it: It was the wand that she had made for Monsieur Chaput.

"So did you kill Monsieur Chaput to get that wand?" she asked.

Bazel grinned. "No, no, no—Miss Laveau sold it to *me*. Of course, she didn't know who I was, thanks to my Transverto spell." Bazel turned the wand over in his hand. "Thank you for making it for me. In combination with Kern's Wendigo wand, it has made us a force to be reckoned with." Raising his wand, Bazel spoke in a low, eerie voice. "I've long ago grown tired of your interference. And as much as I dislike killing one of our own...I feel that I must."

The freezing rain had picked up considerably. Icicles now hung off Ansel and Lavinia's feet as they slowly rotated in the icy wind, soaked and shivering.

Kern positioned himself off to the side of his father.

"Two against one," said Zandra. "Well, it doesn't surprise me that you have become a cheat as well as a greedy thief. The men you deal with tend to be scoundrels of the worst kind. The men whose money keeps them above the law." She pulled out the Piasa Wand. "So much for 'all men are created equal.' What do you get from removing these natives so brutally?"

"Land is power, Ms. Voorhies," said Bazel. "The elite of both sides need control of it to keep the masses in a constant state of dependence. The brutality is twofold. When applied correctly, such as on minority classes of people, it breeds hatred that keeps them separate; working against each other for the scraps we toss them. Thus, they have no thought of rising against us." A dark cloud of a smile passed over Bazel's face. "And I've found that I rather enjoy a little cruelty now and again."

"I had my doubts about your goals when I first met you," said Zandra. "It seems that you have become a twisted old man."

Bazel gave a grin. "A wealthy and powerful twisted old man."

With a flick of his wrist, as though cracking a whip, Bazel shot a spell at Zandra. She raised the Piasa Wand, deflecting it. The tree behind her burst into flames. The warmth from the fire made the ice melt off of Ansel and Lavinia.

Pointing her wand at Kern, Zandra shouted, "Sustringo!"

Ropes shot from the end of the Piasa Wand, wrapping around Kern. Wobbling, he fell to the ground.

Now it was one on one. Zandra threw spells at Bazel in quick succession, pushing him away from Kern, depriving him of the chance to free him. Bazel had thrown up a shield charm to protect himself from her attack, but it was weakening.

Backing into the trees, Bazel disappeared into the forest.

Zandra followed him, weaving through the icy night. Pointing the Piasa Wand into the air, she murmured, "Eum Lux de Caelo!"

A huge ball of light shot out of her wand and hung in the sky, illuminating the forest floor. Pukwudgies scattered.

"Caligo," came Bazel's voice from the trees. A dark fog crept in, blanketing the forest floor.

Eerie orange balls of light appeared all throughout the fog as the Pukwudgies started throwing fire at Zandra and Bazel. Watching where the fireballs appeared, Zandra sent Pulso spells at the Pukwudgies, knocking almost all of them out before they started shooting arrows at her.

The battle had clearly gotten the attention of the people at Potts Inn. A group of men entered the woods with their long guns to see what was happening.

"Integumentum!" Zandra shouted.

Green ribbons of light shot out in front of her, and a shield formed, then turned clear. Arrows bounced off it as she cast a second spell. "Ventus Fortis!"

A strong wind blew through the forest, dissipating the fog. Now that she could see the Pukwudgies, she quickly dispatched them with the Piasa Wand.

Bazel threw another spell Zandra's way as he attempted to circle back around to release Kern. She blocked his spell as a shot rang out from the trees behind him. Turning, Bazel stopped the ball just short of himself. As it sat there in midair, he looked for the shooter. When he had spotted the man, he sent it whizzing back at him.

"Averto!" Zandra said, deflecting the projectile off course into the woods. "Pulso!"

The shooter fell unconscious.

Then a volley of gunfire erupted from the forest behind the first man. Rifle balls bounced off Zandra's shield as Bazel threw a spell at her at the same time, clearly hoping it would overwhelm the shield charm, but the Piasa Wand held strong.

"Pulso!" Zandra yelled, knocking out the group of men all at once.

As Bazel was casting another spell, a man came up behind him and pulled him to the ground, putting a knife to his throat. Pointing his wand at the man's leg, Bazel said, "Flaccidos!"

The man fell limp on the ground.

Zandra threw a spell and brought a tree down near Bazel as he got to his feet. A blue flame shot from Bazel's wand and hit the tree beside Zandra. It exploded into green flames.

Covering her face, Zandra moved away, temporarily blinded by the fire. She stumbled on a tree root, falling to the ground and hurting her knee.

Bazel walked up to her. Looking down, he grinned, preparing to cast a spell, but before he could, Zandra pointed the Piasa Wand at his chest. "Repellere!" she shouted.

Bazel flew backwards with great force, hitting the ground as Zandra got to her feet.

Ropes shot from Bazel's wand, flying toward her with lightning speed.

"Asser!" she yelled. A limb broke off a tree and stuck in the ground between them. The rope wrapped around it.

Zandra hobbled behind a tree. "Percuro," she said. Her knee wasn't completely better, but she could move faster now.

She had lost track of Bazel. She headed back to where Kern, Ansel, and Lavinia were.

When she reached the place, Bazel was already there, pointing his wand at Kern.

"Aversa pars," Bazel said. The ropes around Kern disappeared, and he got to his feet.

"I am not able to subdue her," said Bazel. "We need to kill her together."

Bazel and Kern turned together to face Zandra, who was coming out of the trees. They were back where they had started.

The three of them looked at each other for a moment in silence, waiting for the other to make a move.

Then, in unison, Bazel and Kern raised their wands and shouted, "Neco!"

Dark ribbons of light shot from their wands, heading for Zandra.

She cast her spell, and the ribbons of all three spells met.

Just then, the forest behind them erupted with sound. A Sasq'ets broke through the trees, snapping branches and trunks off, running at a great speed. It snatched Ansel and Lavinia out of the air, dashing into the woods on the other side of the camp.

Then, wand still locked to Bazel and Kern's spells, Zandra saw Omar streak across the sky behind the Sasq'ets.

Zandra jutted her arm out straight forcefully, and her spell shot toward Bazel and Kern. A loud bang sounded as Kern was thrown back. Zandra's spell hit Bazel's wand, making it explode as Bazel fell to the ground, motionless.

Zandra took off, running as best she could through the trees where Omar and the Sasq'ets had gone. When she came upon them, she could see that it was Taug. Omar had already cast the translation spell.

"I was coming back from fishing on the big river when I came across the fight," Taug was saying.

"Thank you for saving them," Omar replied.

Taug frowned. "That man is no friend of me or my troop."

He turned and walked off into the dark, frigid night.

Walking up to Ansel and Lavinia, Zandra produced two blankets and wrapped the two in them. "Are you alright?" she asked.

"I'm cold and hungry," said Lavinia, "but except for the jolt that I got from Taug snatching us, I'm fine."

"I'm fine, too," said Ansel. "But what happened to Bazel and his son?"

They walked back to the scene of the battle. Bazel was still there on the ground.

Omar bent down. "He is dead."

Kern was nowhere to be found.

"I don't remember what spell I had thrown; so much was happening," said Zandra. "But I'm sure it wasn't a killing spell."

"They shot killing curses at you," Lavinia said. "Your spell must have thrown it back at them. It looks like it only pushed Kern back, knocking him out. It must have hit Bazel full force."

Zandra sat down on a log gingerly, careful of her sore bones from the battle.

"Well," said Ansel, "you can thank Bazel for one thing."

Zandra looked at him.

"If it hadn't been for him," Ansel continued, "you might have never made the great wand that you had always sought."

Looking down at the wand in her hands, Zandra traced her finger along the vine growing up the length of it.

"You're right," she said. "I would never have made this."

As she held it in her hands, she felt immense pride in her greatest accomplishment of all:

The Piasa Wand.

CHAPTER 26

PAYBACK

1852

Zandra was now ninety-five. She had not seen Kern since that night at Potts Inn, though the dark hand of the Blackbone family could be seen all over the country.

A lot of good had been done ferrying escaped slaves north to Canada and her friend Elizabeth. Zandra's grandkids had grown; Zara was now in her thirties, and was doing a big part in running the family business. She had also helped her aunt, Lavinia, with her work in helping the Lowell Female Labor Reform Association fight for a ten-hour day.

Although Zandra wished she could end slavery, she took solace in the fact that she had spared so many in her efforts.

She had felt that she had failed the natives greatly, until recent events. She had been in California for what seemed like forever, although it had only been a couple of years. She had managed to covertly help eighteen tribes with a treaty guaranteeing them over eight million acres of land for reservations.[68] Upon returning to Illinois, she had thought she had finally managed to do something important for the indigenous people that she had been fighting for for so long.

On top of all that, she had made two great wands. And fortunately for her, the Piasa Wand had been far superior to the dark Wendigo wand that had fallen into the wrong hands.

Her life had been a great adventure, a lot of which she had never expected. The beauty of this land had taken her breath away, and its magical creatures had nearly cost her her life at times.

But she had enjoyed every bit of it.

As the bill came to the floor, Kern raised his wand. The senators stood there, frozen, as all traces of the treaty disappeared.

He couldn't bring his father back, but he could deny Zandra her victory.

There would be no treaty. The tribes would not get their land.

He would have his revenge.

EPILOGUE

Spring, 1864

It was close to midnight. Ansel was waiting at the mouth of the cavern at Cave-In-Rock.[69] The Ohio River was very turbulent, as a storm had just passed.

The war between the states had been going on for three years, but the Voorhies family had been ferrying escaped slaves to safety before the war even started. There had not been many of them since the war began, but there were occasional groups needing help.

A boat with Lavinia and the runaway slaves rounded Cave-In-Rock Island,[70] pursued by two boats of slave catchers.

"ARHOOOOOO!"

The thunderous Sasq'ets call almost seemed to increase the height of the waves. The escaped slaves huddled in the bottom of the boat at the sound. Now in the channel, Lavinia increased the speed of the boat as the Sasq'ets hurled stones of incredible size at the slave catchers' boats. Finally, a rock hit one and promptly sank it. As the slave catchers swam to the shore of the island, some of the troop of Sasq'ets grabbed them and pulled them into the thick trees.

Screams could be heard from the depths of the island.

The first boat continued its pursuit. Ansel pointed the Piasa Wand—which he and Lavinia had inherited when Zandra passed—at the remaining slave catchers' boat. "Averto!" he said.

The boat turned and headed downriver at a fast pace.

Lavinia threw Ansel a rope, and he pulled her boat ashore.

"I don't know what those Sasq'ets do with those slave catchers—actually, I'm sure I don't want to know," said Lavinia. "But I'm glad they're there sometimes."

As they pulled the escaped slaves out of the boat, where they shivered in fear from their ordeal, Ansel tried to reassure them that they were safe.

As they led them up the bank, Ansel heard something—a faint sound from long ago, echoing in his ears.

Turning, he looked at Lavinia, whose expression told him she heard it too.

He whispered the words that he knew she was thinking.

"The bell."

Don't miss book two in the
Voorhies Wands series:

The KNIGHTS of COLUMBIA

NOTE TO READERS

Some dream of writing a book someday.

I was never one of them.

I have bad handwriting. I sometimes think that the only reason I passed typing in high school was that the teacher was a relative. I can't spell; sometimes Grammarly and Google Docs can't even figure out what I am trying to type, and I can't get close enough for them to figure it out. Punctuation barely exists in my world. To this point, in the process of writing this, there are nine mistakes in my writing according to Grammarly.

In the fall of 2017, my family and I had just signed on a house. Two days later, I was told that my job of twenty-nine years, which had barely kept us afloat, would be ending.

The next couple of months were a struggle as we fought to secure our home, worrying what was going to happen to us. All the job options paid far less than I had previously made, and what I had made before was barely enough.

So, at age fifty-three, I tried to change careers and become a licensed home inspector. As I was training for this, I had decided to start woodturning toy wands to sell, to help us get by.

One day, as I took compost out, I found an amazing stick lying on the ground. Taking it into the garage, I sanded the tip to a point—and the Piasa Wand came into being.

I decided that we needed to write a short description of the wand company to go with the display at the local shop. As my unemployment continued, I started to expand the story into what eventually became this book. I picked the name Voorhies because of an unusual old house in the area, which had been abandoned a lot of my life and was considered haunted. It has since been restored. Hopefully, we will too.

If you enjoyed *Zandra Voorhies and the Piasa Wand* and want me to write more books about the Voorhies family, consider supporting me by leaving reviews online, requesting this book at your local libraries and bookstores if they don't have it, and above all else, spreading the word to anyone you think might enjoy the book. Authors can only succeed through readers like you, who enable us to keep making the books you want to read.

If you want to contact me, or if you just want to hear updates about this and future books of mine, you can like me on Facebook, follow me on Goodreads, follow me on Twitter @AuthorMTFisher, or visit my website at mtfisher.wixsite.com/mtfisher.

ACKNOWLEDGMENTS

Thanks to my diligent beta readers:

Cheryl Lynn Tatum (Ms. T), you have been supportive of us even when you're half a country away. And you always see the wonderfulness in our unique kids.

Rebecca Glenn, my always happy, supportive first cousin. Those family meals that you made safe for us to eat meant so much to us, especially Max.

Gay Amorasak, your kindness has been the light in the tunnel that was not a train.

And thanks to the others who helped give an opinion on the book. You may not have had time to read the whole thing before it was done, but you helped immensely nonetheless.

Thanks to Howard Zinn, who put the names and deeds of the true heroes of this land into a book, so that someone like me could draw from them.

Thanks to the common people who stood up against the odds to move this country to a better place; the ones who truly deserve a monument on the mall in Washington DC.

To J. K. Rowling, for creating the world that inspired this book.

To Sasquatch Chronicles, my companion as I typed late into the night. Yes, I typed while listening to you. If I get rich someday, I will pay for a membership. And, yes, I do believe.

Thanks to all the people, places, and events in my life that I threw into a blender to create this world.

Thanks to Stephanie, my strong, supportive wife, who all too often has to endure the poorer part of her vows, helps me through all my struggles, and encouraged me to keep writing. You help me with everything even when I fight against the help.

Thanks to Sully, my Irish-named, non-potato-eating little superhero. May you always keep the soul and fairness of Batman in your heart. I hope someday you do get to become the Dark Knight. This world needs him now more than ever.

Thanks to Max in the middle, my train buddy. Your good reviews helped spur me on. Your laughs make me smile even when it's hard to find anything to laugh about. Remember, "It doesn't matter where the train is going. What matters is that you get on." [I]

And, finally, thanks to my oldest, Sam: my editor, cover designer, and anything else I needed you to be. Without you, I could have never done this. Thanks for all the times you saved me when I had no idea what I had done with the document on my computer. Thanks for the discussions that got me back on track with the story. Thanks for the hours working at correcting the mess of grammar and spelling that I handed you. Your artistry and creativity in all your endeavors is astounding. Your writing skills would make your namesake, Samuel Clemens, proud.

On a final note, to paraphrase Utah Phillips:
Any mistakes found within were left there on purpose, as some people do nothing but look for them.
I try to please everyone.

[I] From The Polar Express, 2004, Warner Bros.

SPELLS

Ad Designandum

Points the caster of the spell to the desired target

Ambiguus

Confuses and disorients the target(s)

Are Bulla

Creates an air bubble around the caster of the spell or the desired target

---

Asser

Makes stakes or posts from nearby materials

Atollo

Levitates the desired object or person

Auris Silentium

Contains all sounds inside the specified area

Auxilium

Relieves the pain of the target person or animal

Aversa Pars

Reverses the desired spell

Averto

Deflects the targeted object from its current trajectory

Caligo

Conjures a dark fog

Capto

Shoots a ribbon of red light that wraps around the target, picks it up, and moves it however the spellcaster desires

---

Cavo

Hollows out the target object

Commuta Habitum

Disguises the target object or person as something else. Unlike Transverto, this spell also works on objects

---

Concussione

Hits the desired target with a strong impact of force

Delens Odos

Erases the scent of the target

Detego

Reveals the target for what it really is; lifts any disguising or cloaking spells

Dice mihi

Forces the target to respond truthfully to the next question the spellcaster asks of them

Dissimulato Fenestra

Disguises an object, place, or person so that others can only see what the caster of the spell desires

Emarcesco

Shrinks the target(s) to the desired size

Eum Lux de Caelo

Provides an immense light source from above

Excito

Wakes the target

Exsarcio

Repairs the desired object

Flaccidos

Makes the target go limp

Fulgur

Flashes a bright light quickly; usually used to temporarily blind an opponent

---

Indo

Inserts the target object inside another target; usually melding the two objects in the process

---

Integumentum

Conjures a shield bubble around the desired object or person

Invius

Makes the targeted region impassible for intruders

Lateo

Makes the desired object vanish

Lumino

Gently lights up the desired area

Missito

Dispatches letters; upon casting, the desired letter flies off to its recipient

---

Neco

Immediately kills the target

Nubes

Cloaks the desired target (usually the caster of the spell) with a shimmering camouflage; not entirely invisible, but very hard to notice

---

Percuro

Heals the target

Perfundo

Pours water on the target

Propinquitas

Locates other magical people in the nearby vicinity

Pulso

Knocks the target unconscious

Quid hic

Reveals, in the form of purple mist, the events that took place in a specified area

---

Recludo

Opens hidden drawers or compartments

Repellere

Repels the target away from the caster of the spell

Resisto

Immobilizes the target

Revelabo Stultitiam

Reveals hidden doors

Revoco

Retrieves the intended object to the caster of the spell

Segmentum

Cuts a sliver off of the target

Subausculto

Eavesdropping spell; enables the caster to hear sounds which would normally be too far away or too quiet to hear

---

Subterraneis

Creates a tunnel through the ground

Sustringo

Binds the target in magical ropes of energy

Tardo

Slows down the surroundings of the spellcaster

Transferendum

Translates the words of any intelligent life-form into a language the caster of the spell can understand

Transverto

Changes the desired person (usually the caster of the spell) into a different form as a disguise

Truso

Provides a small thrust to set an object in motion

Umbraculum

Creates a spot of shade over the caster of the spell

Uro

Incinerates or burns the target

Ventus Fortis

Conjures up a strong wind

EGYPTIAN/ATLANTEAN SPELLS

Enyscyo

Reinforces and strengthens the target

Epanyri

Removes spells on the target; reverts it back to its original form

---

Epotyfro

Incinerates the target(s) with blue electricity

Faraterum

Shoots electricity

Kadezon

Provides a blast of force and knocks the target back

Kdeyo

Creates a shield around a specified area, so that none can get in

---

Kyrdeza

Removes the wand at the top of an Egyptian witch or wizard's staff

Ni Geni Mykro

Shrinks down the target object or person

Nyrthekas

Wraps the intended injured limb in a splint

Prystet

Creates a temporary invisible shield, protecting the target

Tisynive edu

Reveals who or what has been in the target location recently, and where they went from there

ENDNOTES

---

[1] More on the L'Hermione: https://en.wikipedia.org/wiki/French_frigate_Hermione_(1779)
https://www.youtube.com/watch?v=fakw-bS3ujI

[2] More on Lafayatte: https://en.wikipedia.org/wiki/Gilbert_du_Motier,_Marquis_de_Lafayette

[3] More on Latouche: https://en.wikipedia.org/wiki/Louis-Ren%C3%A9_Levassor_de_Latouche_Tr%C3%A9ville#Service_on_Hermione_and_the_American_War_of_Independence

[4] Salem Street, Boston, Mass., is a real street dating back to the late 1700s

[5] For more on Grace O'Malley, reference *The True Story of Grace O'Malley, Ireland's Pirate Queen* by Anne Chambers or go to: https://en.wikipedia.org/wiki/Grace_O%27Malley

[6] More on Salem, Mass.: https://en.wikipedia.org/wiki/Salem,_Massachusetts

[7] More on Danvers, Mass.: https://en.wikipedia.org/wiki/Danvers,_Massachusetts

[8] More on General Washington: https://en.wikipedia.org/wiki/George_Washington

[9] More on Ipswich Road: https://patch.com/massachusetts/danvers/old-ipswich-road

[10] Many of the creatures mentioned here would not have been known of or believed in by the Mohawk, but for the purposes of the story, are used as magical creatures and are presumed to be known of by all in the area

[11] The convicted ancestors mentioned in this chapter were actual victims of the Salem Witch Trials. For more, visit: https://en.wikipedia.org/wiki/Salem_witch_trials

[12] More on the Leeds Devil legend: https://weirdnj.com/stories/jersey-devil/
https://en.wikipedia.org/wiki/Jersey_Devil

[13] From 1772 - 1780, 4/5 of the Arikara died from smallpox and other European illnesses

[14] More on the legends and geology of Devil's Tower: https://sylvanrocks.com/devils-tower-climbing-legends-history/
https://www.nps.gov/deto/learn/historyculture/sacredsite.htm

[15] More on the Illini Confederation: https://en.wikipedia.org/wiki/Illinois_Confederation

[16] Conkey Tavern was a frequent gathering place for Shays and the Regulators

[17] More on Daniel Shays: http://shaysrebellion.stcc.edu/shaysapp/person.do?shortName=daniel_shays

[18] More on Luke Day: https://en.wikipedia.org/wiki/Luke_Day

[19] More on General Shepard: https://en.wikipedia.org/wiki/William_Shepard

[20] More on Eli Parsons: https://en.wikipedia.org/wiki/Eli_Parsons

[21] More on General Benjamin Lincoln: https://en.wikipedia.org/wiki/Benjamin_Lincoln

[22] More on the Great Valley Road (also known as the Great Wagon Road): https://en.wikipedia.org/wiki/Great_Wagon_Road

[23] More on Harrisonburg, VA: https://en.wikipedia.org/wiki/Harrisonburg,_Virginia

[24] Now known as Piasa Island. https://www.google.com/maps/place/Piasa+Island/@38.9308973,-90.2860894,15z

[25] More on Cahokia: https://www.livescience.com/22737-cahokia.html

https://www.theguardian.com/cities/2016/aug/17/lost-cities-8-mystery-ahokia-illinois-mississippians-native-americans-vanish

https://en.wikipedia.org/wiki/Cahokia

Cahokia Mounds State Park and World Heritage site official website: https://cahokiamounds.org/

[26] More on this theory on the legend of Atlantis: https://www.youtube.com/watch?v=76e-A7RNjKI

https://www.youtube.com/watch?v=oDoM4BmoDQM&t=1054s

[27] More on L'Anse aux Meadows: https://en.wikipedia.org/wiki/L%27Anse_aux_Meadows

---

[28] More on the Haudenosaunee Confederation: https://www.nps.gov/fost/learn/historyculture/the-six-nations-confederacy-during-the-american-revolution.htm

[29] More on Greenthread tea: http://www.itmonline.org/arts/greenthread.htm

[30] More on the Navajo (Dine) creation story: http://navajolegends.org/navajo-creation-story/

The author is not Navajo, but did his best to depict the creation story accurately and with respect. However, the story is depicted differently according to different sources, so any discrepancies are apologized for.

[31] More on Chaco Canyon: https://www.youtube.com/watch?v=A52yWmmHjy0

https://www.youtube.com/watch?v=0h9WlozwiTQ

https://www.youtube.com/watch?v=oVU1PeB6x-Y&t=142s

[32] More on the legend of Egyptians in the Grand Canyon area: https://www.youtube.com/watch?v=lFk6P6FxsJY

https://www.youtube.com/watch?v=soGNyfilZKg&t=103s

[33] More on skinwalkers: http://navajolegends.org/navajo-skinwalker-legend/

https://www.youtube.com/watch?v=iEA1G8efmuc

[34] The word Sasquatch was derived from this, the Halkomelem (Salishan) word for the beasts.

[35] More on the ancient Egyptian birthing bricks: https://www.nytimes.com/2002/08/06/science/ancient-birth-bricks-found-in-egypt.html

[36] More on the legends of Nahanni Valley:
https://www.youtube.com/watch?v=Nb7riuu2yTE&t=341s

[37] The natives in the area called them Waheela.

[38] More on Andrew Jackson:
https://www.youtube.com/watch?v=Yd12Wz6o_KI
https://www.youtube.com/watch?v=LNzDj-EPtgQ
https://www.youtube.com/watch?v=SupNaQeJrq0

[39] More on Tecumseh: https://en.wikipedia.org/wiki/Tecumseh
https://www.youtube.com/watch?v=izBobl1t1fo

[40] The New Madrid Quakes of 1811-1812. More on this and other earthquakes of the area: https://www.smithsonianmag.com/science-nature/the-great-midwest-earthquake-of-1811-46342/
https://en.wikipedia.org/wiki/1811%E2%80%9312_New_Madrid_earthquakes
http://www.new-madrid.mo.us/132/Strange-Happenings-during-the-Earthquake
http://showme.net/~fkeller/quake/mississippi_river_ran_backward.htm

[41] More on the town of New Madrid:
https://en.wikipedia.org/wiki/New_Madrid,_Missouri

[42] More on General Brock:
https://en.wikipedia.org/wiki/Isaac_Brock

[43] More on Tenskwatawa:
https://en.wikipedia.org/wiki/Tenskwatawa

[44] More on Prophetstown:
https://en.wikipedia.org/wiki/Prophetstown_State_Park

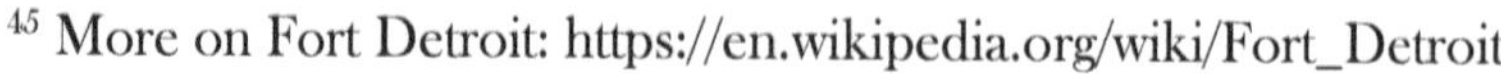

[45] More on Fort Detroit: https://en.wikipedia.org/wiki/Fort_Detroit

[46] More on Frenchtown: https://en.wikipedia.org/wiki/Battle_of_Frenchtown

[47] More on the Maumee River: https://en.wikipedia.org/wiki/Maumee_River

[48] More on Fort Miamis: https://en.wikipedia.org/wiki/Fort_Miami_(Ohio)

[49] More on Fort Meigs: https://en.wikipedia.org/wiki/Fort_Meigs

http://www.internetantiquegazette.com/kitchen_household/2411_clay_general_green_fort_meigs/

[50] More on General Green Clay: https://en.wikipedia.org/wiki/Green_Clay

[51] More on the Thames River, Ontario, Canada: https://en.wikipedia.org/wiki/Thames_River_(Ontario)

[52] Quote referenced from A People's History of the United States by Howard Zinn, Chapter 7.

[53] More on Laffite: https://www.britannica.com/biography/Jean-Laffite

[54] Map of New Orleans, 1850, featuring Rue de L'Union: https://www.loc.gov/resource/g4014n.ct000684/?r=-0.351,0.17,1.909,0.711,0

[55] More on Marie Laveau: http://www.womenhistoryblog.com/2012/07/marie-laveau.html

https://en.wikipedia.org/wiki/Marie_Laveau

[56] A coffee-like drink made from the chicory plant. https://en.wikipedia.org/wiki/Chicory

[57] More on the Battle of New Orleans: https://www.britannica.com/event/Battle-of-New-Orleans-United-States-United-Kingdom-1815

[58] More on the Battle of Horseshoe Bend: https://en.wikipedia.org/wiki/Battle_of_Horseshoe_Bend_(1814)

[59] More on Junaluska: https://en.wikipedia.org/wiki/Junaluska

[60] More on Shawneetown, IL: https://en.wikipedia.org/wiki/Shawneetown,_Illinois

[61] More on the Econfina River: https://en.wikipedia.org/wiki/Econfina_River

[62] More on the this battle: https://newafrikan77.wordpress.com/2016/04/18/new-afrikanblack-seminoles-native-seminoles-defeat-at-battle-of-suwanee-april-18-1818/

[63] More on the Indian Removal Act: https://www.youtube.com/watch?v=qalhDKLrWEQ&t=602s

https://www.youtube.com/watch?v=T8Hd42J-tzs

[64] More on the Lowell Strike: http://historymatters.gmu.edu/d/5714

Labor history timeline, featuring the Lowell Strike: https://aflcio.org/about/history

Or reference A People's History of the United States by Howard Zinn

[65] More on Xolo dogs: https://www.akc.org/dog-breeds/xoloitzcuintli/

https://en.wikipedia.org/wiki/Mexican_Hairless_Dog

[66] More on the Trail of Tears:
https://www.youtube.com/watch?v=qalhDKLrWEQ&t=602s
https://www.youtube.com/watch?v=T8Hd42J-tzs

[67] More on Potts Inn:
http://mysteriousheartland.com/2014/06/20/the-legend-of-potts-inn/
http://www.illinoishistory.com/pottsinn.html
https://en.wikipedia.org/wiki/Isaiah_L._Potts

[68] More on this treaty:
http://www.kstrom.net/isk/maps/ca/caltreaties.html

[69] More on Cave-In-Rock: https://en.wikipedia.org/wiki/Cave-In-Rock,_Illinois

[70] More on Cave-In-Rock Island:
http://mysteriousheartland.com/tag/cave-in-rock-island/

www.ingramcontent.com/pod-product-compliance
Lightning Source LLC
Chambersburg PA
CBHW030423310726
48979CB00009B/1584/J

* 9 7 8 1 7 3 3 2 4 6 2 0 0 *